EVERY HUMAN LOVE

STORIES

EVERY HUMAN LOVE

JOANNA PEARSON

ACRE

CINCINNATI 2019

Acre Books is made possible by the support of the Robert and Adele Schiff Foundation.

Designed by Barbara Neely Bourgoyne
Cover art: *Eighty-Six* (cropped), archival inkjet print on panel by Daniel Alexander Smith, reproduced with permission of the artist

Library of Congress Cataloging-in-Publication Data
Names: Pearson, Joanna, author.
Title: Every human love : stories / Joanna Pearson.
Description: Cincinnati : Acre Books, 2019.
Identifiers: LCCN 2019003781 (print) | LCCN 2019010498 (ebook) |
    ISBN 978-1-946724-19-9 | ISBN 978-1-946724-18-2 (paperback)
Classification: LCC PS3616.E2544 (ebook) | LCC PS3616.E2544 A6 2019 (print) |
    DDC 813/.6—dc23
LC record available at https://lccn.loc.gov/2019003781

The press is based at the University of Cincinnati, Department of English and Comparative Literature, McMicken Hall, Room 248, PO Box 210069, Cincinnati, OH, 45221–0069.

www.acre-books.com

Acre Books books may be purchased at a discount for educational use. For information please email business@acre-books.com.

CONTENTS

Changeling 1

The Private Collection 23

Fox Foot 34

Rumpelstiltskin 48

For the Dead Who Travel Fast 60

The Undead 70

Higher Things 83

Gifts 100

Lucky 116

Romantics 127

Wages 146

The Scare 160

Ouro Preto 176

Every Human Love 192

Acknowledgments 209

EVERY HUMAN LOVE

CHANGELING

When she was feeding him in the wee hours of the morning, Marly would attempt to will her own sleepiness into the baby. She'd close her eyes and concentrate, taking slow, deep breaths, as if by doing so she could channel all the intoxicating powers of her exhaustion into the breast milk, transforming it into a kind of mini–River Lethe. She'd thought of that analogy one night, then immediately questioned the appropriateness of comparing what one fed one's newborn to the river of oblivion in the underworld. Bad brain. Bad mother. But the baby didn't seem to mind. The baby battered his tiny fists against Marly, panting and rooting at her nipple. The baby did not look exhausted. The baby, in fact, never looked exhausted during the hours at which it was normal and customary for humans to sleep. His hunger was indefatigable. And he was indefatigably nocturnal. And his fingernails were surprisingly sharp for being so small. If Marly didn't keep his hands covered, he would rake his own face insistently, drawing blood.

Babies didn't know better. Between their floppy necks and their self-excoriating claws and the soft spots on their big heads like bruises on a peach, babies seemed bent on their own self-destruction. But it was your job, as the parent, to stop them.

In the other room of their overheated apartment, Marly's husband should have been sleeping. Marly longed to join him, to climb into bed and curl against his familiar shape, to breathe in counterpoint—but he was working an overnight shift at the hospital. He wouldn't be home until after his sign-out at 7 a.m., hours away. For now, it was just the two of them: the baby and her. And the baby, his hot-dumpling body wedged against her, sipping the substance of her, slurping up her very cells, hardly counted. She, the baby—they were each alone.

The baby arched his little back against her, repositioned his head on her breast, and kicked off the arm of the couch with one foot like a tiny mountain climber summiting. Marly yawned. Nowadays, her single consuming desire was sleep. She fantasized about surrendering to blank unconsciousness without being awakened by the baby's urgent cry or by her own aching breasts, swollen with undrunk milk.

There were pills a person could take, some of which her husband prescribed to his patients. Marly craved those pills. She wanted the strong ones, pills that would clobber her chatterbox brain into silence.

"I want whatever's the pharmaceutical equivalent of being clubbed on the head," she'd told her husband recently. "I want to be clubbed on the head like a baby seal. Just for a night. Knocked out. One night is all I ask."

"Trust me," he'd said. "You don't. Having a functioning reticular activating system is a good thing."

Marly had disagreed. "I want you to slug me in my reticular activating system."

But her husband wouldn't do that, Marly knew. Her husband was ethical. Scrupulously ethical. He had strong opinions on many things, including the writing of prescriptions for controlled substances for one's wife. Besides, he'd spent far too much time during his residency detoxing people off of benzos and prescription pain pills. It was all poison—Ambien led to sleep-driving on I-95, Xanax was impossible to get off of. . . . Anything rumored to be the good stuff was an addiction waiting to happen; everything foretold a bad outcome. Her husband drank cup after cup of green tea, ate chia seeds and kale, went on early morning jogs, and was generally cautious and consequence-averse. He regaled her with horror stories from his training. He'd seen at least one horrible finale to everything; even the most seemingly innocuous choices, from lighting a scented candle to wearing the wrong pajamas, could lead to terrible outcomes. The world was full of subtle dangers.

"At the very least I could give the baby a little something to make him sleepy," Marly said. Her voice was light, ironic, so that her husband would know not to take her seriously even though she was actually at least half serious. "That would help. You know, like in the olden days? How our grandmothers' generation used to give their babies a whiskey-soaked rag to suck? Or something like that?"

"A whiskey-soaked rag." Her husband snorted at her joke. (She, of course, knew better. Bad joke. Bad mother.)

So, as a compromise, Marly had been taking the occasional Benadryl. Like a criminal. A Benadryl junkie. It was perfectly safe—a fact you could verify on the internet!—but her husband, all bulgur wheat and almond milk, would not have approved. Her mouth and sinuses were now perpetually dry, and yet she still couldn't sleep. Even when the baby did go limp in her arms, finally allowing himself to be put down for an hour or so, Marly remained awake—terribly tired, but awake. She'd tried a glass, or two, or two and a half, of red wine—more than her husband would have approved of for someone breastfeeding his baby son. But the wine had only granted her a solid fifty minutes of unconsciousness followed by the punishment of a banging behind her eyes. The baby, of course, was impervious to the effects of wine-laced breast milk.

And now, the baby stopped sucking for a moment and clung there, his mouth still latched on her nipple, as if lost in a dream state. Slowly, Marly peeled him away from her body, but he startled, his tiny mouth pulling her nipple like it was a piece of taffy. She sighed and let him nestle back against her to resume nursing. He raised one of his tiny eyebrows at her, skeptical.

In her previous life, before she'd become a human milk machine, Marly had been a graduate student. She had started off as a graduate student in comparative literature but had at some point wandered over into the amorphous field of cultural studies, which meant a little dash of everything. It also meant she could never exactly explain to her grandfather what she was doing with her life. "So you're an English teacher?" he'd finally asked, and she'd nodded.

She was ABD. Her dissertation was titled, "Gypsies: Antiziganism as a Literary Trope and the Cultural Legacy of the Roma." What this really meant was that she got to read lots of folklore and stories about tinkers and fortune tellers. It also meant she got to keep up with weird news stories, like the recent one about a blond girl found in the custody of a Greek gypsy couple. The couple was accused of having abducted her, though they'd claimed to have bought her for nine hundred euros from her biological mother. This story had, of course, set off a wave of the old folkloric panic—gypsies! *They'll steal your children!* And of course, this led to the inevitable overreaction: afterward, elsewhere in Europe, two fair-haired gypsy children were briefly—erroneously—removed from their actual biological parents. The Roma and Traveler communities had been righteously aggrieved. There had been a whole political back-and-forth across Europe.

Stories like this (gypsy kidnappings, fairy changelings) had been around for centuries, and Marly collected the most gruesome ones. One young woman in Cumbria in the 1830s had become convinced that her beautiful pink-cheeked, golden-haired baby had been stolen by a traveling tinker and replaced with an imposter, jaundiced and howling. Whether she'd believed the replacement baby was a gypsy or a fairy was unclear, but the imposter sobbed ceaselessly. She'd been so certain the baby was not her own that she'd thrown it into the fireplace. Legend held that if you put a changeling in the fire, he'd be forced to jump up the chimney and return your actual child. Of course, this hadn't happened. So many things led to a bad outcome.

Marly now had pages and pages of notes on the Roma, Sinti, Manush, Romanichal, Irish Travelers; she had pages and pages of stories—both folklore and more recent news items. What she did not have, however, was a dissertation. What she had not done, in fact, was start *writing* a dissertation. When her husband introduced her at parties now, she knew that everyone, nodding politely, interpreted his description of her as a "PhD candidate" as "stay-at-home mom with frustrated ambitions."

Her husband's friends were irritatingly practical. They were doctors. There was something indisputably and unassailably official about this role in the world—even if these doctor friends were mostly all psychiatrists, the vaguest and most hand-wavy variety of doctor. But they didn't have to mention that part. When someone asked what they did, they could just answer with one word if they chose: "Doctor." It was clear-cut. (There was no explaining, for instance, what "cultural studies" consisted of.) They didn't stay at home wearing spit-up-covered pajamas all day (that single fact was delegitimizing). They could say something like, "When I was in medical school . . ." or at least think it reassuringly. No one ever reassured herself by thinking, *When I was in graduate school for cultural studies . . .*

She'd always felt ill at ease among them, like a fake adult. Now she felt like something even worse: a sad housewife—or worse still, a sad housewife with pretensions of intellectualism. When a doctor friend had asked about her graduate work at one of their dinner parties, she'd described the Roma's migration from India, the historical stigma against them, and the evolving trope of the gypsy in literature and popular culture. She'd even mentioned the recent case in Greece about the child abduction, its unfortunate intersection with a long history of prejudice and urban legend.

She'd then told them the story of the woman in 1830s Cumbria, complete with the part about throwing the baby into the fire.

"Postpartum psychosis," said Laurel, an elegant woman who was, in Marly's opinion, too attractive to be taken seriously. She should have been a news anchor, not a psychiatrist. Or maybe the lady behind the cosmetics counter. A cocktail waitress. Someone people's husbands had affairs with.

"Capgras syndrome," said Kevin. He smiled flirtatiously at Marly. Kevin was always smiling flirtatiously, whether you were a man, woman, or child. She felt sorry for his wife, Becca, who was eyelashless and plain. Kevin's amorous energy was like a spigot that could not be turned off. He exuded sexuality, aimed at no one in particular and thus at everyone. You felt your pelvis tilt toward him, magnetized, and then were disgusted at yourself.

Marly wondered how either of these two could possibly do their jobs. They should have been on reality television, not entrusted to care for people's mental health, of all things. It was annoying to have the intriguing aspects of your graduate work distilled by someone else into a smug DSM diagnosis.

"Well," Marly had said, smiling politely. "I'm not so much interested in—"

"You've been to Paris, right?" Laurel interjected. "The gypsies are a real problem. There are swarms of them at the Gare du Nord, the Louvre . . . And they're children. Gangs of children. That's the creepy part. All these beautiful little dark-eyed gypsy children rush you, and you're enveloped by them. The next thing you know, your wallet's gone."

"Well, sure," Marly said, her voice gone slightly huffy. She was aware of this, careful to adjust her tone so it was not hectoring—not the very same admonishing tone she used back when she'd been a TA with classrooms full of sullen freshman boys, dead-eyed, wearing baseball caps and drinking Muscle Milk. "But there are kids in gangs here, too. There's a criminal minority everywhere. That doesn't mean we should assume an entire—"

"The curse!" Jason said. "Speaking of gypsies! Has John told you he's been cursed?"

Marly looked to her husband, John, who maintained the ever-present equanimity his name suggested. Johns were solid, reliable. Thank God she had married a John.

Jason's eyes crinkled with impish delight. Marly liked him. He was a jovial southerner with a big laugh and a slight drawl. Of the handful of John's coresidents who'd stayed in the area after they'd finished residency, he was her favorite. He'd tell Marly hilarious stories of his disastrous dates with all the wrong guys—a stuffy accountant, a way-too-young former frat boy, the gorgeous but dumb bartender from the trendy new club. Of all of the doctor friends, he made Marly feel the most included.

"A gypsy curse, all right. A hex. Black magic," Jason said, looking pleased with himself. "Cursed by Ol' Pants Leg herself."

John was shaking his head. "She's not a gypsy," he said. "I think she's a Lumbee Indian or something. . . ."

"Same diff," Jason continued. "Don't spoil my story."

"Oh, no," Kevin said, laughing. "Not Ol' Pants Leg. You *really* don't want to be on her bad side."

"So what happened?" Laurel asked.

John sighed. Marly knew he hated talking in this way. It was part kindness, part scrupulousness, even if no one ever technically violated HIPAA. He found something horrid about the whole thing: nicknaming frequent fliers in the ER—most of them homeless, many of them schizophrenic, or alcoholic, or both—and telling stories, albeit de-identified stories, but stories nonetheless, wherein these nameless patients were transformed into grotesquely comic caricatures.

Marly understood such stories were probably some kind of psychological defense. A form of gallows humor. If she had to work in the bowels of an urban hospital, in the ER—the psychiatric part of the ER, no less—then surely she too would be telling how Vomit Beard or Prostitute Mamie Eisenhower or Eye Patch had showed up again, or how Heroin Justin Bieber had spat in her face and called her a bitch, or how Snoop Dogg the Homeless Man could actually be extremely pleasant once he was no longer in acute benzo withdrawal. . . . It must serve as a way of coping with the bleakness you encountered.

Even so, it made her uncomfortable—and John, too. This was one of the things she loved about him. She took his refusal to joke about patients as a measure of his fundamental decency. When he did unburden himself to her after one of his shifts, he never played the story for laughs, never gleefully found in one of his patients a tragic celebrity doppelgänger.

John was smiling, but Marly could tell it was a pained smile. He didn't want to be a bad sport.

Jason laughed again. "Ol' Pants Leg cast the evil eye on John," he said. "She's pissed."

John shrugged. "The mobile treatment team couldn't find her for the past several months. She was floridly manic again."

"Fine," Jason said. "I'll tell it. Anyways, so John's right. She's as manic as they come, yelling about Jesus. 'I've got Jesus inside me! Jesus will protect me! I've got Jesus inside me!' And when security searches her, what do they find but the business end of *a cake-topper Jesus* poking out her pants. So John has security take it from her, and she gets *very* upset. Apparently that's her protection. Tiny cake-topper Jesus! And John took Jesus away. That's when she hexed him with the old gypsy curse. The nurses and techs were still talking about it when I came on shift."

"What'd you do with Jesus?" Laurel asked.

"It was a sharp," John explained. "That's what I told her, too. Even if it was Jesus, it was a sharp."

"Look out," Laurel said, laughing. "Ol' Pants Leg holds a grudge."

"She probably does have some kind of voodoo up her sleeve," Kevin added.

"What exactly did she say?" Marly asked. She did not point out that voodoo was something separate entirely from the evil eye—a whole different cultural studies dissertation.

John sighed again. "Oh, she cursed me and my offspring for generations to come. Said she'd destroy what's most valuable to me. That was the gist of it, at least. She phrased it better. More colorfully."

Marly felt herself flinch.

"People say that stuff all the time. It's the psych ER," John said.

Laurel smirked and straightened the bowl of chips on the table. "I don't know," she said, looking meaningfully at Marly's midsection in a way that made Marly flush.

And here they had erupted into laughter, Laurel pouring more malbec into everyone's glass (everyone except Marly's, that is, since Marly had been eight months pregnant at the time) while Marly held her distended belly protectively, as if the words of a psychotic homeless lady actually meant something.

The baby bucked against Marly, his little head bobbing away from her nipple. She looked at her watch. It was after 3 a.m. The baby—his name was John also, which surely meant he would grow into a good, dependable man like his father—had to be finished nursing. Her husband, in the fluorescent glow of the cramped workroom in the back of the ER, would be rubbing his eyes, counting down the hours until the end of his shift, stirring powdered creamer into one more cup of bad K-cup coffee, his single vice.

Maybe she and the baby could get some sleep. A nap, at least, before John came home.

She scooped the baby up to her shoulder, leaving her breasts to drip. It didn't matter. All of her clothes were soaked with milk these days. Who was she trying to impress? Her husband? (She was no longer his anyway; she belonged to the baby now. She was the baby's appendage.) Or Laurel? Fancy Dr. Laurel who nettled her for no reason?

"You should go easy on her," Jason had said to Marly once, back when she'd still been pregnant and had confided her irritation. "She had a miscarriage, you know. Pretty recently. It can't be easy for her. Seeing other people, you know . . . couples, having babies." He'd looked down, studying his hands.

"She told you?" Marly asked. "About her miscarriage?"

Jason nodded, solemn.

"But she hasn't dated anyone since her divorce, right?"

Jason shrugged and looked away. "Things happen," he said. "Not my business to judge."

From the way he said it, Marly knew not to press further. They were friends, after all, Jason and Laurel. No matter what, Marly would always be the outsider.

"Well, I'm sorry for her then," Marly had said brusquely. "For that."

And maybe she was—though Marly had still noted that Laurel laughed a couple beats too long whenever John told a joke (and he was not, one had to admit, particularly funny); noted that Laurel attended to John with a touch of extra care, extra solicitude, whenever they were at the doctor friends' dinner parties.

The baby arched his back in Marly's arms, then spat up violently, a hot stream against her chest. Thankfully, he resettled himself and fell back asleep. Marly moved him to her other shoulder and turned the lights off in the living room. Sleep. They would both sleep.

Someone knocked at the door.

Marly froze, pressing the baby against her there in the darkness. He stirred but did not wake.

The knocking came again, this time louder.

She was aware of her heart now, skittish in her chest. The front of her shirt was wet and her left breast exposed. She clutched the baby tighter, aware of how soft they both were, how vulnerable.

It was most likely a drunken partier. This had happened before. They lived on the same floor with some grad students from the arts institute. The art students had parties all the time—long, boozy parties during which they played bad music too loudly and let the sweet-rotten odor of their pot drift down the hallways. Marly had never complained to the manager, not once. Because she was a good neighbor, she told herself. Because she still remembered what it was like to be young and fun rather than soft-hipped and stretched-out, exuding a warm milky-pee smell.

The knocking again, loud and insistent.

Ol' Pants Leg, Marly thought.

It was stupid (and probably classist and playing into exactly the sort of ethnic stereotype that Marly planned to rail against in her dissertation), but Marly thought of her. The curse. That dumb story.

Marly pictured her there waiting, just on the other side of the door: an older woman, in her sixties, with long, thick gray hair in a frizzled ponytail. A strong-featured, almost Mediterranean-looking face with a large mouth and wide dark eyes. She'd be wearing a loose tunic and big open sweater, her painter's pants cuffed to the knee, the right leg cuffed much higher, like a bicyclist. She'd be waiting there expectantly, waiting to make good on her curse. To steal the baby.

Marly hadn't told John, but she'd seen Ol' Pants Leg once. She often saw people in the city whom she imagined to be the nicknamed characters from the ER stories (terrible, probably, to think of them as *characters*, but that's what the stories turned them into). The cursing man with the brown bag always wandering by the downtown Hilton, for example—Eye Patch? The skinny, grimy, too-young kid pestering people for change between lanes of traffic on MLK—Heroin Justin Bieber? One day, when Marly had been leaving the Whole Foods by the harbor, guiltily clutching her bag of overpriced organic produce and truffles, she'd seen Ol' Pants Leg: an elderly woman pushing a rusted bicycle along the walkway and hurling angry gibberish at the seagulls. Marly had turned and headed the other direction.

There was the knocking again.

Pressing the baby against her, Marly backed away from the door—as if it might suddenly swing open. It couldn't, though. It was locked. She definitely kept it locked.

The baby whimpered, and Marly flushed. She was just as bad as John's doctor friends, with their quips, their dehumanizing nicknames, their brutal efficiency.

Marly tiptoed over to the door and squinted through the peephole.

The person outside moved closer, so close that Marly at first could make nothing out.

A finger jabbed at the peephole. Accusingly, Mary thought, flinching, then reminding herself whoever was there couldn't see her. The floor creaked loudly.

"I know you're there, darling," a woman's voice said in response. "I know you're standing there, just behind the door. I'm sorry it's so late."

Marly shifted, balancing her weight on the old floorboards and praying for the baby's continued silence. The woman's voice was low and raspy and somehow familiar. She spoke with a strange authority.

"Open the door please, darling," she said. "I need your help."

Marly pressed her eye up to the peephole again, and now she could see who stood there.

It wasn't Ol' Pants Leg. Of course it wasn't.

"Come on, darling," the woman said again. "Please, dear. I need your help."

It was a woman she'd seen in and around the building. Marly had passed her in the mailroom earlier that very day.

The woman was older, sallow-skinned with sparse gray hair and watery blue eyes. She was painfully thin—the kind of thin that is the result of either chronic illness or drugs or both. She had the look of someone who'd stopped attending to details. Her clothes were stained and mismatched, and she had dirty fingernails. But one shouldn't make assumptions, thought Marly. Maybe she was an artist—a potter. A starving windowbox gardener.

"Please," the woman repeated. She was so skinny it hurt to look at her. When she lifted her ropy arm, Marly could see every tendon, every scar. "Open the door."

The woman studied the door, waiting for some kind of response. Marly counted silently, peering out the peephole.

"I know it's late," the woman said. "But you owe me."

Marly understood what the words meant: that day the man had grabbed her. This woman had intervened.

There was a liquor store a block down from their apartment building, and a group of loud men often congregated there. Marly usually hurried past them, head down, and wasn't bothered. Once, though, when Marly had been walking home with the baby in his stroller, one of these men had approached her, leering, calling for her. And then he'd grabbed her arm. Marly had shrieked, jerking away, but the man had just gripped tighter. The skinny lady had been standing at the corner, holding a rumpled bouquet of flowers in cellophane and smoking a cigarette. She'd seen what was happening and scurried toward them. "Get!" the woman had ordered the man, who was obviously intoxicated. She'd swung her frail fist at him, landing a feeble punch against his torso, and then swung the bouquet of flowers—a damp, flaccid weapon that the woman rendered somehow threatening—into the man's face, shouting, "You stink like liquor! Get! Leave this poor girl and her baby alone!" As small as she was, there was something fierce and unhinged about her. The man looked startled. He'd released Marly's arm and slunk off accordingly. At the time, Marly had assumed this woman, the Flower Lady, was a benevolent figure—a kind of homeless guardian angel (was that politically incorrect? Insensitive? Marly wasn't sure). "It's no trouble," the Flower Lady had said. "You just make sure that baby boy keeps growing big and strong. A good big strong baby boy." Marly had smiled gratefully. It was only later that she'd started noticing the Flower Lady walking down their block, or standing outside the building, smoking a cigarette. She felt better knowing that this woman was a kind of ally. The city in which they lived was rough; you didn't forget that, even in its nicer parts.

Marly felt a pang of guilt. The baby was warm and heavy in her arms.

"I helped you," the Flower Lady said, "and now I need help."

This woman had stood up for her, had stepped in and protected her. For the first time, Marly risked answering.

"Need help how?" she asked.

"I'm locked out of my apartment, of course," the Flower Lady said. "What do you think? And I don't have my phone. My phone's locked in the damned apartment."

"Can I call someone for you?" Marly asked. "My baby just went to sleep."

"Could you open the door?" the Flower Lady asked bluntly, her voice edged with irritation this time. "Please. For god's sake. Just open the goddamn door. I won't bite."

Marly backed away, pressing the baby against her heart, as if to quell its quickening.

"No," Marly said, whispering at first. "I mean, I'm not exactly dressed." She heard the Flower Lady shift her weight and sigh.

"Oh, darling," she said, her raspy voice softening again. "I've scared you. I didn't mean to scare you."

"Let me call someone," Marly suggested. "How about that?"

"Just open the door a teeny-tiny bit, sweetheart," the Flower Lady said. "Keep the chain on if you like."

The woman smiled, and Marly saw she had the most amazing set of teeth. Her teeth were big and square and white, like a Texas cheerleader's. They did not match the rest of her at all.

"I need to put something else on," Marly said, opening the door a crack but keeping the chain on as the woman had suggested. "And put the baby down."

The Flower Lady smiled faintly and pressed her index finger to her jaw. "Ah, there you are, dear. That's better than talking to a door. I guess we haven't been formally introduced. I'm Lara, but people call me Flip. Childhood nickname. We've seen each other in passing." She tilted her head, indicating the mailroom, it seemed, and smiled again, revealing once more her mouthful of big, toothpaste-commercial teeth.

Marly pressed her forehead against the doorframe. She was so tired. So, so tired. She didn't feel like being here now, having this conversation. The baby was sleeping. This was her chance, her moment to steal away, to go to sleep herself. And it was being ruined.

"Couldn't I just step in for a bit, sweetheart? Darling dear?" the woman said, her voice soft and hushabye now. "I'll call my cousin, and while I wait, I can tend that sweet big boy you've got there. I'm very good with babies. I'll take good care. Like he's my own. And you can get some rest."

The woman's voice was rough but soothing. Again Marly remembered her words after the incident in front of the liquor store: *make sure that baby boy keeps growing big and strong. A good big strong baby boy.* She did seem fond of babies. Taking her time, Marly closed the door again, removing the chain. The baby made a tiny squeak in her arms. She closed her eyes for just a moment. It was possible, Marly thought, that she could go to sleep right there. All of a sudden, after all her exhausted insomnia, she felt that sleep might finally overwhelm her, drowning out the woman's voice, the street sounds, everything. She'd just sleep standing up, like a horse.

She must have waited too long, because the woman outside seemed to think she'd changed her mind. Flip let out a loud sigh.

"How's that for neighborly. You fucking bitch," Flip, said, careful and calm, as if she were merely making a scientific observation. "You selfish fucking bitch. I'm locked out of my goddamned apartment, and you won't even open the door to help."

Marly jolted upright again, a sense of panic triggered by the woman's words. She wasn't selfish, was she? She wasn't. It was almost 4 a.m. She wasn't dressed. There was a strange woman at the door. She had a baby.

"No, no, I'm helping. I want to help you," Marly said. She was a good person, a person who helped others, who believed in the fundamental goodness of her fellow man and woman. "Please. Just hold on. Let me put the baby down. Let me get dressed."

Marly stood there, motionless, her eyes closed for one second. Two seconds. Three.

And then, very quickly, she put the baby down in his bassinet and went to the bedroom to change.

Once she'd put on a clean shirt, she returned to the door, took a breath, and opened it wide.

The woman stood there beaming at her. She threw her arms around Marly.

"I knew it," she said, walking into the living room. "I knew you'd let me in. I knew you would."

Marly nodded, handing the woman her cell phone. The Flower Lady, or Lara, or Flip, or whoever she was, did not smell good, Marly noted. A sour, unwashed odor clung to her—but maybe that was unfair. People had different standards, after all. And, Marly admitted to herself, she felt guilty for having once assumed this woman was homeless. Not that there was anything ignoble in that, but, well . . .

Flip punched numbers into the phone, stepping into the kitchen to talk.

"It's me." Marly heard her say. "Yeah, I need the spare. . . . Yeah . . . Well, hurry up. . . . Yeah, where I said I'd be . . . Oh, yeah, that's great."

When she returned, handing Marly the phone, Marly asked her, "Can I get you a glass of water or anything?"

Flip didn't answer immediately, instead walking a circuit in the small living room, as if appraising the place. She sat down in the blue recliner in the corner of the room as if she were relieved finally to be home after a long day at work. Crossing her arms behind her head, she looked up at Marly.

"No, dear," she said. "I'm just fine. You'll want to charge the phone, though. The battery is low." She nodded to the cell phone in Marly's hand, and indeed, the bar was short. "This is a nice place you have here. Cozy."

Marly was suddenly aware of the squalor of their apartment. Flip had seen the pile of food-encrusted dishes in the sink, the thick film of dust on every shelf, the burp cloths strewn all over the floor. Marly gestured to the phone and walked quickly to the hallway near their bedroom, plugging it into its charger. As she did so, she pushed a pile of dirty clothes to one corner.

"It's such a mess," Marly muttered, as much to herself as to the woman when she returned to the living room. "Such a mess. I'm sorry. It's embarrassing."

"No need to be embarrassed," Flip said, sweeping her arm across the room. "This is just fine. It's perfect, really. You have an infant, for goodness' sake."

On cue, the baby sputtered from his bassinet, and Marly tiptoed over to him. His eyes were closed still, and he appeared to be nursing in his sleep. She was aware now of how awkward she felt with this strange woman in her apartment in the wee hours. She longed to pick the baby back up as a means of distraction from the burden of making conversation.

She paused, uncertain, her hands fluttering just above the bassinet.

When she looked up, Flip was standing right there.

"Let me," Flip said, scooping the baby into her arms. She did it with an easy knowingness. The baby sighed and settled himself into the woman's embrace.

"You sit down," Flip continued. "Better yet, lie down. I'll make you something hot to drink. And you can rest. I've got the baby, don't you worry. You just rest until my cousin gets here."

Marly obeyed helplessly. She was so tired. She sat on the couch, watching as Flip walked to the kitchen and effortlessly put the kettle on with one arm, the baby cradled comfortably in the other. Flip, the guardian angel from the liquor store, had the baby, and the baby was sleeping, and so Marly decided she might as well lie down.

She was reclining on the couch when Flip brought her a hot mug. Marly took it.

"Herbal tea," Flip said. Marly must have looked skeptical. "Sleepytime," the woman added. "You had it in the cabinet."

Marly took a sip. Plain old Celestial Seasonings. She lay back down, her head on the soft arm of the sofa, curling her knees. It felt good just to close her eyes for a minute. She could hear Flip murmuring quietly to the baby. It was soothing, her murmuring, and so Marly let herself rest.

*　*　*

There was a shout outside the window. Marly jolted upright on the couch. Someone—the woman, Flip, she guessed—had put a blanket over her.

The baby let out a howl from the bassinet. Marly went to him and hoisted him up, jiggling him against her. She felt groggy. The room was cold. The baby was cold too, his little fists icy. Marly snuggled him closer, warming him as she walked to the window.

Their apartment looked out on the street. They were on the first floor, just above street level, overlooking a bus stop. People could be so loud there. They heard bus-stop conversations and arguments all the time.

Marly looked out the window and saw children.

One, two, three, four, five of them. No, six. Seven. One more. A gang of them. Eight. An octet.

Romani, Marly thought, shaking her head to clear it. But the children remained. Dark-haired and dark-eyed. Gypsy children.

There was another shout. One of the children whooped, swinging on the bus sign. They wore oversized winter coats, their dark eyes gleaming from under winter hats.

They were looking up at her, Marly saw. They were grinning right at her. They were waving, trying to get her attention. Their grins, Marly realized now, were menacing. Little bandits. A pack of feral kids.

There were no Romani in this city, and yet Marly knew them with unwavering certainty. One of them whooped again. Another shouted. Another answered, in a kind of whooping call-and-response. A war cry.

Marly lifted her free hand and waved tentatively.

She turned to say something to Lara or Flip or whoever she was, but the woman was gone. Maybe her cousin had already come. Maybe she'd left after Marly had fallen asleep.

One of the children outside waved back at Marly, and she felt something—a tiny, terrifying thrill. Real gypsy children! Outside the window! Waving to her.

And then the child's wave changed—he was flipping her off. His face transformed into that of a sneering teenage boy. A kid from the neighborhood. She recognized him vaguely. Now the one climbing the pipe let out a whoop. Marly looked down at him, and he stared back up at her, his mouth jackal-wide, before leaping back to the ground.

Teenagers. Non-gypsy. She'd seen many of them roaming the neighborhood. Realizing this, it seemed impossible she'd mistaken them for gypsy children before—it was the darkness, their bulky winter clothes, her own preoccupied mind. . . .

The tallest kid flung a small rock at the glass, and Marly instinctively ducked. It clattered but did no damage. The windows were double-plated.

The baby shuddered against her. Marly stepped back and stopped, frozen in the center of the room. She wanted either to laugh or to cry. The baby did cry. He melted into sobbing fury in her arms. She bounced him gently, torn as to whether to walk toward the window or away from it.

She could hear them, the pack of teenagers, talking and laughing outside. The baby continued to wail.

She needed to put him down. She needed her hands free. She needed to call John. John. Dependable, dependable John. She would call him at work.

She placed the baby down gently into his bassinet. He lashed his head from side to side, furious. Marly ran to the hallway to get the phone.

With trembling fingers, she called John's cell from the darkness of the hallway. In the living room, the baby screamed, the old radiator rattled, and the teenagers were laughing and swearing outside the building. The phone rang and rang, but John didn't answer. She thumbed through her address book until she found the number John had given her for the physician's workroom. She'd call him there instead.

The phone rang only once.

"Hello?" a voice said. The voice did not belong to John. The voice belonged to Laurel.

"He—hello," Marly stuttered. "It's Marly. Is John there?"

"Oh, Marly," Laurel said. "Of course he is. He's right here. Busy night. He had to call me in for backup. We've got ten people unseen right now. Got patients sitting in chairs out in overflow."

Marly nodded into the phone. There was a ruffling of papers, muffled talking. In the background, Marly thought she heard her husband laugh quietly.

"Hello?" he said into the phone. "Marly? Is everything all right?" He sounded so calm and competent. She'd almost forgotten that about her husband—that he was so competent, so calm, practical. So unmoved by strong emotion.

She no longer knew what to say. *There was a stranger here tonight, a strange woman. Come home, please. Please, please, come home.*

Marly sighed. She was so very tired. It was as though she hadn't slept at all. Not for a minute. It occurred to her she had no sense of how much time had passed since Flip had been there, or since she'd left.

"I got scared," she said, suddenly aware that the apartment was now perfectly quiet. "I missed you."

"I'm here," John said, his voice calm as ever. But different. It was the voice he used with his patients. A voice of practiced but detached soothing.

"A neighbor came," Marly said. "She needed help. She was locked out."

"That was nice of you," John said. He sounded remote, as if he were hundreds of miles away, even though she knew the hospital was just down the road.

She nodded into the phone, as if her husband could see that.

"The baby's all right?" John asked. "How's my little guy?"

The baby. Marly walked quickly, holding the cell phone to her ear, back to the living room. The baby now lay sleeping in the bassinet, his tiny tummy moving up and down. Peaceful as an angel.

"He's fine," Marly said. "He's perfect. He's sound asleep."

"Well, you get some sleep too. Now's your chance," John said. His voice was unusually bright for the tail end of an overnight shift. Laurel said something indistinct, her voice like caramel in the background. "I'll be home soon," John said. "Get some rest."

"I will," Marly said, and hung up the phone.

The room was still cold, so Marly grabbed a swaddling blanket to wrap around the baby. As she walked past the door, she peered out the peephole once. There was no one. All was quiet.

And back in the living room, that's when she noticed it: her laptop. It was gone. Her laptop with all her notes, all her research.

It had been sitting on the small breakfast table, a fresh, blank document open on the screen like an accusation. She'd emailed herself her notes several months ago but hadn't backed up anything recently.

So much work. *Gone.* She almost laughed.

She grabbed her purse from the small table near the couch and groped inside. Her wallet was missing.

Marly did laugh now—a harsh, admiring laugh from the darkest corner of herself. Of course. Who, after all, would want a newborn when he or she could have a wallet and a laptop? She was too tired to weep, too tired to mourn what she had, through her own willful blindness, already lost.

At the bassinet, she bent and lifted the baby. He grunted, a soft, milk-heavy weight. She spread the blanket and repositioned him on it to swaddle him.

He looked different. The streetlight outside cast an orangey glow across his face, rendering his features somehow strange. His cheeks seemed less round, his brow slightly more furrowed, his chin sharper. The nose was off, like it had been recast from a different mold. He smacked his lips once in a gesture Marly did not recognize. It was a trick of the light, she knew. She was smart enough to know that.

There were terms for all of it, the tricks of the brain that caused you not to know the people you thought you knew, that led the world to seem unreal: *agnosia, derealization, Capgras syndrome, Frégoli syndrome, depersonalization.* Her husband had taught her all of this because she'd been interested. This is where she had an advantage over the poor mother in Cumbria; this was what the poor mother in Cumbria hadn't realized.

Maybe the woman at her door had been Ol' Pants Leg, transformed (*intermetamorphosis,* John would say; that was the term). But what did that matter?

The truth was that no pathology was required. Familiar people turned into something strange, something wholly different every day. Bit by bit, we are all rendering ourselves unrecognizable, Marly thought. She touched the baby's cool forehead, stroking his little cheek.

That's my sweet baby, Marly said to herself. *That's my precious boy. My John. My baby. I made you. You are made of me.*

The baby grimaced in his sleep.

Marly shivered.

She realized then why the room was so cold.

Taking care not to wake the baby, she padded quickly over to the window to pull it shut.

THE PRIVATE COLLECTION

There are stories Marvin likes to tell now that he is rich. When you have everything, you sometimes like to remind people you once had nothing. He believes, maybe, that this imparts a lesson of some sort, to his graduate students in particular. *I, too, was once a creature of hunger.* You would not know it from the house he shares with Lucinda, its stunning view of the ocean, the chef's kitchen and marble staircase. So much open space and clean light. It all tastes of success. He and Lucinda keep their walls bare. A deliberate choice. His own art is secreted away in his studio, selling for god-knows-what now, but plenty—figures that, when mentioned directly, almost embarrass him. What's true is that he does not have to teach these occasional graduate seminars; it's a matter of principle.

Near the end of each semester, he invites his students over for a long, wine-soaked dinner on the back terrace. He is generous now that he can afford to be. Lucinda, too, is a gracious host, rising on her soft bare feet to fill everyone's glasses and replenish the plates of charcuterie and cheeses. She is beautiful even now, while he is proud, leonine.

After the sun sets and everyone's eyes have softened with red wine, he tells stories, some from his early days as an artist. Every so often, he tells one in particular. It's a story that Lucinda has heard many times before, a story that makes her mouth tighten, one she'd prefer he not tell. It is a story he knows holds something within it, though what that is, he cannot discern. For years, the wisdom within the story has remained, despite his retelling, opaque.

During Marvin's final term of art school, things were not going well. He was nervous and bug-eyed, overeager, and his professors did not particularly like him. He had just broken up with a girl named Melanie, and afterwards he seemed to run into her everywhere. Melanie was beautiful and wild. She'd been the first in her family to go to college, on a music scholarship. After the breakup, Marvin had heard that Melanie was no longer going to class, no longer showing up to rehearsal, using pills, vomiting up her food. When he saw her, she was busking: a beautiful, bedraggled girl, rawboned and rank, playing her viola on the street. Like a fallen character in an opera. When Marvin spotted Melanie and her viola, he'd turned the other way. The sight shamed him. Yet who could help falling out of love? Or never having loved to start with? It was not his fault, of course, not entirely—but still he understood he was meant to take the blame.

It was time for the senior exit show, and now, without Melanie, Marvin had no guests to invite. His parents were far away in Minnesota, practical people, uninterested in the manner in which he'd chosen to waste his education. He had a few friends, but it seemed an act of self-indulgence to request their presence. So he invited no one, awaiting the show with a sense of resignation, the way one might anticipate a dental procedure.

That night, he wore a white button-front shirt with a blue tie his father had bought him. He wet a comb and tried to press down his cowlick. In the mirror, he gazed back at himself: blinking and idiotic, a farmboy parading in his father's clothes.

When he arrived to the arts center, he headed straight for a small table set up with refreshments and grabbed a plastic cup of red wine.

His work was at the farthest corner of the space, a position that, he understood, meant he was unfavored by his professors. Marvin's preoccupation at the time was the human form, and so his work was filled with naked bodies: bodies strewn against other naked bodies. Landscapes and seas of naked bodies. Naked bodies arranged in such a way as to become almost abstracted, lines and hillocks of flesh. He never had a shortage of volunteers. College students, young and nubile and firm, were never shy about signing up for group nudity, particularly if he provided complimentary beer. They posed en masse, uninhibited, for Marvin, heedless of how briefly perfect they all were.

So Marvin stationed himself in front of his wall of naked bodies with a cup of wine. (He would later tell his students that, in retrospect, his work was really not bad—visually arresting, if a little naïve. These early works were highly coveted now, praised for their formal inventiveness.) Parents and friends of his classmates wandered through, many of them making their way down to his end of the room for a cursory look. Polite. He shook hands perfunctorily with an associate dean. A French professor praised his work sincerely. Most of the time, however, Marvin stood there, awkward in his name tag, watching the passersby mill about, forgetful of him.

The show was almost over when the man in the Hawaiian shirt entered the building. He was loud. His booming voice and laughter cut to Marvin at the far end of the room. He had a bushy yellowish-white beard and wore a jaunty driver's cap and a blue shirt exploding with floral print. He was in a wheelchair, and he moved across the floor like it was a sedan and he was royalty.

"Stunning, stunning!" the man announced to no one in particular as he passed a piece by one of Marvin's classmates.

Now the room was at attention. This man, oblivious of the respectful hush everyone else seemed to honor, was moving through making pronouncements as if he were a visiting dignitary, some of them no more than a "Hmm" or a dismissive shake of his head. Marvin felt himself, his classmates, all tilt toward this strange man like young stalks toward sunlight. They yearned for it—his approval, his critique—just as they'd been trained. Marvin wondered if the man was a critic, a collector, some sort of arbiter of taste. Maybe a gallerist one of the professors had invited? Collectors, gallerists—they too were allowed to be eccentrics.

The man in his wheelchair moved with an entourage now. People clustered behind him, waiting to see what pieces he found of interest. The man helped himself to two quick swigs of wine and a handful of cheese sticks, proclaiming them "Delightful!" And then, he was approaching Marvin.

"My word!" the man exclaimed. He swept one thick hand forward as if to touch one of Marvin's pieces. Marvin blushed and stuttered, stepping to the side. The room was quiet now, awaiting the judgment.

"Mmm-hmm, mmm-hmm," he said, nodding to each of Marvin's pieces individually, as if making their acquaintance. "You, sir. You, young man. This is your work?"

Marvin's throat was dry. He'd gone red in the face, sweating, preemptively tasting humiliation.

"Yessir," he managed to whisper.

"Captivating!" the man bellowed. "Allow me to shake your hand. I'm a collector, see. Always on the lookout for new talent. And this, my God, this!" The man threw his hands up. He spoke in the vaguely transatlantic way of old movie actors, and his handshake was sticky and over-firm. Marvin wanted to wipe his palm off afterward but didn't dare.

Now Marvin's classmates were clustered around, actual envy on their faces. Marvin could barely think. He was accustomed to being overlooked, or, when acknowledged, treated as a mild social irritant.

"Here," the man said. "My card. I'd like you to see my private collection. We can discuss your work. Friday at seven?"

Marvin could do nothing at that moment but nod, dumbstruck, grateful.

* * *

These days, Marvin can tally all his regrets because there are so few: the time he shoved a cousin and broke his collarbone, an early painting he sold for $100 that went on to be worth $25,000, the woman he treated badly before he met Lucinda. And perhaps the man in the Hawaiian shirt. Although how could he have possibly known? Then again, how could he *not* have known?

What he did know as he drove was that he was in the bad part of town. Sad, slumping houses with No Trespassing signs, skinny dogs tied to stakes. The college town they lived in was pleasant and medium-sized, but in its outskirts lived the real locals. Townies. People who often were employed by the university in some custodial capacity. Groundskeepers, cafeteria workers, janitors. This was where, Marvin knew, Melanie's friends drove out to buy drugs— dumb drugs for dumb college kids—pot mostly, occasional benzos.

It did not, in short, look like a neighborhood where an art collector or tastemaker of any sort would live.

Marvin felt silly now, the collar of his shirt scratching him at the neck. He'd dressed up, the way his mother would have expected him to dress for a church supper. He wore imbecilic loafers. He'd borrowed his roommate's car and nestled his portfolio (in the sleek leather case that Melanie had bought for him before their breakup) on the seat beside him like a passenger.

When he pulled up to the address on the card, his sense of misgiving only deepened. The house was small, shabby, with a weedy yard. A full garbage bag was propped next to a rake on the front porch. The air smelled of trash and soot, like someone had been burning things—not the good, clean smell of burning leaves but a toxic smell, gasoline and charred plastic and diapers.

He should have left then, but it would have seemed a waste, a failure. He would have been embarrassed to have returned to his roommates so soon. And there were his nagging midwestern manners. If one accepted an invitation, one showed up. Besides, he still had the tiniest lingering hope that this man, despite all appearances, was somehow legitimate.

When he knocked on the door, he heard the man's voice from within.

"Come in, come in!"

Marvin entered, clutching his portfolio like a shield. The house was cluttered and dark and narrow.

"Welcome! I'm preparing something delectable, my good fellow," the man continued, and Marvin turned a corner, entering the kitchen. "A delicious repast."

The man was stirring something in a pot. Marvin was surprised he could navigate the tight space in his wheelchair. A strong odor of beef and onions rose and mingled with other smells, smells of sweat and unwashed human crevices. Junk obstructed the hallways, old boxes and trinkets piled in odd towers. A hoarder, Marvin thought. He'd been invited into the home of a hoarder.

"Thank you for having me, Mr. Heggerty," Marvin said, remembering the man's name from his card.

"Hans," the man said, ladling grim brownish stew into two bowls. "Call me Hans, please. Marvin." He handed Marvin the two bowls and gestured for him to follow.

Hans moved through his claustrophobic house with impressive ease. Marvin was vaguely disoriented as he navigated the dim hall leading to the back of the house, where they swept through a glass door onto a small deck. Being outside again was a relief. Marvin sank gratefully into a deck chair.

"Bon appetit."

"Oh, no, thank you. Getting over a stomach bug." Marvin blushed as he said it, wondering if he'd offended Hans, who merely nodded, spooning himself up a large bite.

They sat in silence for a few moments while Hans ate. When he'd consumed most of his stew, he set his bowl down and leaned back in his wheelchair, stretching.

"Now," he said, "we talk." He tilted his head toward Marvin, and reflexively, Marvin leaned in closer, like a coconspirator.

"I'm not really an art collector. At least, not in the sense I implied. I do collect art. I have a real interest in it. But unfortunately, with my financial situation, I'm not in a position to acquire more at present." He paused, stroking his beard before continuing. "What I'd like to offer you is an opportunity. I'd like to invite you to take part in an art project. A project of the body. My body."

Hans looked at Marvin intently, and then lifted his shirt. "Behold." His sagging abdomen bore raw pinkish scars like seams. Baggies and tubes of greenish fluid and brown water seemed to extrude, as if his internal organs were leaking out. A few strips of gauze were stuck to his chest, seeping clearish pink fluid. There was a sweetish odor, like rot.

Later, when Marvin had grown older and dealt with the decline of both his parents, he would realize that what he was probably looking at were surgical drains and ostomy bags, but at the time, he could not comprehend what he saw. He only knew it meant sickness, something foul.

"I'm dying," Hans announced rather cheerfully, smoothing his shirt back down over his big belly. "I'd like to invite you to do a series of portraits of my body as I die. A death sequence."

Marvin coughed, nodding slowly. As if to give him time to consider, Hans retrieved his bowl and spooned up another bite of stew. The beard around his mouth was stained reddish.

"Wow," Marvin said slowly. "I don't know how to respond." He was aware of how inane he sounded. The idea was appalling. The idea was also the sort that could make a person's reputation.

"Oh, indeed." Hans spoke with relish. "Imagine how much interest you'll generate. Particularly after I'm gone. And I'll spare you no details—you'll have it all, blood, shit, and viscera."

"Thank you." Marvin did not know what else to say. He wished very much that he had a glass of water, something to wet his lips with, but he didn't trust the dirty plates and cups he'd seen in Hans's kitchen.

Hans laughed now, slapping his knees like he'd just remembered the most hilarious joke. "It's the natural progression, really. I've seen your work—all those kids, splayed out, naked as the day they were born. A body dying. It's the obvious next step."

Marvin nodded again. He could smell the meaty stew on Hans's breath. Something churned inside him, and he felt the urge to be sick. "Do you have a bathroom I could use?"

Hans shrugged. There was a long moment during which he did not answer, and Marvin thought he sensed a shift, a wariness. But when Hans responded, his voice was genteel, jolly as ever. "But of course. Down the hall to the end, on the right."

Marvin likes to pause here. It's a good moment to refresh his drink, which he does, plunking in two ice cubes, just as he prefers. Lucinda is semi-recumbent on the chaise lounge, smiling at him wearily but patiently. The grad students are abuzz, refilling their plates with second slices of the apricot tart Lucinda has magicked from somewhere. Everyone is a little bit drunk. He grabs Lucinda's lovely ankle, proprietary, benevolent, and presses his thumb into her instep, massaging it.

"I'd definitely say yes to something like that," one of the grad students remarks. "How could you not?"

"You did it, didn't you, Marvin?" another asks. "Surely you did it."

They speak to one another as colleagues. He insists on it, though the students are often shy at first. But by the evening of this dinner, they have usually found their ease.

He shrugs, taking a sip of his drink. All this, all that surrounds him, it is his. He looks out to a set of distant red lights blinking from the ocean. The story isn't finished yet.

Marvin slid open the glass door and stepped into the cloying darkness of the house to find the bathroom. He immediately ran into a chair, tipping it over. A woman's brown wig landed on his feet. He shuddered, moving gingerly through that hallway and its towers of knickknacks and old appliances, the sag-bellied mattress propped against the wall. There seemed to be no windows anywhere, giving the house the cramped gloom of a cavern. A few wobbly antique lamps cast dim circles of light here and there.

As his eyes adjusted, Marvin could see that hanging all along the walls were photographs. Bodies: black and brown and white, young and old, men and women. Children. There was something wrong with the photos. Marvin wondered what it was that was so unsettling about the faces in them, and then he understood: they were dead. These people had been photographed postmortem. They were cadavers, the images mortuarial. Marvin knew this with a sinking certitude.

And there, at the end of the hallway, stood a kind of altar. There was no other word for it. An old dresser was covered in little candles and more photos. Marvin lifted one and felt a rush of familiarity. He picked up another photo, and another. The images on the dresser were posed nudes, of living people—people he knew, or at least had seen around town. Faces recognizable to anyone who went to the university: the man who begged for money outside the movie theater, the girl with her scruffy dog who was always camped out at the park, the one-armed veteran who drank endless cups of coffee at the diner. There they were, supine or standing, naked and defiant-eyed.

And there was Melanie: unclothed, sitting cross-legged, holding her viola in her lap.

Marvin's hands shook as he put the photo down.

He'd left the house after that, never even making it to the bathroom. He'd left Hans all alone on his deck, wondering what had become of Marvin. This is how the story always ends.

Is there a moral to this story? After all these years, Marvin does not know, but he still tells it over and over again. And it's a story to which the grad students respond with a kind of recognition. Maybe they are thinking *There are risks one must take for art*, or *Watch out for people promising too much*, or *We all make difficult decisions as creators*. Every time, though, at least one student will remain undeterred.

Tonight, it is the quiet, skinny one with the blondish beard who speaks: "I would have said yes anyway."

Whatever the point is, Marvin understands that this student has missed it—all the terrible awkwardness and foreboding of the situation. This student is not an artist but a carrion bird. Or maybe not a carrion bird but a hero. Marvin is no longer certain he can tell the difference.

Lucinda does not like to hear this story at all. "I feel sorry for him," she says afterward, placing a pile of dishes into the sink. "A dying man. He couldn't help that he was strange. Perverted, maybe. It's still sad."

Marvin nods. How else can he describe the experience? Being young and stepping into the maw of something, something inevitable, too soon. The rot of the man's house, its underworld quality—it has lingered with him.

He is famous now, but not for his figurative work. He abandoned nudes not long after this meeting with Hans. His work became abstract, broad swaths of color and shape.

There is one detail he has never included in the story. Neither when telling his students nor Lucinda. One part he's kept to himself: He did not immediately leave Hans's house after encountering the weird altar and all those photos. He'd realized his portfolio was still out on the deck. He couldn't leave it. He'd walked back to the deck to get it.

And there, he saw Hans sprawled on his back like an upended tortoise. While reaching for something, he'd slipped out of his wheelchair, Marvin understood. His drink had tipped over, and the glass lay shattered on the wood. He was attempting to maneuver himself with one arm back into his wheelchair.

He was weeping.

It was a horrible sight. Grotesque. A red-faced old man, hideous in his very helplessness. Hans's shirt had fallen back, revealing once again the grayish-yellow bruising on his belly, the baggie of brown fluid, the tubing flecked with blood.

"Help me," Hans muttered. "Help."

Gone were his plummy vowels, gone the accent that hinted he was landed gentry.

"Don't leave me," Hans whispered, hand outstretched. "Please."

Marvin stood there, hesitating only a moment.

"You're just like me," Hans muttered.

And Marvin had grabbed his portfolio and walked away. No. Truthfully, he'd run.

For years, even as Marvin has accumulated the world that is now his, gleaming and bright and spare, he has worried about Hans's words, which have rattled in his head like an old curse. It is only now, as he enters his late seventies, with his new high-tech hip and the scars from two stents, that he thinks what the man had offered him was really more of a dark riddle.

This is what he thinks tonight, at least, the muddy moon low over the ocean outside their bay windows, waves breaking into froth on the beach below, and Lucinda sleeping, fragrant and oblivious beside him. He rises from his bed to pace, grateful that the walls are high and bare.

He does not know it yet, but tonight is the last night Lucinda will be present for one of these gatherings. Tonight is the last time he will feel a need to tell this story. A black thread is already tugging, but neither of them could possibly know. And for now, it does not matter. Lucinda is there, sleeping with her long, perfect limbs askew, as elegant as if he'd posed her. She appears so young to him still, especially at rest. Marvin brushes a strand of hair from her forehead before stepping out to their back terrace.

Waves bash the shore below, obliterating themselves again and again, then reforming.

He stands there with a drink in his hand, breathing.

FOX FOOT

I saw the man on the side of the road years after I'd heard about him. So much time had elapsed since that first mention that I had only the vaguest sense of how I recognized him, like recalling something from a dream. *There he is,* I remember thinking. *The man with the cast.* And there he was, leaning with one hip cocked, very casual, against the side of a battered orange truck. He smiled faintly, as if he'd been expecting me. Plaster encircled the entirety of his left leg, toe to hip. I slowed the car to a crawl. The man waved.

It was late June, the evening sky snarled with low tangles of pink and orange. I was almost finished with my intern year in Baltimore, returning home during a rare stretch of time off to attend a wedding. I was preoccupied by a single fact playing over and over in my head like a sick song: I had recently killed someone.

The man in the cast nodded, grinning like we knew each other, like we'd made an arrangement to meet here. I found myself nodding back reflexively.

The person I'd killed was an old lady—bird-boned, terse, in and out of the hospital with multiple medical problems, on opiates for compression fractures in her spine. She'd been admitted most recently for bowel obstruction, and we'd held her Coumadin in anticipation of possible surgery. She had a history of A-fib; she had a history of everything. That's probably why I'd forgotten she also had a mechanical valve. After I'd discharged her with her INR subtherapeutic, she'd thrown a clot and died. Her primary care doctor, one of the attendings who ran the geriatric clinic, called to tell me what happened. She'd yelled at me, confirming every fear I had about myself. I was a fool. The truth was, I'd also been distracted that day. I'd just gotten the email—a group email, friends from college—that Sabrina had finally died.

Later, the attending called back to apologize, but her apology was worse. *You're an intern*, she'd said, sighing. *You have to learn.* I tried not to consider all the other people, all the other mistakes I'd surely made that had gone unnoticed.

The man in the cast kept waving to me. We were at a small clearing on this wooded stretch of rural highway on the other side of Atlanta where it feels, briefly, like you've left civilization entirely. I'd grown up around here. The kudzu and scrub pines and weedy overgrowth along the sides of the roads had a haunted feeling. Stygian gloom. My college roommate, Sabrina, had grown up near here too.

Sabrina was the sort of person who, at age nineteen, lived a life of adventure. This involved many white lies and pushup bras, men buying her drinks while she entertained them with bawdy jokes, laughing, mocking, daring them. *Men love a pretty girl with a dirty mouth*, Sabrina told us. Her father was a genteel country lawyer who doted upon her; her mother, a former pageant queen. Sabrina was a classics major. *Smarter than I look*, she'd say with a wry wink, tossing off a reference to the Virgilian underworld. She could cut a handsy frat boy down to size in Latin. I quickly learned that I could trust about half of what she said, but even her lies were threaded with interesting bits of truth.

When Sabrina learned we were from the same part of Georgia, she'd asked me if I'd ever seen him—the man with the cast. One night, driving home for fall break, she'd spotted a man on the side of the road wearing a big cast that went up the length of one leg. She hadn't stopped. This was unusual for Sabrina, who was rarely hesitant about picking up amiable-looking hitchhikers or sharing her bed with strangers. *He made me uneasy*, she said, shrugging. Two months later, when she'd driven home for Christmas, she'd seen a man with a cast waiting at the exact same spot. The same man? She thought so, but couldn't be sure.

The story, sparse as it was, had given me an uneasy feeling too. Sabrina laughed during the telling, all of us girls gathered at the foot of her bunk bed in the dorm, drinking Boone's Farm and getting ready for a football game. *Bad people out there, girls*, she declared, taking a swig from the bottle and flashing a wicked, delicious smile. Sabrina was an Epicurean, she'd explained to us. She was the only person I've ever known who read Lucretius while taking shots.

I, on the other hand, was risk averse. More of a Stoic, Sabrina had once decided. And I was already late for a rehearsal dinner. My childhood best friend was getting married. She was marrying the top insurance broker in my home county. He'd grown up in the town adjacent to ours. His last name was the last name of county commissioners going back generations. The high school football stadium was named after his grandfather. I should have kept driving, kissed my friend on the cheek, and sat down next to well-appointed relatives in her fiancé's family. People would give toasts, and I would smile wearily, happy for my friend.

Instead, I held the man's gaze. I pulled the car onto the shoulder, and the man slapped a hand on the hood as one might pat a loyal horse after a long ride. I left the engine running, studying him to see if he had the face of a serial killer.

His nose was long and skinny. He had a small chin beginning to slope seamlessly into his neck. His sideburns were graying, and the sun damage on his face made it difficult to tell where he fell age-wise, some ambiguous place between young and old. He was the sort of man Sabrina would have cajoled into buying us all a round of drinks back during our Athens days. Maybe he was handsome. I couldn't tell. Intern year had thrown off my ability to gauge attractiveness. Aside from the leg, he appeared otherwise to be in moderate working order. I'd begun to assess human beings like this: as the sum of their machinery, a series of faulty parts, a disembodied sequence of faces floating above white bedsheets.

I rolled down my window, and the man maneuvered closer with a kind of unsteady hop. There was an old-fashioned quality to his cast, like it was a stage prop. Did they even make casts this big, this white, this bulky, anymore? His leg probably wasn't even broken: this was all a ploy.

"Having car trouble," the man announced brightly. His drawl was deeply familiar and, as such, comforting. He smiled at me again, as if it were some great stroke of luck, him having car trouble and my driving by just then.

"Is that right?" I said. I wasn't sure why I'd stopped, so I was stalling, speaking in a way that always made me feel like I was a skeptical sheriff in an old Western. *Is that right? Gosh. You don't say? Uh-huh. I see.* I'd picked up these little phrases during intern year, useful both in their open-endedness and the fact that you could fall back on them when you were in hour twenty-nine of a thirty-hour shift.

The man hop-dragged himself closer and put his hands on my passenger door, bracing himself on his good leg.

"Where ya headed?" he asked, but I could see he was studying the inside of my car, which was littered with old coffee cups and an embarrassing number of protein bar wrappers.

"I see you hurt your leg," I responded, another trick I'd learned. Deflection.

"Bad break. Needed surgery. Out of work for a spell." He brushed his hair from his forehead, sighing as if the very recollection of it all exhausted him. "Yep, I could sure use some help. Nice lady like you."

"I can call the highway patrol."

"Sure, sure. That'd be great."

He nodded as if this thought hadn't occurred to him. He turned for a moment, looking out across the field that stretched behind him to where the sun was just dipping below the distant tree line. I could acknowledge that this man might be appealing, to the right sort of woman. To Sabrina. Dangerous. I wondered what would happen if I never showed up to the rehearsal dinner or the wedding, if I didn't return for the final weeks of my intern year, never appeared for the first day of PGY-2. I imagined the mournful bleat of my pager going off endlessly, all those unanswered pages for PRN senna or Zofran or so-and-so's blood pressure. I'd be somewhere else, courting trouble. Me and Trouble, his hand in my back pocket. Up to no good.

"You're up to no good," I said, like my thoughts were escaping from the cage of my skull, leaking out of my mouth and into the air around me. My voice was even, but I wondered if he'd think I was joking with him. Flirting, maybe.

He laughed. "I suppose that means you wouldn't be willing to give me a ride to the next gas station. Highway patrol takes a real long time out here."

"How long have you been waiting?" I asked.

"Good while."

I noted he wasn't sweating. His shirt was pale yellow and completely dry. It was hot out, already like summer. Anyone ought to have broken a sweat.

"You're probably a serial killer." It felt like a challenge to say that, something Sabrina might have said. She'd not ended up in a good way. Despite the awards she'd received for translation, despite being the darling of the Classics Department, she never ended up graduating. I lost touch with her after junior year, but I heard from our other dormmates. She'd eventually stopped showing up for classes, all the while accumulating an abundance of nicer and nicer things—designer purses, jewelry, a cherry-red jeep. People saw a dark-haired man picking her up in the evenings. One night, driving back from the bars alone, she'd hit a tree head-on. She had to relearn to speak after that. Her mother eventually moved her to assisted living. You wouldn't have recognized her, people told me.

The man in the cast winked. "Bold one, aren't you." He said this flatly, more pronouncement than question.

I pushed the button and unlocked the passenger door, leaning over to open it. He held the frame of the car, lowering himself in, hoisting the bad leg. He grunted, as if in real pain. His eyes squeezed shut, and he looked older. I almost felt sorry for him. I wondered if I'd gotten the whole thing wrong. Had I become such a cynic, such a misreader of people? Intern year had hardened me. I was always so bone-weary, always craving sleep. Once, doing chest compressions during a hopeless code, I'd closed my eyes to rest them from the ache. You could usually tell which codes were really just practice for the interns. I'd felt relief when my senior resident had called that one. Another code called, one less patient on the census to round on. I could go lie down in the call room for fifteen minutes. It was a way of thinking that no one else in the world would want to hear about.

"You're thirsty," I said, and I handed him the tail end of my gas station Aquafina.

He took a grateful slug. "You're a peach."

I laughed because no one had ever called me that, though I'd grown up in a whole state of peaches. Peach this, peach that. A pretty girl was like a ripe fruit. I was more like a peach pit—the stubborn, hard center of something.

"I'm going to a wedding," I announced. "Assuming you don't murder me first."

Though I'd spent some portion of my time these past eleven months practicing the art of sussing out malingerers, I no longer trusted myself or anyone else. Desperate people claimed stomach pains and suicidality to get a bed, a sandwich, a few cc of Dilaudid. Tricksters, thieves, smiling devils. Had Sabrina really told me a story about a man waiting on the side of the road with a cast? I now doubted my memory. The recollection did feel like a dream, the sort I was prone to having. Déjà vu.

"Oh, I can't murder you," he said, grinning. "I'm headed somewhere special."

I raised an eyebrow.

"Place way out in the woods. Gotta make things right. Bit off more than I can chew, and now I owe some folks. And these are people you don't wanna be owing things to." He winced, shifting, lifting his leg in its cast gingerly to adjust its position. "So I gotta find this place, get what I need, settle things. Party a little bit. Everybody's happy."

I listened, my eyes tracking the tick tick tick of the yellow on the highway.

"They make you wait near exit 19. Somebody meets you and takes you the rest of the way."

He reached into his pants pocket and pulled out something small. I glanced to the side and saw a mass of reddish-gray fur.

"What is that?"

"Fox foot," he said, stroking the object gently. He chuckled. "This was my buddy's lucky charm. He gave it to me. My sign. Gotta show 'em a sign so they know you can be trusted. That somebody's vetted you." His voice had grown soft, almost wistful. For some reason, I shivered.

He noticed, and something speculative entered his gaze. "You could come with me," he said, sounding serious. "New start. New name, new ID, anything you want for a fee."

My eyes were too dry; they were welling up, watering. I blinked, pretending a greater focus on the road than I needed.

"You're a hard woman," he continued. "I could tell when you picked me up. We're alike, you and I."

I swiped at my eyes. He was insane. I'd picked up some kind of country-gothic smooth-talking swindler.

"You're full of shit," I said, but even I could hear the waver in my voice.

"Everybody's hunting for something," he said, his tone jocular again.

I laughed. A barking laugh, too loud, like it was uproariously funny, his suggestion.

My mind flashed to a memory of Sabrina as I'd known her, golden hair pulled back, one arm raised as she spoke, holding forth as she had often done late nights in our dorm—a kind of mock-lecture, a performance. Drunk, surely, entertaining us, regaling us with readings from her classes, translating as she went. She would pause in her monologues, offering us a swig of whatever she was drinking, eyeing us, implicating us each individually. It was a thing she did; we indulged her.

This particular night, though, she was drunker than I'd ever seen her. She'd just learned that her father had been indicted for tax fraud and embezzlement. We knew this meant ruin for her, her family. *"Most of us become like foxes, the sorriest of the lot. For what else is a spiteful, malicious man except a fox, or something even lower and less dignified?"*, she'd recited, waving her fist at the institutional gods, at the fates, at no one in particular. *So said Epictetus.*

The man in his cast sat beside me, silent, the fox foot perched on his good knee. I remembered Sabrina turning to me that night, wild-eyed with her liquor and her books, whispering, *You think you ever understand anyone, you're wrong.* She'd laughed, an empty, shallow sound. She was cupping something in her hand, offering it for me to behold: a tiny diamond on a delicate gold chain. My necklace, given to me by my grandmother. The one I kept hidden in a drawer beneath all my balled-up socks.

Can I borrow this, Emily? Sabrina asked, her voice still quiet, lacking her typical bravado. *I'll get it back to you. Promise.*

I wasn't sure what she intended, but the urgency in her face frightened me, repelled me even. I shook my head no. She let the necklace pour into my palm like liquid before turning, her voice going loud, confident again, resuming her performance.

We drove the rest of the way to my hometown quietly. It made me appreciate this man as a traveling companion. He even offered to pay for a quarter tank of gas just outside the city limits. Gentlemanly. *Serial killers don't do that,* I told myself.

We were passing storefronts now, sad chain stores and fast food restaurants, bleak in their bright colors, their pleading two-for-one deals and desperate exclamation points. It was all lullingly familiar, humdrum in a way that punctured any sense of mystery.

The man told me his name was George. So ordinary. I decided I was unbothered by him. Possibly even fond.

"Hungry?" I asked him.

We were getting close to the small country club to which the groom's family belonged, the location for the rehearsal dinner. I wasn't sure what to do with this man with the cast. George.

He rubbed his belly like a cartoon character and winked. I laughed.

"Come on," I said. "You'll be my date. But you need something else to wear first."

We drove to the Walmart because there was no other option. I left him in the car and jogged inside, choosing a stiff white shirt that seemed to be his size. I paid for it myself.

"Here," I said. "Put this on."

I turned away while he changed shirts but stole a glance. He had tattoos, smudgy and blue, just like I knew he would. I thought of my ex-boyfriend, clean-shaven, his skin unmarked by ink—the one who was supposed to have been my date to the wedding. We'd broken up a month ago, another casualty of intern year.

"How do I look?" George asked me, grinning rakishly.

I didn't answer. He looked exactly like what he was: a man of questionable character I'd picked up on the side of the road, wearing a new shirt. *Bravo*, Sabrina would have said. *Watch out*, the little bird-boned lady I'd accidentally killed would have cautioned. I could feel them, all my mistakes, all the people I'd ever loved or hurt, hovering around me like benevolent or vengeful ghosts.

He retrieved a small flask from the breast pocket of his old shirt, took a swig, and offered it to me. "To new friends."

I drank quickly. The liquor burned in a way that was both gratifying and punishing. We sat there, in the country club parking lot, passing the flask back and forth. By the time we walked in together, I felt loose-jointed and warm. I let George take my arm.

"You can stop the pretense now," I told him. "With the cast. The leg. I know it's not broken."

He winked again, and then we both broke into giddy laughter.

"Gotta let it heal," he said, still grinning. There was an energy between us now. I could discern at this point that George was not handsome, not really. His teeth were too small, too ratlike, and despite the leanness of his limbs, a softness at his belly hinted at the old man he'd become. And yet the way he guided me lightly into the main hall of the country club, two fingers at the small of my back . . . I liked that. I was a little bit drunk.

When we walked in, I saw that we were indeed very late. The guests were at circular tables covered in white tablecloths, spooning up their chocolate mousse. Across the room, I caught the eye of my childhood best friend, Marissa, the bride, and she ran over to us.

"Emily!" she exclaimed, clasping me around the neck and pulling me close. "You finally made it!"

As I hugged her back, I wondered if she'd smell the alcohol on me. George stood patiently in his stiff shirt, his bad leg jutting to one side.

"And you brought a friend," she said, her smile unfaltering. Marissa had excellent manners, always had. You could not throw her socially; she was masterful. The perfect wife of a county commissioner.

"This is George," I said, holding in laughter. The whole situation seemed farcical. "He's my guest."

"Enchanté," George said, offering a hobbled but courtly bow.

"Welcome," Marissa replied, her brow barely furrowing. Already she was leading us to a pair of open seats and beckoning to a cummerbunded teenage waiter. I'd missed her brisk, pleasant efficiency.

"The dancing will start soon," Marissa said. She waited while we sat and the waiter set plates of roast chicken before us. Then, kissing my forehead lightly, she was off to mingle and entertain, like royalty. George and I began eating ravenously, without speaking, and the food was salty and very good. We were both so hungry, this stranger and I. I sipped the red wine, and the teen waiter refilled my glass. Maybe I would move back here, where everything was recognizable, the rituals and seasons a comfort: crop cycles, people getting married, local festivals.

Guests were dancing by the time George and I finished dessert. It was too loud to have a real conversation.

"What do you want?" George asked, his mouth purpled with wine now, against my cheek. He had to lean in close to be heard.

"What do you want?"

He shrugged. Maybe the wine was wearing off, or maybe the full effect of the long drive was finally hitting me: my head was starting to hurt, and I felt tired.

Then there was a commotion on the dance floor, a collective gasp followed by a circling of people. I stood, but the crowd obscured my view.

Marissa's nephew, the DJ, stopped the music, his brow creasing with concern, and a lady in a spangled dress rushed toward him, whispering in his ear.

"Is there a doctor in the house?" the nephew asked into the microphone. He said it just like that, a bad joke adopted from a lifetime of bad television.

My stomach dropped. I willed myself deeper into the background, willing myself to disappear, while I waited for someone else, some older gentleman, the local internist, maybe, to step forward.

Marissa in her beautiful fuchsia dress twisted her hands. She looked across the room, catching my eye. "Come on," she mouthed, beckoning.

George watched me as I stood up slowly, smoothing my skirt, brushing the crumbs from it. I felt his eyes slide over me, assessing me in a new way. I hadn't told him what I did. We knew nothing about each other. I saw now that he had put the fox foot on the table, and he was stroking it slowly, as if it were a treasured pet.

I moved toward the knot of people, and they parted to let me through. A middle-aged woman in a teal skirt was lying on the floor. Her eyes were closed. She took quick, shallow breaths. This was good news. It couldn't be too bad if she was breathing. A wave of relief passed over me.

"Are you a doctor?" asked an older man.

I shrugged. "Sort of," I said. "Yes."

He nodded gravely.

"Carol felt like she was going to pass out," he explained. I gleaned that he was her husband.

"An ambulance is on its way," another lady said.

I reached for Carol's wrist, pressing between the narrow bones to where I could feel her pulse: a hummingbird thrum.

Carol's eyes fluttered open, terrified.

I smiled at her, grateful she was alert.

"Try this," I whispered. "Bear down. Like you're having a bowel movement."

She nodded. I watched her Valsalva, a sheen of sweat on her forehead. She bore down once, twice. A third time. I kept my hand on her wrist, more to comfort her, to comfort myself, than anything. I felt her pulse slow to something I could count, steady, regular. She smiled at me, and I helped her sit up. I wanted to weep.

"Better?" I asked, my tongue thick and dry in my mouth.

"My God, Charlie," Carol said. "She did it. She saved my life."

"Oh, no," I said. "Not at all. I didn't—"

But Charlie, her husband, was already clapping me on the back, jolly-good-fellow-style, helping me up, and the people around us were breaking into a tentative smattering of applause.

Marissa grabbed the microphone from her nephew.

"That's my friend Emily," she announced, her eyes sparkling. She lifted her glass of wine.

What I wanted to say was that the tachycardia might have broken anyway, that suggesting the Valsalva maneuver was a lucky shot, the illusion of effect in a world where things are preordained.

* * *

The festivities resumed after Carol was ushered away by the EMTs. The incident over, tension eased from the room. Marissa was dancing with her soon-to-be husband. Couples dipped and turned around them. I headed back to the table to get my glass of water.

George was gone.

I looked for him by the bar, by the bathrooms. I walked outside to the clubhouse porch, where I expected to find him smoking a Marlboro Red. A row of white rocking chairs sat empty, still. The stretch of golf course beyond the porch appeared wide and flat as a body of water, bounded on the sides by sloping green hills. The crickets chirred like machinery. I'd forgotten that sound.

And that's when the obvious thought occurred to me. Of course he was gone—and my car with him. I'd left my keys at the table where we'd been sitting. Now my keys were gone, too. He was no more serial killer than I was, but he was a common thief. *When you hear hoofbeats, think of horses, not zebras.* It was what our attendings said when we missed the obvious in our attempts to be clever.

I moved quickly from the porch to the parking lot. It was empty, quiet save for the soft splat of warm rain starting to fall on the cars. I wove my way between the vehicles, feeling strangely out of time, like no one, a shade of my former and present selves.

But my car was still there, parked exactly where I'd left it. George must have caught some other ride out to exit 19, the fox foot clutched tight in his hand.

Something caught in my throat, and I realized it was disappointment. Plain and ordinary life, with its plain and ordinary choices. I would return to Baltimore and finish my final weeks of intern year, swallow my humiliations, plod forward, dutiful.

I would go back inside and hug Marissa, raise my glass, dance with a country boy who smelled like the clay I'd grown up on, while somewhere, deep in those woods, were people caterwauling and free, lost in a rollicking dark mischief. There was danger there, and in that danger, a letting go. Shadow-faced men and cackling, foul-mouthed women, like Sabrina. The thought gave me a terrible thrill, a ping of sadness.

But first, I walked to my car. It was unlocked, my keys visible on the dash, and I was glad for a place to sit a moment, alone.

I saw then what else George had left me: in the passenger seat was the long cast, slit down the side, eerily empty of its occupying leg.

And written inside: *Put this on.*

My fox foot, I thought. *A sign so I'd be known.*

A door opened somewhere, and sounds of music and dancing, a celebration, spilled into the darkness.

RUMPELSTILTSKIN

Bree began to dream that the doctor was placing a small silvery fish inside her, always with the promise that it would turn, eventually, into a human baby—a tiny version of her husband and herself, their darling replica. In the dream, she could see that the doctor held a minnow, or possibly one of those iridescent fishing lures her father had used throughout her childhood. She remembered the lures as dangerous objects of great beauty, tantalizing her with their feathers, their shimmering gunmetal grays and dragonfly blue-greens. They lay nestled in her father's tackle box like jewels, barbed hooks just waiting to snag flesh. *Noli me tangere.* In the dream, Bree would wince at the moment of insertion, but the doctor always spoke in such a calming voice that Bree felt reassured. This was how babies were made, scientifically speaking. You stuck in a fish, like the Thanksgiving Indians had done when planting corn. Fertilization. She remembered some fact like this from elementary school, so when the dream-doctor explained it this way, it made a certain sense. She would wake with the pleasant sensation of having taken definite action toward a goal.

The point of the dream was that Bree was willing. She was willing to do it all. Stick fish or fishing lures up inside herself, suck down protein smoothies and wheatgrass, purchase healing crystals and naturopathic supplements, take special yoga classes. Pinch an inch of belly fat and inject herself with supraphysiologic doses of hormones each evening. Inject progesterone into her buttocks until they flowered with soft lavender bruises.

And so far, nothing. You pay money like that and you expect something.

Bree had a good job, but not *that* good a job. The same was true for her husband, Owen. This was not a thing they'd done lightly. She'd stopped counting at this point—all the cycles, all the failures, all that money dumped into a gaping pit.

A friend of a friend of Bree's had been in a support group in which a woman announced she was planning to write a humorous memoir about the whole experience titled "Inconceivable!" Bree had laughed when her friend, Lisa, told her this story, not because the book title was funny, but because it wasn't. It was exactly the sort of sour anecdote she craved. She had just seen another pregnant woman pass outside her office window and felt a convulsion of jealousy—these pregnant women, so shameless with their big brazen bellies! Rubbing it in everyone else's face. Meanwhile, here was Bree, her uterus rattling around like a dried gourd.

Lisa was the one person Bree could confide in, and they'd already talked through all the acupuncture recommendations, massage therapists, specific brands of Coenzyme Q10, and the SART success rates for the various reproductive endocrinology clinics. Lisa had finally, after years of frustration, had a baby herself, and she had recently emerged from the cloister of new motherhood more tired-looking and less triumphant than Bree would have imagined. The baby was at home napping with his father, and Lisa whispered this like being away from her infant was scandalous. Babies, they consumed you. Literally. Lisa had the hollowed look of someone fleeing disaster.

"There's one thing you still haven't tried," Lisa said, stirring her coffee carefully with a spoon. Her eyes when she looked up at Bree's were those of either a prophet or a lunatic. "The thing that finally worked for us."

Lisa looked side to side to see if anyone else was in earshot, then spoke so softly that Bree had to lean closer to hear.

"It's not scientific or anything, but we have Hartley now. I've still got the phone number."

Bree was nodding so furiously she couldn't focus. "Please. Anything."

Lisa paused, frowning slightly. She seemed to hesitate before pulling out a crumpled yellow paper from her bag and passing it to Bree.

"I can't quite explain it to you. I mean, I couldn't if I wanted to, but I'm also not supposed to."

Lisa looked apologetic, but Bree merely nodded. She would call. She would do anything. Make every bargain, give up what she had to give up, sell what she had to sell. If it was some kind of hocus-pocus, she could accept that. Fertility spells. It was no weirder than the rest of it. She would go deep into the forest, to the witch's house. She would do all of it, without complaint. Whatever it took.

Bree grabbed the sticky note and stuck it in her pocket. "Thank you," she said. "Thank you."

The problem with Owen was that he was a good man, a decent man—a man of faith, even. This had been exactly what had drawn Bree to him in the beginning. She knew herself, knew the sharp edges of her own longings, well enough to understand that she would benefit from matching with a more generous soul. Placid. Owen had a placid quality. He had the same eyes one saw on faces in old, religious triptychs—not the faces of the martyrs, eyes turned heavenward in holy subjugation, but the faces of the observers, the ones who stood there calmly and said to themselves, *Well, I suppose this is how it's all meant to be. I suppose this is just the divine plan.*

Owen taught at a very competitive private school—the school to which they could send their hypothetical child, for free, unless they were overcome with conscience. They lived in a pleasant neighborhood where people owned nice things but tempered this with an appropriate measure of guilt. Little girls in the neighborhood had truck-themed birthday parties and little boys were given gifts of baby dolls, and parents took their toddlers to vigils in the name of causes righteous and good. Owen's school was the same way. He loved teaching there. He had a gift for it. He also volunteered on weekends. He was very handsome, to boot; people said he looked like Jon Hamm. The only person people said Bree looked like was her mother.

"I'm happy with things as they are," Owen had told her, had been telling her from the beginning. "But I'll support you. We'll play this thing out as far as you want. All the way to the end."

Bree had just thrown a small temper tantrum over having to make a meal for the couple up the street who'd just had a baby. They got the baby *and* the home-cooked meals? It seemed grossly unfair.

"Of course it's not fair," Owen responded evenly, splashing balsamic vinegar onto the salad he was finishing in its Tupperware bowl. "The world isn't fair. Look, look at all we have here."

He gestured to their home, which was, Bree had to admit, nice enough. She had a nice house and a nice husband; meanwhile, people were getting shot by police officers, and police officers were getting shot by snipers, and children were being kidnapped and forced to be child soldiers, and refugees were drowning in their flimsy boats before they could make it ashore, and in Syria the last hospital for miles was getting bombed. Just yesterday, she'd seen a heartbreaking photo from Aleppo: an injured child, soot-covered and staring. The list went on. And yet so clearly was she focused on her own particular grievance with the universe that these greater woes did little to make Bree feel appreciative. All of it just made her even sadder. *Farewell, little no-baby. It's a bad-sad unfair world anyway.*

Owen snapped the lid on the salad and pulled out a loaf of bread from the oven with his mitts. He'd made the whole dinner for the couple up the street himself while she'd sulked.

Bree watched him and found herself inexplicably resenting his goodness, his even temper. It was lonely to be so miserable by herself. She wanted to drag him down into the murky depths of her sadness like a mermaid drowning a sailor.

Lisa had warned her: a want like this could strangle a marriage. There was an art to managing thwarted expectations. The whole thing made Bree hate herself—at least the twisted version of herself she'd become.

"I'll practice gratitude," she said now, wanting very much to mean it. "I want to be grateful for all these things. For our good life."

Owen smiled at her so thankfully that she wished her heart were more authentic. She wanted to be the woman he deserved.

"My sweetheart," he said, pulling her toward him, kissing her and then nuzzling the back of her neck.

The paper Lisa had given Bree seemed to burn in her pocket, alive with a kind of animate heat. She felt false, self-conscious, and pulled away from him.

"We may still get our good luck yet," she said.

"We've already had such good luck," he replied, not unkindly. "No matter what. Remember?"

The woman's house was set back from the road down a long gravel drive. Bree had driven out into the adjacent county, a good twenty-minute trip. She'd passed a farmhouse, and then a stable advertising horse-riding lessons. She'd passed a little white clapboard place with a wide porch. *Rustic.* That was the word. Bree could imagine the sort of woman she was going to meet: an older lady with smile lines at her eyes who smelled of homemade bread, someone who knew home remedies and had herbs drying in her kitchen. The thought comforted her.

When Bree pulled up to the address, the house was bigger than she'd expected, but also more run-down. There was a visible sag to the roof, and a brown speckled couch losing its stuffing sat in the front yard.

Bree parked and walked to the front door, but before she could even knock, someone opened it.

"Yvonne?" Bree said, blinking from the bright day into the dimness.

But the person opening the door was a child, a scraggly little boy wearing shorts but no t-shirt. His chest and abdomen were practically concave, and his scapulae protruded sharply like denuded wings.

"I'm here for Yvonne," she said, and he beckoned her inside.

The interior of the house had a damp ammonia smell. As her eyes adjusted, Bree could see there were cats crouched everywhere: an orange tabby perched atop a shelf, a black-and-white cat sleeping in one corner, a fat brown one darting under her feet. There were heaps of things everywhere—junk, as far as Bree could tell. Piles of fabric, empty boxes, a grandfather clock open to the guts as if someone had tried to fix it but then abandoned the job.

Bree paused, taking it all in.

"Mama collects things to sell on eBay," the boy explained, clearly taking her hesitation for admiration. His voice lower than she'd expected. He gestured to an old stereo with a large dent in the side.

Bree nodded, almost tripping on what turned out to be a toddler.

"That's Maisie," the boy said. "Scoot, Maisie. Get out of the way."

Maisie wobbled away on chubby legs, heavy diaper sagging.

The room was hot, the air stagnant, and Bree felt queasy. She'd begun to second-guess her decision to come here. Maybe she'd found the limits of what she was prepared to do.

When the boy opened a back door, she was relieved. He led her to a cement patio upon which sat a large inflatable pool. After the dimness inside, it was too bright. Bree squinted. More children, more cats. The cats skittered and skirted her legs, and the children dashed around barefoot, calling to one another. A couple of the younger kids splashed in the pool, where, presiding over the scene, a large woman in a flowered one-piece sat on a plastic raft. She floated, immense and queenly, over to Bree, waving to her.

"Well, hey," she said as if they were old friends. "You made it."

Bree wet her lips before answering. She needed a glass of water. "Hi," she said. "You must be Yvonne."

"You want a baby," the woman said. She had on big heart-shaped sunglasses, and Bree could sense the woman assessing her from behind the shaded lenses. "No luck so far, huh?"

"None," Bree replied. "My friend, Lisa, said you could help."

"Oh, yeah," the woman responded calmly. "Gonna cost you, though. A thousand bucks. Then you get your baby, guaranteed."

Bree wanted to laugh with relief. A thousand dollars was a bargain at this point! She'd paid for prescription medications that cost more. Bree was already pulling out her checkbook when the woman put a wet hand on her arm. She pushed the heart-shaped glasses atop her head so that Bree could see her eyes, which were tired and brown but winning, like a loyal dog's.

"Before you pay," she said, "you should know up front. No backsies, no refunds, no blabbermouthing."

Bree nodded furiously. "Of course," she said. "As long as I get a baby. My own." She felt nervous all of a sudden.

Yvonne pulled down the sunglasses again. With one hand, she paddled her float over to the other side of the pool, where a glass of what appeared to be lemonade sat. She took a drink.

"Write it out to Y. B. Miller Plumbing," she said. "It's the hubby's business, so." She flung a hand to the side as if indicating her absent husband.

When Bree had written the check, the woman smiled.

"Give that to Horace," she said, and as if by magic, the skinny, shirtless boy appeared beside Bree.

Bree awaited further instruction, or to be handed some potion or poison.

54

"That's it," Yvonne said, chuckling. "It's already in motion. Whether you like it or not. Millie, come show this lady back around to her car."

A scrawny girl-child emerged from the other side of the pool, where she must have been crouched, playing in a patch of dirt. Obediently, she walked over to Bree and made a practiced mock curtsy.

There were even more children, Bree saw. The longer she stood there, the more they seemed to emerge, like camouflaged moths from a patterned background. She noticed another little shirtless boy in overalls standing by the side of the house, where he was assisting a larger stooped boy. They seemed to be working at something—a stretch of gutter or a bit of siding—and it was only when the bigger boy turned to look at Bree that she realized she was staring. Something about the angle of the sun made the boy look deformed and ancient, with a leering old man's face. He wore a jagged silver chain of sorts around his neck that caught the light, sparkling like knives. He winked knowingly at her—she could have sworn he did—and she turned quickly away. It was nothing. A trick of the sun.

"How will it work?" Bree asked. "How will I know?"

"You'll know."

Yvonne began to paddle to the other side of the pool, and Bree knew her audience was over. The bright afternoon had given her a sharp pain behind her eyes. Millie, scrawny and mute, tugged at the hem of her shirt. Bree followed the girl back around to the front. She was trembling when she started her car.

When nothing happened in the coming days or weeks, Bree was not surprised. As soon as she'd gotten home, any illusions she'd held about her visit to Yvonne's had vanished. Another thousand dollars lost: at this point, pocket change. She wouldn't tell Owen. She'd cut corners in other ways, make frugality her penance.

"You should have married Clara," Bree said to Owen yet again one evening. It was her preferred form of self-torture. Clara had been the long-term girlfriend who preceded her. Clara—perfect, goldenlimbed Clara—with her three beautiful children. Bree and Owen were friendly with Clara and her gentle husband. Lovely, nonjealous Clara. Kind, fecund Clara.

Bree was leaning into their bathroom mirror, digging at an angry red bump on her chin, and it felt painful and correct: something Clara would never do. Smiling, unblemished Clara. She would become the anti-Clara. Another form of self-abnegation, another punishment.

Owen put down his toothbrush and sighed. He'd made some reassuring remark to this statement at least fifty times before.

"Bree," he said. "Look at me."

She turned to him, catching the full reflection of the two of them in the mirror now: Owen's even, handsome face; her own, with her tired eyes, her chin inflamed.

"Stop it," he said softly. "Please. You have to stop it."

She did not answer him, but later she cried. She cried because she knew it was true: she should stop but she couldn't. She'd made herself into the dark fairy at the christening, her heart an ugly knot of brambles. She'd formed a bad habit she now inhabited so deeply it was unbreakable.

A few weeks later, Bree saw Lisa at the local food co-op with baby Hartley strapped to her chest in an Ergo. Lisa's husband, Richard, was nearby, testing the ripeness of the avocados, while Lisa trailed her fingers over the lettuce. The first moment Bree saw them, she felt a pang of envy—Lisa had left her behind and joined the club of mothers, and now, here she was, perfect husband and baby in tow. A pretty picture. But you could swallow your own bitterness, Bree had found. You could swallow it, and it was poison, but it was a poison you became used to, by degrees. So she swallowed and moved toward them to say hello.

But there was something wrong. Bree hesitated, watching them from a display of cheeses, trying to figure out what it was.

They weren't speaking, she realized. They wore the silent faces of the stricken, the stunned. Even Baby Hartley. His small mouth hung slack, and though his eyes were open, he seemed only dully aware of his surroundings. Richard wore a similarly glazed expression. Lisa lifted a head of lettuce and placed it in their basket. When her arm brushed Richard's, he seemed to shudder involuntarily and pull away.

Things were not right. Bree could see it clearly now: a sort of sickness had befallen them. She stared at them, their ordinary faces gone monstrous in the produce section lighting, then backed away.

Hurrying to the exit on the other side of the store, she left without the milk or the cheese or the special local jam she'd intended to pick up. She left with nothing but a heavy sensation encompassing her whole chest. She was feverish, queasy.

Bree couldn't quite focus the whole ride home. A cloud passed over the sun, and she felt an incipient sense of dread. She would make things better. She had to. She would start by making dinner for herself and Owen. They would eat together. They would sit on the porch with drinks the way they used to, and he would tell her funny stories from his day. They hadn't done this for so long. Owen would remember to squeeze just the right amount of lime for her. She would kiss him and knead the knot he always got in his right shoulder. They would laugh. She couldn't remember, now that she thought about it, the last time they'd so much as smiled at one another.

When she pulled up to the house, there was a battered old truck parked up front. They were not expecting anyone. Something fluttered in her, but she took a deep breath. At the door, fumbling for her keys, she could hear voices inside. Owen's and a stranger's.

She walked to the kitchen. A man sat with his back to her at the table across from Owen. She saw that Owen had poured them both glasses of iced tea. Owen caught her eye. He was looking at her in a new way. The muscle of his jaw flickered, but he pressed his lips into a tight line. Unreadable.

"Bree," he said, and his voice had such a practiced calm that it chilled her. "We have a guest."

She frowned. The visitor, still turned away from her, was a small man. He looked older, too thin. Emaciated, really. There was a hitch to his shoulders, an unevenness she could see from where she stood. His hair fell to his neck in oily ringlets. She caught Owen's eyes again and shook her head furiously, but he just held her gaze, implacable.

"Come on over and sit down," Owen said, rising from his seat. "He's explained it all. We'll play this thing out. All the way to the end."

She stepped forward, careful not to look at the visitor directly.

"No, Owen," she said, but her voice came out very weakly, like a whimper. "This isn't what I meant."

"I'll let him introduce himself," Owen said, picking up the jacket he'd draped across the back of the chair. "I'll let you two talk." He was leaving now, Bree understood. He was leaving her alone with the strange man.

Putting on his jacket, Owen moved around the table toward the door. She caught his arm, her fingers digging into the flesh, but he jerked away, rougher than she'd ever known him to be with her.

Bree stood, immobilized, next to the visitor sitting at her table. She could see his profile in her peripheral vision. He was not a man, no, not really. She saw the odd hump to his back, his concave chest, and suddenly he was very familiar to her. The body of a misshapen boy, the face of a wicked old man. She could not bear for him to look at her. She could not bear to look at him. He cracked his knuckles, and she saw his hands, knobby and callused but strangely adorned. Each of his fingers was knobbed with unusual silver rings, sharp and geometric, spiky in their stalagmite complexity.

"Please don't leave, Owen," she whispered.

Owen stood, pale, watching her from the doorway. She wanted to throw her arms around him. She wanted to cry out. But she stood there, saying nothing.

The man at the table gave a slight nod, and Owen looked to Bree, as if for confirmation. She thought that if she could just call the whole thing off, they might still go back to how they'd been before. But she did not. It was irrevocable. She knew that by now. Owen's face tightened, and he turned from her.

Too late, Bree whispered, "Wait."

But Owen was already gone, the door to their beautiful house clicking softly shut behind him, and she was left with this troll, this manikin, who turned slowly to Bree, lifting his glass of tea as if making a toast. She had the odd thought that he was vain in his way, with the manicured fingers of a dowager.

"I don't know you," Bree said, her mouth gone completely dry. "I don't know you at all. You shouldn't be here." She sank to the chair next to him, though, so close that she could hear the faint whistle of his breathing.

The little man just looked at her peaceably with his pitted cheeks and toothless grin. His touch was damp and cool, but she let him take her hand. When he rose, she followed him.

FOR THE DEAD
WHO TRAVEL FAST

It's around the time my sister gets involved with this guy who's leaving bruises all over her, around the time of yet another one of those shootings, around the time I start to think there's something wrong with men in general—myself included, something rotten and dismissive and violent in the piddly tails of our Y chromosomes—that I hear about it.

A missing girl. A girl I've never met. I can't stop reading about her.

"Have you talked to your sister?" my mother asks. "I'm worried about her."

My sister has stopped answering my calls.

"I'm worried about you, too," my mother adds. She has a way of making everything into one big crisis she's directing.

There is something rotten at the core—maybe in all of us. I don't trust myself in a great many things. I don't trust my sister either. Or my mother. We're all fools, in our way.

But I'm stuck on the story of this other girl. Cecelia.

*   *   *

The hotel where Cecelia goes missing is on the wrong side of town, a rougher part of LA. It doesn't look like the sort of place where nice young people go, certainly not nice young girls—correction: nice young women. Outside, men hunch under awnings, their beards grizzled and flecked with grime. They sprawl on cardboard boxes. Someone sour-smelling in a bright blue tank top is yelling at someone else from the back of a moving van. A bottle arcs through the air and then shatters. Everyone is idling, leaning against buildings, watchful. The air is damp and heavy with the scent of rotting onions. Still, there is the hint of old glamour. Once upon a time, this place was not so squalid. The hotel was upscale, ornate. You can see it still in the art deco lobby, the old statues looking out blank-eyed into the mirrored walls. Now there are water stains in the corners of the ceilings, cracks in the cornices. A cluster of Belgian backpackers drink coffee out of paper cups.

Cecelia was traveling on the cheap, documenting her exploits: photos of her having fancy cocktails with a friend, a lunch at an outdoor café, on a hike somewhere near the canyon. What she lacked in money she made up for in charm, in Instagram followers. Her photographs are moody and lovely—supersaturated and smeary on the edges. Life as a beautiful adventure.

"But I love him," my sister says the last time I talk to her, after I drive her back from the ER, after I give her ice packs and let her sleep on my couch. "He's trying to change. Besides, I was egging him on. I was saying awful things. We'd had a few drinks." She sighs, touching the necklace of fingertip-shaped bruises around her throat. "Things are always so beautiful between us, except when they're not."

She gives me a pointed look before continuing. "I bet you know about that. You and Trinny."

I don't answer. My girlfriend, Trinny, left months ago, taking our daughter with her. An extended trip to her parents' house. To think, she said. I get that. We all need to think sometimes.

My sister looks at me, a scratch like a question mark on her cheekbone. I glance away, choosing to consider instead my baby daughter, how I miss pressing my face against her and inhaling, how I miss her soft frog belly, the good part in me she summons.

Better angels of our nature, blah, blah, blah.

I am a fraud, I am thinking. But who among us is not?

My sister is crying softly, prodding gently at the bruises on her arm as if she's in the produce aisle testing fruit, as if her body is a separate entity.

It probably goes without saying that the disappeared girl, Cecelia, is pretty. Or maybe not pretty, but young, which is often taken for the same thing. She appears even younger in her photos. It's in the way she tries to look older. It's how she tilts her face in her selfies, knowing how to suck in her cheeks just so, which filter to use. Kissy-mouthed and serious-eyed. And though she aims to project a certain worldliness, she's still devoted to her parents. Every day, she checks in with them. Until the day she does not. They hear nothing. This is so unlike her. Something is amiss.

"It can be as subtle as a shift in atmospheric pressure—the wrong tone of voice, or maybe he thinks I'm laughing at him. I say the wrong thing. A joke I make lands wrong. And then it's like I'm talking to a different person." My sister sighs. "They say impulsive aggression is associated with lower levels of serotonin." She is studying to be a clinical social worker, ironically enough, and believes the world can be broken down into solvable problems.

"Don't make excuses for assholes," I say.

"You're an asshole," she says.

I nod, devil-made-me-do-it style. "Most of the time."

In the hotel, there are fourteen floors, quieter as you go up. There are shared hallway bathrooms. It feels more like an old dormitory than a hotel. A hostel. There are two rickety old mirrored elevators that go up from the lobby. And that's where they got the footage. I've watched it over and over. Cecelia.

She enters the elevator. The time stamp shows it's very late, or very early. She presses the buttons—not one floor, but all of them. She leans in close, as if terribly nearsighted. Maybe she's intoxicated. Maybe she's been drugged. Then, as if struck by something—a sudden sound, maybe—she backs away. Pressing herself into the corner of the elevator, she appears to be hiding, trying to make herself invisible to someone passing by. A few beats pass, and then she moves to the door, peering out. She looks to both sides, careful, checking. Then she's back inside the elevator, stabbing at the buttons. It is only grainy security footage, but you can tell she's frightened. Something is happening, something bad. She steps out of the elevator again, making strange motions with her hands, flapping them like winged things. She steps forward, out of the frame. Finally, the elevator door closes. She is not on it.

My mother calls and leaves a voicemail about a study she ran across, one about aggression in chimpanzees. "The sexually aggressive males tend to sire more offspring." She leaves this message as if it's an explanation, or an accusation.

My mother leaves more messages.

"Your sister's back with him, isn't she?" she asks, her voice savage. Like it's my fault. "Neither of you is returning my calls."

I haven't heard from my sister in weeks. I haven't heard from my ex-girlfriend in months.

I think of how my daughter will recoil the next time she sees me, a stranger.

Of course, the story blows up on the internet. I'm not the only sleuth. There's the security footage, begging for speculation. Everyone has a theory.

Also, a body has been found.

Here is where you think the story ends. The grisly finale. Because the body appears to be hers. Cecelia's. Though by the time they discover her, she is bloated beyond recognition. Her parents give no statements. They retreat to the town from which they came. The restaurant they run is boarded up for weeks, and people leave flowers, notes, candles at the door.

Time passes, and eventually a report is released: no evidence of foul play.

There is more talk, information shared in an interview with a close family friend: she wasn't well.

At a certain point, it's your own fault. Your own fault for doing nothing. There are choices. There are things you let happen and happen and happen . . .

I start to feel that if I were to look directly into my daughter's eyes, it would be like staring into the sun. I would smile a smile that would threaten to split my face in half, into a cataract of tears.

Every smile is this close to a threat. The baring of teeth. That's just evolutionary biology. All this stuff written into our genes. Maybe my sister is right. Maybe I'm onto something. I send an email to Trinny trying to explain all this, as if it will make her understand.

But this is not the end, I promise you. There's an addendum.

Cecelia comes back. Reappears. Or maybe she never left.

The first time someone sees her it's actually in a coffee shop in a neighborhood adjacent to the one with the hotel, and there she is, hunched over a laptop, half-grown-out bangs swept over her eyes. The barista notices her. He brings her the tiny cappuccino she ordered and is caught by her watchfulness, by the reluctance with which she seems to take the cup from him.

"I know you," he says, although he is far from certain. "From the—from somewhere." He feels himself stumbling over his words.

She looks up at him evenly. "People say that," she says. "I get that all the time."

Hello, you've reached the voicemail . . . Hello, you've reached the voicemail . . .

This becomes something of a lullaby.

I imagine my daughter as the tiny singing hollow of a seashell, miles away. I imagine my sister as a broken bit of coral, washed ashore. I don't know what I imagine Trinny as—nothing, the darkness when I squeeze my eyes shut.

Next it is a pair of Australian backpackers staying in the hotel, arriving late from a night out drinking. There she is, flustered, in the elevator. She's kneeling, as if she's looking for some tiny object she's dropped.

When they enter, boisterous with drink, she rises, her eyes large and startled as a deer's. It's 3 a.m. They feel enormous and loud, bawdy, with big clumsy paws. But instinctively, they know not to alarm her. They quiet themselves and slow, as if approaching skittish wildlife.

"You all right there?" one of the Australians asks in the overloud quiet voice of a drunk person. "You lose something?"

She shakes her head, inching away. She turns and runs down the hallway and is gone.

One of the building's tenants is taking a bath when he hears someone padding softly across the room. It's her. A cruel joke. The tepid water he's in is suddenly unbearably cold. She walks just up to the bathtub, staring at him with a worried expression. He shouts, and she runs off.

Soon, it seems, she is everywhere. All over the hotel, all over the neighborhood. She is not a ghost, people insist. She is decidedly not a ghost but solid flesh and blood. There must have been some mistake. The whole thing, the whole ending—it was told wrong.

* * *

I think I see my sister wearing a motorcycle jacket in the frozen foods aisle, holding the hand of a stocky older gentleman, but when she turns around, she has the face of a grimacing hag.

The world is haunted by doppelgängers.

Then, I really do see Trinny. She's getting a sandwich across the block from her office, but she pretends to laugh very hard at something her colleague says so as not to see me. I have to clutch at my chest because I feel an actual pain there. Trinny is gone by the time the pain passes and I can straighten back up.

An old man stops, touches my shoulder. "You okay, son?" he asks.

I don't know how to answer.

A French backpacker holds up long strands of black hair to prove he's seen Cecelia. A patron of a nearby diner has a paper cup marked with her lip gloss. An Israeli tourist has cell phone video of a woman's small, wet handprint on his bag. A man wakes up from what seems like a dream with a pair of cheap earrings left by his bed. Always, always, she is damp-haired and serious.

"Let's go swimming," she says. "It'd be such a lovely evening for a swim."

A sick joke. That's what people say in response. What kind of Reddit troll would make that up?

Or she says, "I know a place. A place we won't be found."

People in the hotel still have a superstitious awe of the showers. They reach up to test the water pressure, cautious before stepping in.

And then someone is posting photos on Cecelia's Instagram account—the same half-darkened, empty hotel room, posted every night right around the time Cecelia was last seen.

#creepy.

There are new posts on her blog, filled with cheery paragraphs and too many exclamation points.

That's just cruel, people say. Unless, of course, there was some mistake. A fugue state, someone offers. An amnestic fugue. Disassociation. And a body wrongly identified. It could happen, maybe.

It's the stuff of soap operas.

The voice inside the seashell sings *gone gone gone.*

About a year or so after all this, I meet a woman in Tempe, where I'm spending way too much money on bad habits, chasing whoever gives me a smile and the time of day. Trinny has moved with my daughter back up to Seattle. My sister goes and marries that guy, first name Bad, last name News. At least, that's our best guess. We don't hear from her anymore. She's cut off communication with us for good. Done.

"Could be dead for all we know," I say to my mother, and her mouth snaps shut.

"How's Trinny?" she asks a moment later, sly in the way that mothers are sly.

"She's dead to me," I say, and my mother flinches.

I've decided to freelance and travel. The entire Southwest is filled with hippie chicks. Girls who go to sweat lodges and have mandala tattoos and attended massage therapy school but really want to practice energy work. Bullshit, but I'm a sucker for that type, so convinced of themselves. I love Tempe. I love a winterless college town. I love a place that pretends to be thoughtful, where you don't actually need to have a thought in your head.

And that's where I meet her.

We're both a little drunk on too-sweet prosecco at a friend's backyard party, and she turns to me and says, "I'm a living ghost."

Her hair is cut short, dyed a reddish color. I don't recognize her at first

"Oh, yeah?" I say. I assume she's flirting with me, speaking in metaphors. "I'm a living ghost, too." Which feels true at that point. I smile my well-worn chimpanzee smile.

She laughs. "No, seriously. You'll know me when I tell you who I am." She twirls her hands in front of her the way people do when they're spaced out on something and suddenly their own fingers are strange, elongated worms, the most interesting things in the world. That's how I take it at first, but when I sidle up a little closer, I'm hit with second thoughts. It's her eyes. The way she can't quite seem to focus her gaze—it makes me think there are unopened bottles of prescription medicines she's supposed to be taking.

Still—and I'm not proud of this—there's the way her hand is moving up my arm, and she seems laid-back enough, if odd, and I'm thinking we could get along just fine, for the night at least, so I let myself move in closer.

"I went missing," she says. She mentions the hotel in LA. "The woman in the water tank?" she adds.

She laughs madly, a supervillain in a comic book movie, pulling me toward her by my shirt collar. I get this weird prickling on the back of my neck. She's cute, this girl, but there's something off—the way she smells, damp and mossy, the faintest hint of mold. And her skin is cold against my hands. Maybe it's the evening air, but I swear to God she's cool to the touch, her skin like lake water.

"It'd be such a lovely evening to go swimming," she whispers, taunting me, her words against my throat.

And that's when I back away, my mouth clotted with lame excuses.

She cocks her head. "You had a sister once," she says, studying me the way a gambler might, waiting for my tell. "A daughter." She swirls her hands, shaman-like. The hocus-pocus of a beautiful flirt. "You're a black hole."

I nod because what else could I do? I am a black hole, and she has said it out loud.

"I tried to save you," I stammer. "Her. I mean her." I mean my sister. I mean my little daughter, who still looks at me all large-eyed and joyful because she doesn't know better yet. I mean Trinny, Trinny and me. I mean us all. I want to open my mouth again to explain, but it seems like she is right and my smile is too wide, my teeth too bright, as if I have eaten all the stars. That inescapable gravitational pull.

"Save yourself," she says wryly. "We all have to save ourselves."

She slips away from me then, melting into the darkness and twinkling lights and drinks and laughter, the smudgy press of other partygoers.

I'm sweating. I go inside, where my buddy pours me a whiskey so I can collect myself. My hands are shaking.

When I tell him what happened, my buddy hints that maybe I've been talking to myself. That things hit me harder than I realize. He slaps me on the back and pours me another whiskey, saying I sure know how to spin a line.

I give him a jangled smile and shut up. My buddy and I clink glasses and drink. The news is full of disappearances, missing people, the dead, their names cluttering the white space. I can't keep up with them all. But now I know better than to speak of them. I tell no one about the specific chill I feel, how certain I am it is the cold rush of souls, how convinced I am we are all fleeing something terrifying and animal.

THE UNDEAD

Melanie's daughter Isabel was obsessed with vampires, not unlike many girls her age. Yet it was different with Isabel. She was preoccupied with the undead more generally. Vampires, zombies, succubi, etc. Melanie figured it was her fault. She, the parent, must be doing something wrong.

"*Moroi*," Isabel announced, studying the book in her lap. "That's what they're called in Romania." Her daughter was terribly precocious, people always said. Terribly. "And I would become one, according to them. Anyone born with a tail or an extra nipple would become a moroi," she continued proudly, pointing meaningfully to her small torso.

Melanie and her husband should never have mentioned that the small dusky spot on Isabel's chest was probably the ever-so-slight hint of an accessory nipple. They could have called it a birthmark and left it at that. Accuracy was so rarely worth it.

And yet Isabel seemed to demand it—had demanded it from the earliest age, in fact. Calling an animal *doggy* or *birdie* or *ducky* had never been good enough. Even as a toddler, Isabel had wanted to know what specific *type* of dog, what specific *type* of bird.

"What's a caul?" Isabel asked, her forehead puckered into a frown.

Melanie paused, unsure how to answer. "A membrane," she said. "Why do you ask?"

"Oh," Isabel answered. "If you were born with that, you'd also become a vampire." She turned back to her illustrated pages. What kind of children's book was this, Melanie wondered?

Isabel was just *that type of child*, David said. They should be glad she was interested in things. They should be glad she wasn't some empty-eyed dud, sticky hands glued to a video-game controller. Isabel was all quicksilver curiosity and third nipple instead.

And now she was curious about vampires.

"It's totally normal," Melanie's new friend, Claire, had told her over cocktails. Claire's husband's work had brought them recently to the city, and so Claire was doing locums work also. Both she and Melanie considered their lives here to be temporary. Claire was an emergency medicine doctor, brusque and opinionated, the kind of person who'd rather be putting in a chest tube than making conversation. "All the girls are into vampires. Ever since those books. And zombies too. They're everywhere." Claire swept her hand through the air quickly, as if she were gathering in all of popular culture only to dismiss it.

Melanie had shaken her head. "But it's not *that* kind of vampire. Not a sparkly vampire-boyfriend. A *vampire*. She's interested in . . ." Melanie was at loss as to how to describe it. "I don't know. It's not like the other kids. It's like she's interested in the sickness, the near-deathness."

"Is she goth?" Claire asked. "Is it a phase?" Claire's children were teenagers.

"She's in the third grade. She shouldn't be having phases."

"I've seen a goth third-grader before. Dyed-black hair and all. Kids do everything earlier these days."

Melanie laughed.

"I'm not joking," Claire insisted. "It's all the fertilizer runoff and estrogen in the water supply or something. Kindergartners are having periods, and second-graders are getting bellybutton piercings, and fifth-graders are reproducing. A third-grader can definitely go through a goth phase."

Melanie shook her head again. "It's not like that. Not with Isabel."

Claire stirred her drink and looked at her knowingly. "Everyone thinks that about her own kid."

They had moved to this city for one year, and everyone knew moves were hard on children. It was a truth held to be self-evident. But really the move was hard on Melanie. They had left the comfortable college town she was used to and had moved north— to a city with a reputation for being dirty and dangerous. David had taken a visiting professorship.

"But what about Isabel?" Melanie had pleaded. "Her school? And what about my practice? My patients?"

David sighed. "I told you we didn't have to do this. You said you were okay with it. The plan's already in motion now."

Melanie swallowed. It was always easier to agree to something in theory. It was easier to do everything in theory, including uproot one's career, start anew, apologize, live a moral life.

Isabel, of course, had adjusted without a problem. They had ended up sending her, somewhat guiltily, to a private Quaker school. The public schools in the city were too daunting—investing in the public-school system yet another thing Melanie found easier to agree with in theory rather than practice.

The teachers at the Quaker school were charmed by eccentricity and so adored Isabel. Her evaluations (there were no grades, of course) were glowing.

David loved the visiting professorship. Worse, he'd become enlightened. First, he had taken up meditating. Then he'd signed up for a psilocybin-and-spirituality study. Now he walked around with the contented look of someone who saw the larger picture, someone who had witnessed the face of God, someone who wasn't so caught up in the mundane details.

It would have been enough to make Melanie lonely in the best of circumstances, and these were not the best of circumstances. As it turned out, it was Melanie who had trouble adjusting. She missed the small quotidian things: the local grocery co-op, her book club, the friendly man at the gas station who always told her knock-knock jokes, her well-intentioned friends who gathered to write outraged letters or protest on behalf of worthy causes outside the state legislature. She missed what she was used to.

Melanie had taken a locum tenens job at a behavioral health center. People referred to it as a methadone clinic, but it was not *merely* a methadone clinic. They had emphasized this to her during her interview. There was Suboxone too, and not all of the patients were in treatment for opioid dependency. Nor was it one of those irresponsible, gas 'n' go clinics that were so notorious in the city—the ones with people bartering pills just beyond doorways, nodding off at bus stops right outside.

Her clinic was a multifaceted behavioral health center, equipped to address substance abuse and other psychiatric comorbidities in a sensitive and respectful way. At the time she had taken the job, it had seemed like a grand adventure. A recruiter named Mimi had sweet-talked her into it, paid for her trip up for the interview, and negotiated a bonus.

Melanie hadn't worked in addictions since residency. Her second day on the job, they made her the interim medical director. The previous director had lost his license quite suddenly for something related to inappropriate dispensation of controlled substances.

"Someone's got to do it," Cheree, the head therapist, said, her voice more resigned than anything else. "And you've got the highest degree here."

Melanie had flushed. Cheree had thirty years of experience. Cheree had outlasted five previous medical directors. Cheree had a way of quietly clucking from behind as you fumbled something, then huffing softly when she stepped in, wordlessly, to fix it.

"So," Melanie had said to her. "What do I need to know? About how things work around here. About the patients."

Cheree patted at her braids absently, raising an eyebrow. "Well, in theory, it's easy. . . ." Her mouth twisted into what one could almost construe as a smile.

On her third day, Melanie went to the bathroom, leaving her office door ajar. When she'd returned, she'd found Cheree standing there, one hand cocked on her hip, the other holding Melanie's purse.

"Better me than one of the patients," Cheree said, handing the purse back to Melanie. "Hold everyone to a high standard," she added, "but don't be stupid."

Melanie was careful to lock her purse in her drawer after that. She couldn't bear for Cheree to think she was a fool.

"What exactly *is* rabies, Mom?" Isabel asked.

In the rearview mirror, Melanie eyed Isabel, her seatbelt securely fastened and her hands clasped primly on her lap. It was Friday; in their new life, Melanie had decided to take Fridays off, and so she was the one to pick Isabel up from school. The car windows were beaded with rain, and the sky, the city, the buildings around them, were awash in gray. It was dreary, like Isabel's preferred topics of conversation these days.

"Why do you ask, honey?"

"Vampires," Isabel said. "Apparently people with rabies were mistaken for vampires."

"Well," Melanie said. "Rabies makes you foam at the mouth."

"What about porphyria?"

"Porphyria makes your pee turn red."

These were accurate oversimplifications suitable for a third grader. "You can imagine how that might scare people," Melanie added.

"Vampires aren't real," Isabel mused. "They're myths. Ms. Kathy at school said myths arise out of things we don't understand. But I think I've seen them."

"Where did you see a vampire?" Melanie asked, vaguely alarmed. Isabel was her baby—her sweet, smart, odd, wonderful baby. Vampire-ish people should not be lurking around her, whatever the explanation.

"Oh, everywhere," Isabel said, gesturing out the car window. "Since we moved here. Every time we drive around."

As if cued, a bedraggled man staggered toward their vehicle. They were stopped at one of the larger intersections, one where panhandlers gathered with signs written on flaps of cardboard and approached the stopped vehicles.

This man was skinny and missing his front teeth. He rapped on Melanie's window. She reflexively moved her hand to the automatic lock button, but the car doors were already locked.

Isabel opened her window and thrust one small hand out, waving. "You're all wet," she said. "Mom? We could give him a ride to a shelter?"

"Isabel!" Melanie hissed. The crossing traffic had stopped, and their light was about to turn green.

"Here. A granola bar," Isabel offered.

The man took the granola bar, eyeing it dully, seconds before the light changed and they drove away. In the mirror, Melanie could see him staggering back to the median, out of the flow of traffic.

"Sweetheart," Melanie said, her voice alarmingly high-pitched. "What were you thinking?"

"The golden rule," Isabel said, her face stricken. She was a child who recoiled as if struck from the slightest note of disapproval. "It's rainy out there, and we had room. And the granola bar. We have a boxful at home."

"I'm sure he appreciated the granola bar." What Melanie wanted to say was, *Next time throw the granola bar out the window; don't get too close.* "But you can't invite people into our car. We can't give rides to strangers. It's dangerous."

Even as she spoke, Melanie was aware of being an Awful Person, clumsily crushing the rare bloom of her daughter's innate goodness. The type of person who flinched at a benign, rain-drenched panhandler, caring more about boxes of Costco granola bars than about the homeless, the suffering, the afflicted. The type of person for whom the scrabbling instinct for self-preservation, for perpetuating one's own gene line, outweighed basic kindness.

In the backseat, Isabel, curled forward, orchid-pale and delicate, had begun to cry.

That evening, Melanie and David fought, whispering fiercely at one another behind their bedroom door. They had not quarreled in some time—not since David had become preoccupied with mandalas and breathwork and achieved an irritating level of calm.

"How could you yell at her for that?" David asked, his voice quiet, stern. "How could you make her feel bad for showing empathy? For appreciating our connectedness? For demonstrating fundamental kindness to another person?"

Melanie lifted her chin. "There are other ways," she said. "She has to learn what's reasonable and what's not. You can't just roll down your car windows for every person asking for money and invite them to hop in your car."

"Jesus," David said. "Listen to you. Of course not. Of course not—but it's the way you handled it. You made her feel terrible. I'm proud of her. The kid actually thinks about other people. We want to encourage that, not nip it in the bud. There are ways of having that conversation."

"Take her to volunteer at a soup kitchen, then," Melanie hissed. "If you're so worried about it."

David reached with both hands to rub the back of his neck. "Look at you, Melanie," he said. "You used to have ideals."

She flinched. "Look at you, David," she said. "You used to live in the real world. Now, you do magic mushrooms once in a research study and turn all holy."

David sighed and walked away from her, presumably to meditate.

"I help people," she called out to the back of David's head. Her voice came out tinny and desperate. "I help people for a living! I don't just sit there and philosophize!"

Psilocybin Can Occasion Mystical-Type Experiences Having Substantial and Sustained Personal Meaning and Spiritual Significance—that was the title of the journal article he had shown her months earlier, before he'd signed up to participate in the psilocybin study. Even though she was a psychiatrist, somehow this study, the quick-and-easy promise of it, felt like cheating. David had called her a hypocrite.

What was the point of philosophy, she'd asked him, *if all it took to reach the ineffable were a few mushrooms? What was the point of psychiatry,* he'd countered, *if it rejected the mind's capacity for revelation?*

Melanie stared at a spot on their bedroom wall until her eyes blurred. She could hear David's weight shift in the other room. She kept staring, her body tensed. Was this meditation? She felt angry, then unspeakably weary. She closed her eyes.

A few days later, after she and David had reconciled and the argument seemed like the sort of thing one could weave into a humorous anecdote, she told Claire.

Claire, who was coming off a stretch of nights, making her extra-brusque, had said, "Honey, first of all, what's David do? Philosophy? He's a *philosopher?* I don't care how damn *at one with everything* he is. Has he even *met* a homeless person? Please. Donate to a charity. Roll the damn windows up."

On the day things went wrong, Melanie was distracted. She should never have brought Isabel to work with her in the first place. Who, after all, brings an eight-year-old to a methadone clinic?

Of course, she thought this only in retrospect. She and David had forgotten it was a teacher workday. Their usual babysitter already had plans. Isabel, presented with the choice of going to Claire's house or sitting with Mrs. Schenck, the philosophy department secretary, had pleaded (somewhat unusually, it should be noted), "Mommy, Mommy—I want to go with you!" Melanie had been, well, a little bit flattered.

Desiree, the twenty-something with blue-streaked hair and a stud in her nose who worked reception, said that Isabel could sit near her and color. Desiree's desk was near the employee break room, which opened to a small patio in the back. Isabel could eat Goldfish crackers and draw to her heart's content. She could sit there with a nice view out the window and Desiree right there in earshot, and it would be fine.

Throughout the morning, Melanie saw patients, managing for once to keep on schedule. Already she knew so many things about them, facts that often made her behold them with a kind of horrified respect. Mr. Pleasants, whose seventeen-year-old son had been shot a few months ago and left quadriplegic; Mrs. Kandell, whose husband had recently broken her jaw; Ms. Kemp, whose toddler daughter had swallowed a baggie of heroin and died; Ms. Marshall, whose twenty-year-old son needed hemodialysis for end-stage renal disease. They moved with a kind of slow dignity, Melanie thought, under the mantle of sorrow.

How did one even begin to cross the chasm of experiences like that? And yet, she had learned to approach everyone with a firm professionalism, stern and practical-minded. When Mr. Simpkins's urine came back dirty, they discussed it calmly. When Mrs. Watts lost her take-homes, they came up with a new plan. And so the day progressed as a series of discrete micro-dilemmas to be solved. Mr. Pleasants needed his SSRI uptitrated. Mrs. Kandell was oversedated and needed her methadone decreased. Mrs. Watson needed to see her ID doctor because she'd run out of her antiretrovirals. Ms. Smith wanted to switch from methadone to Suboxone.

It was fairly simple, in a way. Cheree was right. The problems—at least the problems she was equipped to address—were, in theory, the easier ones.

"I still got withdrawals, Miss," Elon Jones said. He was a relatively new patient. "I got 'em bad. I need my dose increased."

"Let's give it a little time," she said, studying the man. He demonstrated none of the telltale signs of opioid withdrawal. He looked comfortable, pupils neither dilated nor constricted. "We just increased it. I promise, we'll get you where you need to be."

Mr. Jones coughed. He was painfully bony, the shirt he wore torn at the collar so that she could see his knobby shoulder bones and clavicle. He had the sunken cheeks and temporal wasting of someone chronically ill. Tuberculosis, she thought, or hepatitis C. His initial lab work was still pending. When he lifted his arms, Melanie was overcome with a sour smell of body odor and dried sweat.

He coughed again, and Melanie reflexively backed away a little. He gazed up at her, waxen-faced and strange, like some twilit creature from Isabel's folklore book.

"You're not treating my anxiety either," Mr. Jones said. His voice was robotic, flat. "I need something for anxiety."

Melanie sighed. "We'll get there," she said, her voice sharper than she'd intended. "It takes a while for this medicine to work."

"Won't help," Mr. Jones said. "I need the little pills. The Xanax. It's the only thing that helps me."

"We don't prescribe that here," Melanie said. "It's just a temporary fix. Like a shot of liquor. What I've prescribed is much safer in the long term."

"Well, fuck," Mr. Jones said, clutching his ropy arms and rising from the cheap plastic chair. "I want out of this shithole of a clinic then. If you don't wanna help me, I want the fuck out."

"Listen," Melanie said, attempting to make her voice soothing.

He cut her off. "You and the rest," he said. "Treating me like I'm already dead. Like I'm contagious."

"Sir, I'm trying to help," she said, but she was already speaking to an empty room. Mr. Jones was gone, the door swinging shut hard behind him.

She exhaled loudly, suddenly overwhelmed by a throbbing headache. She'd never gotten a coffee that morning, and now her head was pulsing. The exchange with Mr. Jones had drained her. She didn't used to be this way—so weak, so susceptible to the things people said. It was the nature of the job.

Cheree poked her head into the room. "Your baby girl's digging in the dirt outside. Might wanna get her. There's rats in that alleyway."

The way Cheree clicked her tongue at the end let Melanie know she disapproved. Disapproved of her mothering. You wouldn't catch Cheree bringing her kids to this clinic—work was work, and it was no place for a child.

"I'm doing it all wrong," Melanie said, weary of this clinic, weary of her own incompetence. "How do I keep doing it all wrong?"

Cheree sucked her cheeks in and shrugged. "You're gonna want to get your baby out of that trash. No telling what's back there."

Melanie rose quickly, the blood still beating in her head as she walked down the stairs to the waiting room. Desiree was chatting on the phone, laughing at whatever the other person on the line had said.

"She's outside," Desiree told Melanie, covering the receiver and bobbing her head in the direction of the back patio.

"I thought you were watching her," Melanie answered, making no attempt to hide the irritation in her voice.

"She asked to go play." Desiree turned her attention back to her phone call.

The clinic building was old and cramped, and the back patio opened onto what was little more than a glorified alley between the other nearby structures. Their trash cans were back there, tucked against a fence on a small patch of weedy ground. The ground itself was festive with bits of broken glass, bright fast-food wrappers, and limp condoms like spent balloons.

Melanie opened the door from the break room and walked out onto the deck. She couldn't spot Isabel at first, but then she saw her crouching by the fence. She was fully absorbed, her small hands shaping and pressing something.

"Isabel!" Melanie called. "This isn't a good place to play."

Hearing her mother, Isabel turned and looked up, her small face pleased. That was one thing Melanie wished would never fade—that look of eager delight to share some new astonishment. This would change, Claire had assured her, in only a few years. That sweetness would dissipate in a flood of bitter hormones.

"What are you doing?" Melanie asked.

She could see a patch of dirt in front of Isabel with something in the center, partially covered.

"A burial," Isabel announced, pointing to the object in the center of the dirt. "A vampire burial. I'm putting the stake in the heart."

"What is that?" Melanie asked, a sick feeling welling up in her. She stepped closer, making out the damp gray of feathers. "A dead bird?"

"A laughing gull, I think," Isabel said.

Her smart little daughter and her books. Melanie felt a lurch in her chest that was part squeamishness, part pride.

"It was here. I found it. See?" Isabel scooped away the dirt and bits of trash to reveal more of the corpse.

And that was when Melanie saw the small stake Isabel had found to pierce the bird's heart—a broken intravenous needle. It rested in the bird as innocently as a pin in a pincushion.

Melanie jerked Isabel's shoulder, pulling her away. "Isabel, no. Where'd you get that? The needle."

"I found it," Isabel said, clearly pleased with her resourcefulness. "There are lots of them. All over the place. People just threw them out, I guess."

It was true, Melanie saw. The ground was littered with discarded IV needles, glinting silver in the late sun. "You don't touch needles," she said. "There are germs. You'll catch things."

Isabel looked down, tucking her hand behind her back. "I just wanted a stake," she murmured. "For the vampire burial."

"Come here," Melanie said sharply, grabbing Isabel's arm and yanking it forward.

Isabel gasped. "You're hurting me, Mommy," she said, her voice more scared than it should have sounded.

Melanie flinched but didn't let go. Her fingers were clenched hard around Isabel's soft, babyish wrist, which was smeared with a streak of blood.

She understood then that everything would always hurt her more than it hurt Isabel. Something flew up into her chest, frantic and beating. It was panic. Panic transmogrified to its most animal form. All those pathogens, furious and tiny and alive, that might or might not be replicating inside her baby, her Isabel—how could she stave them off? By what force of prayer or potion or magic could you save your own flesh and blood? By what charm or chant could you protect anyone?

She could hear Cheree's voice, muffled behind her, and she could see a cluster of patients gathered to smoke cigarettes around the side of the building, but they all seemed unreal and distant, like a great flock of bodies on the far side of a river.

HIGHER THINGS

Mara heard the animal their first night in the rental—a skittering of claws followed by a small crash overhead. Then, more clicking right above where they lay on that old-fashioned canopy bed with its lumpy, ridged mattress (listed as a queen in the rental ad, but definitely only a full). Benny slept beside her, his whiskered jaw slack, lips slightly parted, his chest rattling. His sleep was never interrupted by such things—a wonder, really, and indicative of his general unflappability.

She nudged him, gently at first.

"Benny!" she hissed, and he shifted, resettling the heft of himself against her. She was sitting upright at this point, her arms hugging her knees. The house was cool even though it was summer, and her arms were goosebumped. Mountain summer, mountain nights.

"There's something in the attic."

"Go back to sleep," he murmured, his eyelids fluttering.

There was another thump, followed by the thud of something soft but heavy toppling. It, *he*, sounded large, Mara thought. Already, she found herself referring to the animal interchangeably as an *it* or a *he*. It had a male energy—those impudent sounds, that brash thumping across the floor.

This summer rental outside of Boone had been the cheapest option they could find that still had an internet connection. Slow internet, dial-up, but internet all the same, which wasn't a given in these small mountain coves, these between-town hideaways tucked into the ridges. Benny had argued against internet altogether—wasn't the whole idea to have a summer without distraction; time to themselves?—but the thought left Mara feeling strangely bereft. What would she *do*, she moaned, without it? What if people were sending her email, or Facebook messages? All that, of course, could wait, Benny had replied. Mara knew her reaction meant that she was a weak and uninteresting person, someone lacking adequate inner resources, but Benny had eventually relented, and they'd found this house—pale yellow planks with a narrow porch in front and a larger screened porch in the back. No cell reception, but a landline in the event that someone really needed to reach them. In the online photo, the house had appeared modest, appealing in its unassumingness, like a plain-faced country girl at the Saturday night dance. In reality, the house needed a paint job badly, and someone ought to trim the wisteria that threatened to overtake it.

"It's perfect," Mara had said when they'd first driven up the long dirt drive. By perfect, she'd meant it perfectly suited Benny's vision of himself. He was enormously wealthy—family wealth, inherited—but did not like to think of himself as such. His life had been hard-scrabble, whether buffered by the fallback of money or not, and he insisted that no one forget this. It made him the worst sort of cheap-skate, a quality that Mara could still manage to find quaint, even endearing. He fancied himself the sort of person who taught in order to make ends meet so that he could devote the rest of his time to his art.

Mara, on the other hand, had a habit of referring to herself as a *layabout*, meaning that she worked three different part-time jobs, none of them impressive or desirable. *The opposite of a layabout*, Benny, ever a champion of the proletariat, had pointed out. *It's called irony*, Mara had responded. What she did not say was that she worried she was dull, particularly in comparison to him, and so had adopted a defensive strategy of self-deprecation.

Benny loved the ramshackle, the run-down, the struggling-to-survive. Benign neglect, disrepair—these only indicated a devotion to higher things. Mara sometimes suspected this was what had drawn him to her.

"Not bad," Benny had said, pulling Mara toward him. She'd let herself be dipped back, like a ballroom dancer or a bride. His lips against hers were delicate and papery-dry. She reached up to his throat and felt his pulse throbbing there. *Alive, alive, alive*, his pulse said. When he pulled away, he coughed hard, loosening something viscous at the center of him. He was always coughing, *mucking out the slugs*, he said. *Slugging out the muck.*

Phlegmatic, in every sense, Benny had said not long after they'd first met. This was the kind of cool humor he allowed himself, this detached amusement at the body and its failings. Mara had laughed, later looking the word up just to make certain she understood.

The rental meant a summer alone, finally. Finally, the two of them, free of their recent counterparts: one bad boyfriend (Mara's), and a jealous wife with two sullen, skinny boys, twins adopted from the Ukraine (Benny's). Mara was Benny's mistress. She was the mistress who had triumphed, the woman a man had left his wife and kids for. *The woman commonly referred to as the villain*, her friend Lu had pointed out.

Benny was already snoring again beside her, the curve of his back jammed too close to where she sat, cold, in nothing but a ribbed tank top. There was a thump up above, the long scratch of something hard on wood. Whatever animal lurked up there sounded too big to be a raccoon or opossum. He was heavier than that, more substantial. There was a creak, and she thought that it—*he*, the creature—was definitely trying to enter the main part of the house.

The rental was all one floor: an open layout, with the master bedroom and bath in the rear opening onto a screened porch. There was a large living area with a stone fireplace and adjoining kitchen, and one extra room that was well-lit enough to serve as Benny's makeshift studio. The walk-up attic was off-limits; the owner used it for storage. Mara had climbed the stairs earlier and found the door padlocked. A little guidebook left by the hearth informed them about the nearest grocery store and gas station, along with various features of the house.

Mara slid out of the bed and grabbed Benny's sweater from a chair, pulling it over her head. Benny sighed in his sleep, the persistent rustle of his breath like tissue paper crinkling. She didn't want him to wake again. Slipping out of the bedroom, she headed back to the stairs that led up to the attic. Her feet were cold on the wooden steps, and she stepped the way she imagined a primitive hunter might when stalking prey.

She did not want it to hear her. It, him—the animal. She did not want it to know she was coming.

There was silence except for a pounding in her own head as she climbed, pausing between each step. When she got to the attic door with its padlock, she pressed her ear against the wood and waited.

Nothing. Nothing except the hum and creak and buzz that wove together to compose the present silence. Her heart slowed, and she focused on her breathing, counting each inhalation and exhalation the way her old therapist had first taught her to manage her anxiety.

A boom resounded, and she jumped back, stumbling but catching herself. The animal, as if aware that she was there listening, had slammed itself against the door.

A purposeful scratching followed—a painful noise, that long, slow drag of hardened keratin against wood.

She half-toppled down the stairs, back to the bedroom, back to the lumpy mattress. She pulled up the sheet and pressed herself, fish-cold, against large, warm Benny, her wheezing genius, her phlegmatic ticket somewhere. Somehow, some time later, it was morning.

* * *

Benny had told her on their first date-that-was-not-quite-a-date that he was dying. A lung disease. Genetic, autosomal recessive, but not cystic fibrosis.

He laughed, defusing her response. "Heck, I might be dying more slowly than you. People live with this thing for quite a long time now."

She'd nodded. He was large and captivating, a man who carried the bulk of himself handsomely. The word *rugged* kept coming to her mind, and yet he was a teacher. And a painter. He had won awards— was famous in a minor sort of way, famous among the cognoscenti.

"CF gets all the buzz, of course," he continued. "And what I've got, well, similar, same end result, but no glamour." He chuckled, then broke into a fit of coughing.

They'd met in AA. Benny was an AA veteran, whereas she was a relative newbie, still white-knuckling it, still doubtful of whatever guiding force all the others seemed to have found, still teetering through the first of the twelve steps. *And already working that thirteenth step,* her friend Lu, also an AA old-timer, had declared in her singsong voice when Mara told her about Benny.

True, she'd been drawn to Benny. She couldn't help herself. And yet she should have kept her distance. Reasons included: Benny was married; she had a boyfriend, Raoul, who made good money working as a mechanic; she had one year of semi-fragile sobriety; Benny had twins with his wife.

And yet, and yet.

When he'd asked to paint her after a meeting, she'd cackled at the cliché. She'd been aware of his presence for some time at that point, had sensed the way his eyes followed her, how he tracked her movement through the church basement.

"That's the line you're using?"

"You assume I'm using a line."

She'd smiled, waiting for this to prove to be a joke, but he'd cocked his head, pressing his hands together. He had large, dry, capable-looking hands—hands you could imagine fixing things or punching someone in a bar fight. It was harder to imagine these same hands holding a paintbrush, making fine strokes across canvas.

"Please. Nothing improper."

And that was how she had found herself naked, reclining on a plush blue bath towel in a pool of sunlight in his converted-garage studio. Naked on the first date—but it wasn't a date, really, was it? She lay there, feeling herself go into a trancelike state while the sun warmed her limbs and Benny worked. The silence was punctuated only by the sound of his brush and an occasional cough. She had the strange feeling that he was seeing something in her that no one else yet had—some potential or insight, something that suggested she was more than a recovering alcoholic who worked days as an administrative assistant in an office and nights in a diner for tips.

When he was finished, he wrapped her in a big white bathrobe, made them both cups of tea, and they talked. She noted how careful he'd been, averting his eyes as he'd put the robe on her shoulder like he knew that once he was no longer painting her, the normal social boundaries again applied. He was scrupulous to avoid touching her directly.

"I'd like to show you something," he said, gesturing for her to follow. She padded quietly behind him to the far corner of the garage studio, waiting as he pulled out three canvases and uncovered them, then stepped aside. He watched her for her reaction.

She recognized herself immediately: the first painting, blue-tinged and moody, showed her in profile, lost in thought. The second was a figure depicted at a distance in a smudgy woodland dusk, and yet she could tell by the slight hitch in the shoulder, the angle of the head, that it was she. And the third was a straightforward portrait, Mara looking head-on, something troubled and mysterious in her eyes, suggesting either imminent confrontation or tears. The woman in the painting contained a depth and seriousness that left her feeling unspeakably grateful to Benny—grateful that he'd somehow seen past all her nervous failures and unstarted ideas to this, whatever *this* was. It was there, in the paintings: proof. He'd been painting her already, painting her all along.

"I have a tendency to paint the things I want," he said. "I paint things into being. Nature has had her day."

He smiled, half joking at first, but then, from the way he looked at her, she decided he meant what he said. He had, she'd noticed already, a magpie's love of language, cribbing bright bits, stealing shiny phrases. She'd often sense that he was quoting something, as if from a big invisible book. He continued to hold her gaze until her cheeks burned, and she found herself admiring his utter confidence.

"Do you believe in fate? Destiny?" Benny asked. He could deliver words like this—words that would be mere tin coming from anyone else, but from him, they were gold.

She couldn't tell if he was spinning another line, reeling her in even harder. She studied him for a moment, his kind brown eyes. Later, when she confided the exchange to Lu—mentioned the portraits already painted in the garage—Lu had shrieked with laughter and declared this either the most romantic story she'd ever heard, or the most stalker-ish.

Mara had looked at those portraits of herself in Benny's garage once more before answering. "I guess so."

"I think you're meant for something more," he announced solemnly. "I think you're meant for me."

She felt something large and bursting rise up between them—a ripe peach splitting, warm and inevitable as the sun—but still they had not touched. It ran deeper than that with them; she knew this already. He'd seen something promising in her, something she'd dreamed might be there all along.

Mara slept hard into the next morning, long after the summer heat had intensified in the bedroom. She was sweating by the time she walked into the kitchen. Benny had left the pot of coffee on, and she saw that he must have gotten supplies from the nearest store, fifteen miles or so away. She poured herself a mug and wandered toward the spare room, out of which spilled a cello concerto. Benny liked music while he worked.

She tapped on the door and pushed it open just as he turned to look at her.

"Sleepyhead," he said, paintbrush poised in midair.

"I got woken up last night. Remember? The animal in the attic?"

He shook his head, smiling at her fondly, as if she were an inventive child.

"We should call an exterminator. Or animal control. I don't know. Who do you call for an animal trapped in an attic?"

"It's probably a squirrel. Or a raccoon," Benny said. "We can let the owner know, but for now, I think it's all right. It's happy up there. It won't bother us."

She sipped her coffee and glanced at the ceiling, almost unconsciously. True, the animal was completely silent now. But probably it was nocturnal. She envisioned it, vague and brown-furred, nestled in a corner between a box of Christmas decorations and a plastic container of old sweaters.

"It's peaceful here, isn't it?" Benny remarked, turning back to his canvas. "I'm on a mandatory schedule," he declared. "You are, too. No more talking until after lunch. Go write."

He raised his palette with a flourish, and she nodded, turning and closing the door behind her.

She had already wasted half of their first morning. This was no way to start. In addition to having an interlude together, finally free from the tearful remonstrations of Raoul (who'd yelled at them, obviously intoxicated, outside of Benny's studio) and the icy messages from Benny's wife, this was supposed to be a time for her to tap into some dormant creative force. She would write something. For so long, she'd felt a sensitivity to things. In school, her teachers had made note of it, the way her ear was tuned to language, how she noticed little details—the flicker of iridescence on a pigeon, the chortle of plumbing at night. She was a too-sensitive girl born into a loud, chaotic household, destined to be either an artist or simply a sufferer.

So she'd grown into a person who thought of herself as creative but who was always ever just on the brink of creating. Then: all those blackout years, evenings blurred with laughter and cheap wine, bad boyfriends, and that constant worry-cloud of debt, the ever-present menace of poverty that kept her with those bad boyfriends.

And now: Benny. Heavy, broad-shouldered, capable Benny, who was frugal by principle but did not know the true specter of privation. She was finally sober. He saw something soulful in her, something he wanted to draw out. She would write poetry.

She took her notebook and laptop along with a second cup of coffee back to the screened-in porch. A trio of deer, dark-eyed and bold, bolted across the backyard. Her mind was like those deer. She wondered when Benny would stop for lunch, when they would lounge like lizards in the sun, when they would make love lazily on that too-small lumpy bed. She felt pleasantly drowsy already, the morning shot. She let her eyes close and knew she would get nothing done.

She woke to Benny nuzzling her shoulder, and only then did she realize she'd fallen asleep in her chair. The long shadows cast by the trees in the yard showed it was later, much later. The afternoon.

"Sleepy girl," Benny said fondly. "The bird is on the wing."

The notepad on her lap was empty. Benny was kissing the length of her neck, nibbling as if it were an ear of summer corn—sumptuous, a short-lived delicacy, but wasn't that just everything? He had a way of savoring it all.

"Come with me," he said, and she let her notepad fall off her lap, let herself be guided inside with his big rough hands, let herself be pulled against him, his consuming warmth—always distracting her from some thought, some sound in the distance that she could never fully discern.

When Benny had told her that he was being referred for the lung transplantation list, he spoke as if it were merely a precaution, like getting a flu shot or taking a multivitamin. He told her when they were sprawled, flushed and naked, on his bed back home, a photo of his snaggle-toothed twins grinning at her lewdly from a nearby shelf. Her impulse was to turn the frame facedown, but she didn't want to be the sort of person who was flustered by such things. Your boyfriend's children, your boyfriend's ex-wife, your boyfriend's chronic lung disease, your boyfriend's impending lung transplant. The glistening lungs of a dead person being lifted by gloved hands and placed gently into the maw of your boyfriend's open chest.

"That means your lungs are very bad," she said without inflection, staring down the twins in their frame.

"I told you that when I first met you." He coughed, then reached for an inhaler on the bedside table and took a long, slow drag.

"But that's worse than I thought."

She felt something pass over her like a shadow, a tightening in the corners of her eyes that she recognized as tears forming. If there was one thing Benny couldn't stand, it was weeping. Weakness and self-pity. Benny would gobble up weakness with his great life-loving jaws. He had no use for it.

He laughed his big, hoarse laugh. "Moving up the list can take time. I qualify, based on my lung function. My doctors insisted. My *parents* insisted. I've told you what they're like—at every hospital fundraising event, waiting at the heels of my pulmonologists whether I like it or not."

She'd heard about Benny's parents, who embarrassed him. He avoided them for the most part, but she'd seen photos—stiff-lipped people with careful hair and worried eyes, dressed always in formal attire. They were gala-goers, charity ball hosts, alumni donors. Benny said they'd been this way since he was a child—throwing money at the institutional gods, an act of appeasement meant to save their only child. Caution was their religion, money their burnt offering. They were the eponymous donors of the new wing of the children's hospital where Benny had spent intervals during his youth.

Though Mara had never met Benny's parents, in a way she felt she understood them better than she understood Benny. Benny, with his careless ease, his unworried cheer, haunted by neither the past nor the future, was unfathomable to her.

"Okay," she'd said cautiously, studying his face for any further clue of something dreadful. "It's no big deal then."

"No bigger deal than all the rest," he said, opening his palm to her as if with some offering. "Time's winged chariot hurrying near, et cetera. True for us all, my darling. Gather ye rosebuds, Mara. I'm gathering mine."

He spoke like this, in allusions she might have easily recognized had she lived a different life—grown up with book-loving, moneyed parents, gone to college. And yet, always, she felt she got what he meant anyway. So she let herself melt against the warm bulk of him, comforted by the steady rise and fall of his chest. *Alive, alive, alive.*

They had a summer feast that evening, and Mara realized she had not heard the animal for the entirety of that day. Maybe it had left the attic. Maybe she'd imagined the whole thing: invented a creature out of snatches of country sounds. *That* took a kind of creative ingenuity, she thought, cutting the last fragrant tomato that Benny had picked up from a local farmer's roadside stall.

"Just a hint of salt," Benny cautioned as she arranged the sliced tomatoes on a plate. He loved food in the way of a man who took all his pleasures seriously. Real tomatoes, summer tomatoes, he'd instructed, should not be adulterated.

Mara shucked corn next, letting the silk fall to the sink and stick to her fingers. "You got good work done today?" she asked.

His attention was on the okra he was frying on the stovetop—a childhood favorite he'd insisted on. "Oh, yes," he said. "It's a series that's important to me. I'm closing in on it."

He offered her a secretive smile, giving the okra a little stir with a spatula. He did not like to show her his work before it was finished. He was very private this way; perhaps the only way in which she felt he held himself at a distance from her.

"Take a bite of this," she said, offering a triangle of watermelon. He bit, and the juice ran down her arm, and he smiled at her.

"Sweet to tongue and sound to eye," he said, then kissed her while the okra popped and spit in the pan.

He gave Mara this feeling like she would surely rupture if she did not make something. She would wake up tomorrow and start writing. She would prove herself to be the person he saw: a person who dreamed things into reality, sweet to tongue and sound to eye.

She even admired the way he ate, with such gusto and relish, closing his eyes in pleasure at each precise flavor. It made her feel timid, a woman of blanched winter supermarket tomatoes and bagged white bread. But she vowed to be more like him. More alive.

That night, long after they'd washed the dishes and gone to bed, Mara could not sleep. The animal, so far at least, remained quiet overhead, yet she found herself anticipating its movements. It would walk soon. It would prowl. Benny lay beside her, sleeping the peaceful sleep of a man contented with himself and all around him. The little bedroom seemed suddenly stifling, so she got up.

She walked to the screened porch and sank into the rocking chair, listening to the steady, mechanized whir of crickets and frogs; the loudness of country quiet. She sat there, attempting to be contemplative but shivering.

Back inside, she busied herself drying dishes and putting them back in the cabinets. She still felt a restlessness, a discontent verging on fear, and the fact occurred to her: she was nothing without Benny.

In the daylight hours, this fact was obliterated by his all-encompassing presence. She glowed with his reflected light, borne into luminescence by proximity to him. But when he was asleep, absent, she felt herself sink into a deep, familiar terror. A nothingness. She'd made it this far, and without the radiance of his being, she was nothing.

This was the old terror, she recognized now, that led to the drinking. Drinking blunted the sharp edges, blurred the outline of her fear. And now, she faced nights like this with nothing to help her.

She wandered to the room Benny had designated as his studio, opened the door slowly, and turned on the light.

The space still smelled of Benny: paints, turpentine, his deodorant. He was an athletic painter, often sweating through the t-shirts he wore while he worked. She picked up a clean brush and flicked it under her chin. A stack of stretched canvases was propped against a wall. She thumbed a canvas forward and tilted it back. The first was blank. But the second appeared to be finished.

It was a country scene, with a long, winding road and a large tree in the distance—an oak, maybe. The colors indicated dusk. The scene was almost idyllic except for the car Benny had painted accordioned against the tree. Crushed. She could see minute brushwork indicating smoke, flames. When she examined the car closely she could make out the smallest indication of a figure—just a shadow, really, some black gesso hinting at a profile—crumpled against a steering wheel.

A coldness seized her, and she almost dropped the painting. There was the smallest thump overhead, and she knew that the animal had awakened; perhaps she had summoned it. Instead of walking away, she felt compelled to look at more of Benny's recent work.

The next canvas appeared to be an elaboration of the initial scene. The car was in the foreground and surrounded by the smudgy yellows of headlights of emergency vehicles. She squinted, trying to make out the driver, but could only see gestural figures scurrying around, attempting a rescue.

The animal was above her now. She could hear the slow scritch-scratch of claws. Although it made no sense, she had the queasy feeling the animal knew what she was up to, knew that she was engaged in a violation of some sort.

Another canvas showed the same country road, darker now, a full moon out, with the debris of the smashed car still against the tree and the rear lights of an ambulance speeding away.

The final canvas sat on Benny's easel, and as she turned to it, the cold feeling settled into her bones. It took her a moment to make out what this painting was—a departure, it seemed, from the initial triptych. She moved closer, realizing as she did that what at first appeared to be two large blobs were actually a delicately rendered set of lungs. Nothing more. The lungs took up the entire canvas. She could discern now the thready indication of the bronchial tree, the alveoli. The image had the excruciating accuracy of a medical illustration. Healthy lungs, she knew immediately. New lungs. Lungs for Benny. The lungs he wanted and would get.

Mara felt a catch in her own chest and backed away slowly, turning off the light and closing the door.

All night, she listened as the wild thing above her dragged itself, heavy-knuckled, across the attic floor. All night, she wondered what the creature might want from them—from her—but she said nothing. She did not wake Benny.

When morning broke and Benny kissed her, Mara felt as pale and lightheaded as a Victorian lady in one of his old art illustration books.

"I see a lily on thy brow," he said, pressing one hand against her forehead.

But she shook her head, said it was nothing that ibuprofen couldn't take care of, ignored the thought of whose lungs those were in the next room.

The animal grew bolder as weeks passed and the summer days deepened. He moved in the daytime now, alert, it seemed, to where they were in the house. Mara heard him now when she poured her coffee in the morning—a barely perceptible snuffling just above her. It, he, unnerved her; she could hardly think. Her hands shook in the old way, the way she used to know how to cure with a drink.

"Surely you heard that?" she asked.

Benny was already finishing his breakfast, his hair still wild from sleeping. She, of course, had spent another restless night roiling in the sheets like a tiny sailboat in a rollicking ocean. She hadn't slept well in days, weeks. Not since they'd gotten here, really. She was exhausted. It was the animal's fault.

"Definitely a squirrel," he said peaceably.

"I don't like it."

He shrugged, taking a last sip from his mug.

"I can hear it breathing over us at night," she added.

Benny raised an eyebrow at her. "You can hear me breathing at night. I'm a very loud breather."

"I know how you sound. This is different."

"After the transplant, it'll be so much quieter you won't know what to think. You'll think I've stopped breathing and shake me awake. How's that for irony? I'll finally breathe so quietly you'll think I'm dead."

He smiled like the thought amused him. She'd noticed by now that his sense of humor was often not really a sense of humor at all but rather a way of saying discomfiting things with great satisfaction.

"You sound so certain," Mara said.

He shrugged again and kissed her. "Like attracts like," he said. "Remember that book that was so popular awhile back? *That* was the big secret. One I've known all along."

She did not find his kiss, his flippancy, to be charming. Her eyes held an ache under them, puffy with nights of sleeplessness. And still, she had not written anything. She spent the rest of that morning daydreaming of the perfect gin and tonic, glass sweating in her hand, the first sip so cold, very cold, while Benny painted to a swooping piano concerto in the next room.

When Benny found Mara after lunch, she'd just about managed to pry the lock off the door to the attic with an old hammer she'd found. She was sweating, one of her thumbs already swelling from where she'd accidentally bashed it.

"Jesus, Mara," he said. He almost sounded frustrated, and he was never frustrated by anything. Imperturbable, her Benny.

She brushed a damp strand of hair out of her eyes. The animal had sensed her presence and retreated to a corner of the attic. She could envision it crouched there, its matted fur exuding a thick must, eyes flashing narrow glints.

She did not answer Benny, even though he stood there, arms crossed, awaiting a response. Instead, she gave the lock several more hard whacks. When the padlock finally broke, she lifted it above her like a trophy, triumphant. Benny sighed loudly, but this did not stop her. She pushed, and the attic door opened with a groan. The light, when she found it, illuminated stacks and stacks of dusty cardboard boxes. There was no animal in sight.

"Mara," Benny said.

"If you aren't helping, then—" She shoved him away. It was a gentle shove, but her voice was so brusque she surprised herself. Usually she didn't talk like that to Benny. He looked stung for a moment, then chastened, like a little boy. She was already shifting aside the first few boxes when he turned to go.

"I'm not having any part of this," he called over his shoulder. "It's pointless."

She wasn't listening. Her ears were trained instead for the faintest scuttle. She strained to detect the soft thump of a tail against the wood floor. She would find the animal—and what? She hadn't thought that far. And yet she had the unshakable certitude she'd know what to do once she found it.

The trouble was that there were so many boxes: boxes the size of wardrobes, square boxes, rectangular boxes in every size. It was a wonder that the owner could have so much he needed to store. Decades and decades' worth of boxes, a pointless accumulation of stuff. She moved through the boxes as through a dusty brown forest—a landscape of hidden nooks and dead-ends and perfect hiding spots. Her hands were shaking again, she noticed. She would simply have to search in and around every box, one by one.

Mara did not stop searching the attic when Benny called up to her for dinner. She could smell basil and something spicy, a hint of lime. He did not call for her again. Her stomach grumbled, but she was unwavering. A yellow disc of light through the one attic window dwindled and then ultimately dissolved.

Benny called up that he was going to bed and she should too, but she was digging through a pile of old clothes on her hands and knees with no intention of stopping. She didn't answer. There was only so much space up here, and she would go through every inch. She would meet this animal, eye to eye, after so long—a lifetime, it seemed. Yes. She'd been waiting an entire lifetime.

When the landline rang in the wee hours, splitting the rural quiet with its obscene cry—after weeks during which no one had called them, weeks in which she'd nearly forgotten the landline's existence—she was so close to where she was certain the animal crouched, hidden, that she didn't even pause to wonder who might be bothering them at such an hour.

"Mara?" Benny called, her name bouncing against the looming piles of boxes. "Mara? It's happening. It's all happening."

But she did not answer, hunched and waiting herself, every muscle coiled—so close that she could hear the creature's frightened breath, picture its curled claws, its sour odor sharp in her nose and almost human.

GIFTS

Lynn Drucker was the sort of woman who had made me reluctant to join the group in the first place, and now she wanted to be my best friend. Again. I could tell in the way she lingered by the coffee urn while I stirred cream into my cup, in the way she followed me, slow and placid as a cow, her eyes flickering to catch mine. Whenever I entered that church basement, she would beckon me to the seat she'd saved beside her, her broad face heartbreakingly eager, like we were allies in a school cafeteria. It had been back in elementary school, after all, that I'd first met Lynn Drucker. I am regressing, I thought. I am moving backward in time. I am sitting on a plastic chair in a church basement that smells like canned tomato sauce in the desperate hope of mending myself. With Lynn Drucker.

Parked at the far end of the church lot that first Tuesday evening, I'd hesitated with the engine running. I could still change my mind. But I hadn't. I'd entered the building and found my way to the meeting room downstairs.

The other women gathered were, as I'd unfairly expected, dowdy and plain. The few who had taken some care with their appearance were expending their efforts the wrong way—their highlights a garish yellow, their tropical-sorbet-colored cigarette pants intended for a much younger set. These are my people now, I thought. This is what I have become.

"Janey! Hi! Welcome!" A woman was approaching me, clasping my arm. She was the dowdiest of all, wearing a shapeless black shirt and an ill-matching navy skirt. She was heavy-bodied and heavy-faced, the delicate skin around her eyes dry and red. When she sniffed, her whole upper lip retracted, revealing a set of unbeautiful teeth. She looked sturdy, built for hard labor—someone with chafed hands and thick, practical arms meant for milking. I stared at her, not because I didn't recognize her, but because she looked exactly the same, only larger, more fully realized, more herself.

"It's me, Lynn. Lynn Drucker! From Harvell Elementary? Remember?" She smiled at me with genuine warmth. "Janey Whitmore! You're back!"

"Lynn!" I said, masking my surprise as enthusiasm. It was hard to believe she was only in her thirties—my age. But Lynn Drucker had always looked middle-aged. Maybe Lynn Drucker was finally reaching the age she'd always been meant to be. And maybe thirty-something was older than I'd wanted to admit, anyway.

"Welcome to the group!" she said. "I'm sorry about your divorce!" She added this brightly, like we were discussing a bake sale.

"Oh, we're not divorced yet," I said, as if the distinction mattered. "Rob and I are separated. We've got a little boy, Tommy, so, you know . . ." I let my voice trail off, because when I spoke of Tommy, only eight years old with big, liquid eyes, I'd get an ache in my throat and my own eyes would start to water.

Lynn's forehead crinkled. "I understand," she said. "You've come to the right place."

"What about you?" I asked. "How long ago were you divorced?" We'd only recently moved back, so I wasn't up to date on these things.

"Oh, no," she said. "I wasn't. I never married. My father thought the group might be good for me." She cocked her head. "Come on, let's get you a snack and a seat."

Before I could protest, she led me to a table covered in a white paper tablecloth, set with tea cookies spread fanlike on a plate. She filled a Styrofoam cup of coffee for me and placed a handful of cookies on a napkin, and like that—like it had been foreordained—I followed her.

She introduced me to the other women with her arm inked in mine, proprietary. They nodded, friendly and encouraging. Lynn Drucker held a certain authority, I understood. I'd been taken under her wing.

Back in elementary school, Lynn Drucker had been similarly stolid and slow-moving, a sea mammal surely graceful in water but plodding on land. She came to school wearing quaint hand-sewn blouses and pinafores, heavy woolen skirts, and old-mannish black socks with thick-soled shoes. Even as early as first grade, we knew, little pack animals that we were, that her smell was off, that she was not one of us. Our parents dressed us in bright t-shirts emblazoned with cartoon characters or unicorns. We laughed along with sitcom laugh tracks and got punch lines easily. Lynn once inadvertently revealed her family did not believe in celebrating Halloween. Over time, we also learned that she did not know who Bart Simpson was, had never tasted Kool-Aid, didn't know Michael Jordan from Michael Jackson, didn't even have a television. This struck us as outrageous.

Very often, I was partnered with Lynn. I think this was because of some teacherly instinct to pair a "good" child with a misfit. I say "good" meaning I was quiet and serious, too hesitant to say very much at all, especially not when Ashley-Claire Thompson and Rebecca Kerr started calling Lynn "Augustus Gloop," or when, a few years later, they told her that the letters OPP shaved into the back of Derek Lovegood's buzz cut stood for "Opportunity!" then howled with laughter.

Back in third grade, when Lynn and I were desk partners, I started receiving strange little gifts. Once, it was a small speckled chicken's egg, unlike the type I saw in cartons from the grocery store; another time, a long, sleek feather, oil-black and iridescent, tied with a red ribbon; another time, a chunk of homemade toffee wrapped in wax paper. It never occurred to me to question my good fortune until one day, after all the other kids had gone out for recess, I sought the new tiny treasure left for me: a halved geode the size of a baby's fist. I looked up and saw Lynn waiting in the doorway, watching me.

"You like it?" she asked, the tips of her ears pink with pleasure.

"Yes," I answered, abashed for some reason, unsure what social transaction had taken place.

"You're my best friend," she said, looking away from me, a smile like an open wound across her face. "You're the nicest girl at school."

Even then, I'd known that this was untrue. Lynn fled the room while I stood there, sick with guilt, the geode heavy in my fist. I was embarrassed by Lynn, embarrassed by her openness, her oddness, her affections. And yet now, because of the gifts, I was bound to her. We would be inextricably linked. Never would I flit about, a big bow bouncing atop my sleek ponytail, with Ashley-Claire or Rebecca.

The geode was beautiful, but I stuffed it down to the bottom of the wastebasket by the teacher's desk. I wanted to be rid of it.

Then the gifts stopped. I noticed one day that the geode was tucked in Lynn's desk. She had found and rescued it. This shamed me even more.

Some weeks later, Lynn arrived late to school wearing a lumpy sweater even though it was late spring and warm. She smiled at me in such a conspiratorial way that I knew I'd been forgiven. Finally, she gestured for me to come close. Pulling forward the neck of her sweater, she revealed her surprise. There, nestled against her chest, was a tiny, perfect piglet.

"He's a runt, like Wilbur," she said, angling the opening of her sweater toward me so I could admire him. She leaned down to kiss his snout. "We can share him. He can be ours."

Our whole class had cried at the end of *Charlotte's Web*. Everyone wanted a real live baby piglet.

"Where did you get him?" I asked her.

"The farm," she said. "Our farm. We have lots of pigs."

Later in the day, inevitably, Wilbur the piglet got loose to the mixed horror and delight of the class. The vice principal called Lynn's parents, two stern-looking old people dressed all in black. Her mother wore a cloche hat in dark felt, the brim pulled over her face. She marched her daughter to our desk to gather Lynn's homework assignments. We all hushed, studying her. Mrs. Drucker had the rounded shoulders and quick, uncertain steps of someone willing herself to disappear. When she turned for just a moment, I got a clear view of her face: her jaw and cheek on one side were a taut, corrugated red. Burned. I looked quickly away. Mrs. Drucker hurried, head down, out of our classroom.

When Lynn returned to school the next day, she was limping. She wouldn't meet my eyes. When I asked her what happened, she told me she broke her toe. She accidentally dropped something heavy on it.

"My father says that's what happens to stupid girls," she told me, still not making eye contact. "Clumsy girls."

What happened to Wilbur, I wanted to know, still tantalized by his tiny perfection, that sweet, animal adorableness, by my love of Charlotte and her web.

He was dead, Lynn explained flatly. That's what happens to runts.

Lynn was a presence in the support group, albeit a mostly silent one. Though she didn't say much, she was a vigorous nodder, and she was the first to rush to whichever woman was crying, the first to comfort her, to stroke her head. She'd often arrive with delicious baked goods to share during the meeting.

"I just made this, and there's no way we could finish it all," she'd say, beaming over a loaf of apple bread or a chocolate pear cake. "It's my father's favorite, but it's too much for the two of us."

Her mother had died years earlier, so it was just Lynn and her father left on the farm. They hired in-season help sometimes, she explained, but only ever temporary. Lynn never mentioned her mother or her mother's death. She referred to her father only in passing, the way one would a benign but forgettable roommate. Her life outside the farm, it seemed, was the group.

No one ever commented on the fact that Lynn had never gone through a bitter divorce herself; she was too stalwart, so this fact was elided. She was single; we were single. Same, same.

I never saw Lynn be anything other than supportive, except once, when Liz Harrington tearfully announced that she and her husband were trying to reconcile.

"We're giving it a shot," Liz said, dabbing her eyes with a tissue but smiling.

The response was mixed. Some women cheered for her. Daphne Parsons lifted her cup of water and proposed an impromptu toast. Clementine Brown gave a little whoop. There was also a smattering of grumbles, murmuring—it had been a bad situation between Liz and Mike Harrington, after all, and we'd heard all the details.

I noticed Lynn, pallid, her mouth twisted in disbelief. She cleared her throat, letting the paper napkin she'd been working into fine shreds fall to the floor.

"You can't go back," she said, her voice quavering, quiet at first. She rose on her heavy haunches, moving toward the center of our circle, and her voice grew more firm. "He *cheated* on you. It's not right. You can't."

I wasn't sure what to say. The room had grown hushed. Lynn's forehead was beaded with sweat, and she was swaying slightly.

Liz flinched, visibly embarrassed. "Well, I . . ." she began, her hands shooting up to her face as if she might reflexively cover it. She rubbed hard at her jaw as though massaging a bad tooth. "I thought it was worth a try. He says he's changed."

The mood in the room had shifted from overall celebration to dismay. Almost as suddenly, Lynn retreated.

"I'm sorry," she said, stepping back and lowering herself gently back into her chair. "I shouldn't have said that."

Liz shook her head furiously. "Oh, no," she said. "No. Please, Lynn. I understand—I hope you do."

"Of course," Lynn said, quiet but decisive. "Of course. I understand. . . ." Her voice trailed off, and someone eagerly changed the subject.

When Lynn invited me to spend the night at her house in sixth grade, I didn't want to go.

"But it'd be nice of you," my mother said. "She's a good girl. You should."

"Hoity-toity Janey," my stepdad said.

My stepdad accused me of being hoity-toity whenever I objected to anything, like him dipping Skoal and spitting at the kitchen table or cutting his dirt-grimed nails in the living room. He was a good man, my mom always reminded me. Never raised a hand to her, and a provider too—*unlike other deadbeats I could mention,* she would add. He also tolerated with good humor my mother's occasional nights out with coworkers for strawberry sparkletinis at Applebee's. *Bonding with the girls,* he'd say. *I get it. You need your time with the women-friends.*

My stepdad was the one who ended up driving me out to the Druckers' farm, miles out on rural Highway 18, in the middle of nowhere.

The road was narrow and dual-lane, and large fields opened like two broad hands on either side. We finally came to a dirt drive, which we drove up, and there sat a plain, clapboard farmhouse. It was larger than I'd thought it would be.

Lynn ran outside, wiping her hands on the sides of her shirt. "You're here!" she sang.

I climbed down from the cab of my stepdad's truck with my sleeping bag and backpack. Lynn hugged me. She smelled like hay and woodchips. I saw the lean silhouette of her father hunching to fix a bit of machinery around the side of the house. He didn't stop what he was doing to greet us.

"Y'all have fun," my stepdad said, leaning over to close the passenger door instead of waiting to speak with Lynn's parents.

I stood there uncertainly, watching him back his truck out of the drive until Lynn grabbed my hand and pulled.

The Druckers' house was cold and dark inside. There were no photos on the walls, I noticed, everything bleak and anonymous. A pile of old quilts sat on a hairy brown sofa. Lynn's mother was nowhere to be seen.

"Come on," Lynn said, gesturing for me to follow her up the bare wooden stairs.

Lynn's room was small and would have been similarly bare were it not for dozens of torn-out magazine photos of laughing girls taped to the walls: girls in jaunty yellow raincoats, heads tilted back, laughing into the rain; studious girls in plaid skirts with pencils pressed against their cheeks, lost in thought; and pretty girls with shiny brown ponytails grooming horses. Catalog photos, I thought. Catalog friends. A ratty-looking afghan was spread across Lynn's twin bed. Despite the wall of eager, smiling girls, her room seemed lonely to me.

"Look," she said, handing me a framed photo of a stern, slender woman.

"Oh," I said, uncertain how to respond. The woman was not beautiful, but I heard in Lynn's voice her need for me to admire the photo. "Wow," I added.

"Yeah," she said, her fingers brushing over the woman's face in the glass. "That's my mom. She was so pretty. That was before her accident." Lynn gestured to her face. I felt she'd given me the opening to ask, and so I took it.

"What happened to her?"

"Cooking grease," Lynn said, her tone doleful, almost angry, and I understood I shouldn't press further.

"Afterward she took down all the photos. They made her too sad. But I kept this one." Abruptly, she brightened. "Come on," she said. "You want to see the horses?"

I spent the rest of the afternoon trailing Lynn around the farm while she showed me the animals. She cradled the chicks, holding their soft fluff up to my face so I could feel. She had names for all the pigs, even the meanest ones. I followed her over ruts in the fields, and she pointed out how far out the cows went to graze, guiding me all the way back to the tree line, where she had a special hiding spot in the hollow of a big oak. She went out there when she grew tired of chores and wanted to escape into her own head.

We'd gravitated back to the horses and were feeding them mushy crabapples when Lynn's father called us in for dinner. Lynn jerked to attention, and I saw cheerful enthusiasm fade into something more wary.

We sat across from one another at a long table, with Mr. and Mrs. Drucker on either end. I tried not to stare at Mrs. Drucker's face.

Mr. Drucker said a blessing, and then Mrs. Drucker went to the kitchen to bring out the food. I was prepared for a country feast—a steaming bowl of mashed potatoes, cornbread, green beans, ham. Instead, Mrs. Drucker brought out a pot of baked beans and hot dogs. Beanie weenies. There were slices of white bread to help soak up the meal, and Mr. Drucker took his with extra Heinz ketchup.

The meal took place in silence. Our chewing sounds seemed amplified. I could hear the very twitch of Mr. Drucker's mustache, the ends of which appeared bloodied with sauce. He drank an entire glass of milk in one gulp, wiping his mouth with the back of his hand. Mrs. Drucker was silent, neat, and did not look up from her food.

Across from me, Lynn ate quickly and ferociously. She was finished several minutes before anyone else, and sat there, eyes down. I could feel her swinging her feet underneath the table.

Finally Mrs. Drucker cleared away our bowls. Mr. Drucker then went to the living room and came back with two boxes, which he set upon the table with some ceremony. I recognized the boxes: Welton's Candy, a local delicacy, something people gave to one another for hostess gifts or housewarmings.

Mr. Drucker opened the first box and plucked out two candies, offering them to his wife. He then opened the second box and plucked out two candies, which he placed at his end of the table. He turned to me.

"Janey," he said. "Can I offer you a Welton's for dessert?"

I nodded, then remembered my manners. "Yes, please," I added. "Thank you."

He took a candy from each box and handed them to me. I waited for him to give some candy to Lynn, but he didn't. He took his seat and began unwrapping his own candy. Mrs. Drucker did the same. I looked at Lynn, but she said nothing.

"Um," I said. "Lynn didn't get any candy?" I let my sentence curl into a question, as if this were a simple omission.

Mr. Drucker sucked the piece of candy over to one side of his mouth. "Oh, Lynn had her candy already," he said. "Each of us got a box, but Lynn ate hers. She didn't save any." He tipped his head meaningfully toward her.

I glanced at Lynn, whose lips were pressed together hard. I felt queasy, too aware of the bits of hot dogs stewing in acid.

"She can have one of my pieces," I said quickly, sliding a piece over to where her fists were clenched into tight little balls. "I don't mind. Really."

Mr. Drucker jerked his chair back across the wooden floor. His hand swept down like a flash, batting the candy out of Lynn's. It spun off the table and landed on the floor.

"No," Mr. Drucker said too loudly. "No." He turned to me, his mouth tight. "She's had hers already. You get what you get, and that's it."

I could feel the heat off Lynn's face from across the table. She would not look up at me or her father.

This was the only time Lynn invited me to her house.

Rob and I were meeting for coffee while Tommy spent the weekend with his grandparents. This would be our first true conversation since Rob had moved out at my request over three months ago; we had barely spoken other than to arrange logistics regarding Tommy. Rob still kept a key to the house and often came over to watch Tommy if I had a late meeting. He'd been nonetheless reticent with me, careful to avoid protracted talk, scrupulous about giving me space.

I wasn't sure why my hands shook when I applied mascara, why my mouth tasted of sand and grit. I'd taken extra care blow-drying my hair, even putting a dab of perfume on my wrists. I puckered my lips, inspecting myself in the mirror. Maybe I still wasn't half bad. We were meeting like strangers on a date, like there was the possibility of something thrilling happening. The day was bright, early autumn, and gave me the hopeful feeling of a new school year, things starting over again.

I wondered about Liz Harrington and her husband. Were they happy again now that they'd reconciled? Did they laugh over private jokes, touch each other gently when they passed one another in the kitchen? Was it like it had been before the rupture, before Mike Harrington had been caught in flagrante with Brit Turnbull at the Cavalier Inn?

Neither Rob nor I had cheated. Instead we'd experienced—I'd experienced—merely the long unraveling of affection, the slow build-up of irritation, like so many motes of dust. I didn't know if this made things easier or harder. In a way, I wished for some great blow, some huge fight or infidelity from which were wounded but could then recover. Something cathartic, a conflagration.

Throughout our separation, Rob had communicated with me through a series of little benevolent gestures. Though he had done nothing wrong, he was trying to make amends, to win me back. I'd come home to find the toilet that wouldn't stop running finally fixed, or a bag of bagels from the new bakery sitting on the counter, or a small vase of fresh flowers arranged on the kitchen table. I liked the thought of him sneaking into the house while I was away to do these small kindnesses. This gave me hope. He knew me. He knew me better than anyone. Maybe that was really worth something. And there was Tommy to think about, after all. Didn't we at least owe him the effort?

But then I thought of Lynn at the meeting the evening before, biting viciously at a hangnail on her index finger. "Some people are weak," she'd said to me afterward, "and others are strong. It's just as true for us as it is for animals." I knew she was talking about Liz, who had just sheepishly returned Lynn's springform pan. As Lynn watched Liz walk to her car, her eyes burned like bright embers in the dull slab of her face.

Rob had arrived at the coffee shop first and claimed a table. I saw him run one broad hand through his dark hair, a gesture so utterly familiar that I wanted to weep. He glanced up and caught my gaze. I waved tentatively, gesturing that I would order, then join him. As I turned toward the line, the bell on the door jingled, and I found myself almost face to face with her. Lynn.

"Lynn!" I said, my voice rising with helium giddiness. Guilty-sounding. Like I had been caught at something.

"Janey, what a pleasant surprise!"

I watched her scan the room. Was I imagining the chastising look on her face? Surely I was.

"We should have a coffee together," she said warmly, overly warmly, as if it were a performance. "Unless you're already meeting someone?"

"I am," I said. "I mean, I'd love to, but I'm meeting Rob." I gestured to him.

"Oh, of course!" she said. "But listen, I'm not sure if you heard—" She leaned in, gesturing for me to come closer. I did, and I could feel her words, warm and milky, against my face.

"About Mike Harrington?" she whispered. I shook my head, and she continued. "He and Brit Turnbull were in a car accident last night. They're both in critical condition. Poor Liz . . ." She let her voice trail off, her eyes searching my face for a reaction, eager for something I could not name.

"Oh, Janey," she said. "You're so sensitive. I forget." She embraced me so hard it hurt. "Things balance out. Fate has its own ways of making things right. It just takes time," she whispered against the nape of my neck, as if she were comforting me.

Lynn Drucker was smart, a good student, so it was something of a surprise when she began attending fewer and fewer days of middle school. A week would elapse without her presence, and then she would show up again, often with some odd injury—a jammed finger, another broken toe, a fractured clavicle—all byproducts of growing up on a farm. One day someone put a dead squirrel in Lynn's locker. Everyone knew about it. When Lynn found it there, she was silent, unfazed. She simply went to the bathroom, wrapped the squirrel up in paper towels, and disposed of it. Lynn had once told me how she'd learned to wring a chicken's neck, to drown a sack of mewling, taffy-colored kittens. That was her life. She was accustomed to disposing of things.

Lynn and I still spoke at school, but I was distancing myself from her. Kate Turner was my new friend, who, with her black fingernail polish and thrift-store clothes, was the cool-girl alternative to Rebecca and Ashley-Claire. Lynn felt like an anachronism.

It seemed appropriate, therefore, when we learned that she would be homeschooled.

During junior year, we heard that Mrs. Drucker had died when the tractor she was driving overturned. Number one cause of farm injuries, my stepdad said. *Poor Mrs. Drucker*, my mom said. I thought of the woman: quiet, with her red-raw face. I thought of Lynn, alone now on the farm with her father.

Rob moved back in about six months after our initial separation: a relief. It was better to be with him than to be apart from him. True, there was no new magic, but things with us were warm and steady, and there's solace in that.

I dreaded telling the group. As if sensing my betrayal, Lynn had already shifted her attention. A new woman, Caroline, had joined us, and Lynn coddled her with the same possessive kindness she'd once employed with me.

At the coffee break on my last evening, Lynn smiled at me archly. "How's Rob?" she asked.

"He's good," I said quickly, warily. "I think it's going to work out."

"Oh?" Lynn said.

"Yes." Defensive, I added the bit about the flowers Rob had brought me, the toilet he'd fixed. He was a good man, my husband. I didn't know why I felt it necessary to prove this to Lynn Drucker, of all people.

"The toilet, huh?" Lynn repeated. "He fixed the toilet?" Laughing softly, she walked away.

Later that night, I thanked the group and told them I'd stop attending now that Rob had moved back in. The other women in the group were warm and seemed sincerely happy for me. Lynn sat quietly in the corner, her face inscrutable.

Escaping into the parking lot, I felt strangely triumphant. My marriage was intact. I was free. The night air was mild still but autumnal, the first of the yellow leaves already underfoot.

When I got to my car, I saw that my back tire was completely flat. A nail. I had to call Rob to pick me up.

That was just the beginning of a sequence of little bits of bad luck—our poltergeists, we said. The toilet that had so recently been fixed started running again, even overflowing once in the middle of the night. The sink got clogged. We poured just-bought milk onto our morning cereal only to gag when we took a bite—it had gone bad. We found a dozen eggs we'd just purchased all cracked, as if someone had systematically pressed a thumb into each shell. Jars of raspberry jam and mayonnaise conspired to crack and spill inside our refrigerator. Our thermostat would magically reset itself to 98 degrees overnight. And there seemed to be an abundance of nails in the road—Rob got a flat tire next, and then I got another. Then our old retriever mix, Brutus, ran away, which was strange since our backyard was fenced and he'd never before gotten out.

"It's like a country song," Rob said. "Except I got my wife back."

Everything was funny at that point, everything tolerable, even our bad luck limned with gold.

One Saturday, I asked Rob if he would go get bagels again from that new bakery. Sure, he told me, he'd been wanting to try that place.

"But didn't you go that one time—when we were apart?" I asked.

He frowned, then shook his head. "Let's not talk about the time we were apart," he said, pulling me close, kissing my mouth to hush me.

I saw Lynn Drucker only once more. Years later. After Tommy, so bright and well-adjusted I could hardly believe he was my own child, had gone away to school out of state. After Rob and I had separated a second time and then, finally, divorced. Some people, I'd learned, are meant to be alone, solitude so intrinsic to their being that there's a pull to it, a magnetism that draws the self inward while repelling others. Maybe Lynn and I were not so dissimilar after all, I thought when I saw her there in the fluorescent-bright aisle of the Super Walmart. The miraculous thing was that Lynn again appeared exactly the same. Like those portraits by the Dutch masters, her face existed outside of time. I looked older than she did now that whatever ephemeral prettiness I'd once had had passed. I could be her older sister, her mother.

Lynn was studying packages of paper towels. She too was here at midnight on a Wednesday, the lonely person's shopping hour. In a true feat of maneuvering, she was pushing a cart with one hand and an old man in a wheelchair with the other. Her father. Of course. He was tiny now, shrunken, thin-limbed and shriveled, hair white and wispy as dandelion fluff. By contrast, she radiated ruddy good health, broad-shouldered and powerful. She seemed taller. Maybe it was just in the way she moved, almost regal, down the aisles.

I thought of how terrifying Mr. Drucker had once seemed. I recalled Lynn rubbing at her bruised shins, the implicit terror behind her raisin eyes. And now? She was his caregiver, duty-bound to the old tyrant, helping him on and off of the toilet, pushing him through a big-box store for paper towels and store-brand peanut butter.

"You want cookies, Papa?" Lynn asked. She'd pulled down a bright package of rainbow chip cookies, the sort of junk food a child would clamor for. Lynn turned, and I feared she'd see me. I ducked behind the end of the aisle.

Mr. Drucker grunted, noncommittal. Lynn put the cookies back on the shelf. Her hand moved to her father with surprising gentleness. "Oh, Papa," she said, stepping back, studying the floor. "Oh, Papa, look what you've done."

I saw now what Lynn saw—a puddle on the floor beneath the cloth seat of the wheelchair—and I waited to hear her lash out, to use this opportunity to berate him. I waited to see him turn toward her, humiliated, her supplicant.

Instead, she murmured to him so softly I couldn't hear the words. Then she leaned down and kissed him gently, quickly, consolingly on his whiskery cheek. She scanned the aisle for passersby, daring anyone to question them, daring anyone to comment, and then, seeing no one, she simply pushed her father and the cart away, leaving the guilty puddle on the floor.

I watched Lynn check out, efficient, shoulders squared. I watched her push her father out the yawning automatic doors, the two of them moving like a single organism.

There are some currents that run harder and deeper than love, I thought then. Some things calcify in a way that can't be easily broken. And the universe, tectonically slow but indefatigable, maintains its own destined frictions. Let love try to compete with that.

Lynn never saw me. Of that, I was almost certain.

When I finished up my own shopping, I walked with my purchases into that empty parking lot, vast as a football field and smelling of asphalt in the August rain. And for the first time in years, I had a flat tire. I knew that if I looked for it, there would be an embedded nail, its head glinting silver—a semaphore, a coin tossed into the darkness like a wish.

LUCKY

Jess preferred to say she'd been attacked. It better captured her sense of violation. *Mugged* sounded too benign, too reminiscent of a hot, cozy beverage, whereas *attacked* had teeth to it. It was so much more bitingly intimate. True, she hadn't been injured. And she'd only lost what little cash had been in her wallet at the time. He hadn't even taken her cell phone—she'd forgotten it at home that day—and cell phone theft had been a huge problem throughout the city recently. "How lucky," her roommate had said. "You were barely mugged at all!" As if there were gradations of mugging—though, yes, of course it could have been much worse. But real luck, Jess thought, would mean not being mugged in the first place. Real luck was another vision of life entirely, something with more champagne flutes and sheath dresses.

She'd been walking home after her shift when it happened. It was one of those still-warm fall evenings, the sky just dim enough to prove that summer had ended. The pastel dregs of sunlight softened the edges of the rowhouses. Jess didn't live far from the hospital where she worked; she was on the close side of the park. It was not an unreasonable walk. She was wearing her scrubs, and at least back then, she'd half-believed this conferred on her some sort of battleground immunity—proof that she helped people for a living and therefore should be exempt from petty crime. This was exactly the sort of subconscious tenet her father would have teased out of her and mocked had he still been living.

Once, running into one of her former patients, someone she knew had been convicted of armed robbery, she'd feigned obliviousness, but he'd waved at her, enthusiastic as an old friend. "Lookin' good, doc!" he'd called out cheerfully. "You eat it up," the guy she was quasi-dating, a financial analyst, had said. "Just because you work in the emergency room. Like that makes you Jesus or something."

He was wrong, though. That was the last thing she'd ever think. There was a giant statue of Jesus in the old entrance to the hospital that people touched for solace and luck. They left flowers and notes there, as if it were the local Lourdes. Jess passed it every day on her way to work without stopping. She couldn't bear the detritus of wilted petals, the hopeful crayoned drawings of children, all those earnest supplications.

And yet she'd still somehow expected, well, not to be celebrated, but to be left alone, to be granted a kind of protected neutrality. So when someone jerked her back into the alley, she'd felt at first like she'd been wrongly inserted into another person's bad dream. When he jammed a cold metal barrel against her throat, she'd almost laughed—the sheer absurdity of it! *No, seriously!* she wanted to say. *You don't know the things I've heard, the things I've seen, all the graham crackers I've given out with a smile! I've been so nice! I've wanted nothing but to help!* She had, she suddenly recognized, been operating under a childish assumption. Every story of human depravity her father had ever told her, his attempt at inoculating her against naïve optimism, flashed through her mind.

"Give me whatever you've got," the man said. He spoke low and warmly into her ear. She'd once taken a self-defense class, learned ways of jabbing her elbows, kicking at groins, but this all vanished from her mind. She went limp-limbed, her heart jabbering wildly in her chest.

"You can have it," she whispered. "Here. Take my wallet." As if in a dream still, she handed it over. She didn't want to see his face. She'd heard bad stories about what might happen if you saw the person's face.

The man laughed, a harsh bark. "That all you got?" he said. "That ain't nothin.'"

She swallowed. The metal against her neck shifted, and then she felt his hand. It was callused but tender, grazing the line of her cheek, down the curve of her throat to her clavicle, down, down between her breasts to the waistband of her scrub pants.

"I could hurt you," the man whispered. "You should be more careful. You got lucky this time." And with that, he'd shoved her back out to the sidewalk.

She'd staggered forward, panting. When she dared gaze into the alley again, all that remained in the dimness were two large plastic trash bins and a rat.

She hadn't even called the police at first. Once she'd made it back home, she simply wandered around the apartment, dazed. The police already had their hands full, she figured. Her roommate, Aubrey, a practical-minded medicine resident who was working a stretch of nights, had been the one to insist Jess report the crime.

A female officer had arrived to take the report, but Jess could tell that when she told the woman what she'd lost—twenty dollars and some change—nothing would ever come of it. When Jess had mentioned the threat, the officer had looked up.

"Well, did he?" she had asked impatiently.

"What, hurt me?" Jess had responded. "No, no. He told me he *could have*. If he'd wanted to. He whispered it in my ear." Jess felt herself tearing up at the recollection.

"Sorry, miss," the woman said, her voice weary and faintly condescending. "We'll do our best."

Jess knew by the distracted look in the officer's eyes, the way she'd scribbled down notes—an act, something to placate Jess—that no one would find this guy. No one would really even look for him.

When the officer shoved her notepad into a pocket, Jess blurted stupidly, "My dad was a cop." As if this would make a difference. As if this fact would matter to the officer. It was a hard moment to celebrate police work. People were filled with scorn and mistrust. One bad apple, etc. Though now it was more like two bad apples, three bad apples, a whole bushel of bad apples. Jess rarely mentioned her father's line of work to friends, so now maybe she just wanted to tell someone else about her dad—someone who would be sympathetic.

"Oh, yeah?" the officer said, her voice bored. "Here?"

"No," Jess said. "Pittsburgh. Where I grew up."

"Well," the woman said, not even looking at Jess. "Good for him. But it's not like it is here. Nowhere is like here. Take better care of yourself."

Jess felt chastised. Foolish.

And that's when she had decided to start carrying the knife.

It was a large Buck knife her father had given her for her sixteenth birthday, a gift she'd considered terrible and thoughtless at the time, a consolation prize after she'd refused to accompany him to a firing range and learn to properly handle a firearm. And now? It was sentimental. A Buck knife in a city full of guns! *Would you bring a knife to a gunfight?* Yes, apparently she would.

She was working another shift in the ER, and the man in bed B seemed vaguely familiar. Jess refreshed the computer screen so that his name popped into the field—it meant nothing to her: Augustus Johnson.

Of course, she didn't know the name of the man who'd attacked her. She wouldn't recognize his face either. When she'd felt those hands gripping her shoulders, heard that voice, commanding as a malevolent god's, her eyes had rolled back in her head like those of a spooked horse. Useless. She'd been useless.

Jess was a person who prided herself on her calm competence. She was unflappable. Usually. That's why she didn't mind working her shifts in the ER.

She went ahead and put in the routine lab work for the guy in bed B: CMP, CBC, U/a, Utox, BAL. It was always a surprise when someone's tox came back negative—almost everybody's urine was dirty with something. Everybody who showed up here was up to something, but at least in this little universe of the ER, Jess was in control. She liked to believe she brought a touch of human kindness, of dignity, to the people she saw. An extra blanket here, a cup of cranberry juice there—it made the shift go better.

She'd meet Mr. Johnson later, after she finished her note on Ms. Thaxton. Ms. Thaxton believed herself to be pregnant with kittens.

When she'd first decided to go to medical school, her father had been thrilled. *My daughter, she's gonna be a surgeon*, he'd told his buddies at the dark-paneled bar where they drank shots of Jameson after work. Later, his vision grew even more specific. *Can you believe that?* he'd say. *A blue collar guy like me with a daughter who's gonna be a heart surgeon? My daughter, the heart surgeon.* Her cheeks had burned whenever he'd said it. She'd wanted nothing more than to please him. Of course, she had never planned to be a surgeon, had never trusted herself to be deft at anything other than listening.

She'd applied for residency in psychiatry not long before her father passed. He'd died on the job suddenly—not in the line of duty, but sitting in his patrol car, hands clutched against his side, a half-eaten burger wrapped in wax paper on his lap, a victim of a massive myocardial infarction. A victim of a cliché.

Sheila, one of the nurses, popped her head into the workroom. "Chalmers is looking a little shaky," she said. "We may want to go ahead and give him something to stay ahead of his withdrawal."

Jess ordered a dose of Librium. Chalmers was well known to them—a heavy drinker who came in frequently, making all kinds of provocative statements until he sobered up. He had a history of withdrawal seizures. Sheila was right to watch him.

"We can start with fifty," Jess said. "Although I'm sure he'll need more soon."

Sheila nodded. "Oh, and let me know what you make of the new guy in B," she said. "Not sure what he's after." She threw her hands up in an exaggerated gesture of frustration. "I tell you, every day's a lesson in gratitude!"

Sheila had a way of inventing aphorisms.

Jess was used to talking to all kinds of people: the flagrantly psychotic, career criminals dodging upcoming court dates, sad old alcoholics, intellectually disabled eighteen-year-olds who'd just gotten kicked out of their group housing, sharp-tongued young heroin addicts selling themselves for their next hit, weary homeless guys who'd say they were suicidal just to get a cranberry juice and a sandwich. First it shocked or saddened you. Then it made you calloused, practical. You battened yourself down with efficiency. You learned the art of kicking people out.

Jess pulled her hair back into a ponytail and stood up. She took only a blank piece of paper and a pen with her as she exited the workroom and headed to bed B.

"Knock, knock," she said. There was no door—only a thick curtain. "Mr. Johnson? I'm Dr. Reilly. I'm here to talk with you."

The man in bed B smiled up at her. He wove his fingers together, letting them rest on his chest, a gesture that struck Jess as professorial. Augustus Johnson then nodded to a chair as if he were her host, as if she were a business associate and he were inviting her into his office.

"How are you, sir?" Jess asked, pulling a stool close but not too close. Her voice was carefully calibrated to be pleasant but detached, like a reporter in a strange, war-torn city.

Mr. Johnson shrugged and studied her, impassive.

"Can I get you anything?" she asked. "Water? Juice? Graham crackers?" This was another one of her standard openers.

"That all you got?" Mr. Johnson said, inspecting his left hand as if he'd just been the recipient of a French manicure. His voice was low. "That ain't nothin.'"

The pen slipped from Jess's hand and rolled to a stop on the floor.

"Why don't you tell me what brought you into the Emergency Room today? How can we help you?" she asked after a momentary pause, speaking by rote as she leaned to pick up the pen. Her hands were numb, too stiff not to be clumsy.

Mr. Johnson leaned forward too, so that their heads almost bumped. The knife, which Jess had tucked in the shirt pocket of her scrubs, fell with a thud to the floor. Stupid, she thought. *Always respect the blade*, her father used to tell her. *Always appreciate the fact that you're holding a weapon.* She never should have had the knife with her during her shift. But the cold heaviness of the folded blade in her pocket had pleased her. She'd been reassured by its quiet proximity to her heart.

Her hand scrambled away from the pen, fingers fumbling toward the weapon instead, but Mr. Johnson got to it first. He picked up the knife, lifting it appraisingly. Opening it, he pressed the tip gently against the soft meat of his palm. Respectfully.

And then the blade flashed. Mr. Johnson waved it in front of her face. For one stupefied moment, Jess considered calling for security. That would be the correct response. But then she'd have to explain. By the time she'd finished debating, he was pointing the tip down again.

"You should be more careful," he said, extending the knife back to her, handle first, more gingerly than necessary. "You could get hurt."

She had less than an hour left on her shift, and then she was going out tonight with the financial analyst. The financial analyst wore subtly expensive clothes and always had a good haircut. He took her to nice restaurants, the kind where your bread was served with a tiny bowl of olive oil dotted with a glob of garlicky stuff. The financial analyst kept up with things that were going on in the world. He asked Jess if she'd invested in her Roth IRA. He wore a pedometer—one of those high-tech wristbands that also tracked your sleep. Every now and then during their dates, Jess would catch him glancing down at it.

The financial analyst was scornful of many things: macarons, acupuncture, good deeds. All loads of crock, he said. Boutique junk food, voodoo, people trying to make themselves feel better. The financial analyst had more respect for a world in which people scrabbled over things openly. There was more honesty to it.

The financial analyst didn't put a lot of stock in psychiatry either. He'd told Jess that. Psychiatrists were merely the current socially acceptable version of psychics or fortune tellers, he said, but with the ability to prescribe sedatives. Jess often wondered why she continued seeing him. Her roommate Aubrey also wondered why Jess continued seeing him. She'd told Aubrey she found him tart and refreshing, like balsamic vinegar. Something to sting your throat and make your eyes water.

In reality, there was something else. Jess had discovered it twice accidentally: once, on her father's birthday, and once, just after the man attacked her. "So he only got twenty dollars?" the financial analyst had said. "Yes," Jess had answered, "but he *attacked* me. He pulled me into an alleyway, where no one else could see, and he had something against my throat. He threatened me." She'd begun crying, her whole body racked by big, hiccupping sobs. Both times, the financial analyst had held her, wordlessly, stroking her forehead as if she were very young again. He held her that way for a long time, patiently—more patiently than Jess might have imagined, more patiently than he had to. Afterward, they didn't speak of it. If Jess thought about it too long, it was embarrassing. She preferred the financial analyst gruff, matter-of-fact, and complaining, ill-tempered with everyone else around him.

Mr. Johnson's lab work had all been within normal limits, and surprisingly, his tox had been negative. He had retracted his suicidal ideation and asked to leave in time to make it to the nearby Code Blue Shelter.

Jess nodded, the knife heavy now in her pants pocket, more secure and easily within reach. "Just as soon as the attending comes by and clears you we'll get your discharge papers and get you out the door," she said.

It seemed like he winked at her. A wry wink. Or a lazy eye.

Jess wondered if she was losing her clinical aplomb. She was turning into the sort of person who carried a knife, who slept with it under her pillow, who grew skittish when she passed old men licking fried lake trout from their fingers at bus stops.

When the shift ended and Jess had signed out to her coresident, she gathered her bags and headed for the main ER entrance. The waiting room, as she left, was crowded with bedraggled figures sleeping on plastic chairs or moaning under blankets. One man hunched in the corner was vomiting into a plastic basin. An obese woman in pink capri pants clutched at her side. A sign in handwritten marker said the current wait was eight hours. The room smelled of urine and unwashed feet, the multitude of ways a human body can rebel against itself.

She walked into the late afternoon sunlight like someone fleeing a leper colony. It was the time of day when you could almost mistake the neighborhood for beautiful. Even the low-rise projects nearby seemed gilded.

Jess looked at her watch. She was meeting the financial analyst at a tapas place. Small portions had become a luxury item, he said. The plates gave one a sense of accrual.

She walked briskly down the block, noting that the trees were starting to turn.

A hand clamped down on her shoulder. She startled, her relief ricocheting into panic.

"Hey!"

She jerked around, grasping the knife reflexively and flipping open the blade. Muscles tensed, she stared up at the man behind her and wobbled, her balance off. He grabbed her hand to right her. His palm was large and warm and rough. She let herself be steadied, squinting into the sunlight, one hand in his and the other still clutching the knife.

He was tall, a dark silhouette backlit with late October sunlight, a figure ablaze. Mr. Johnson. He seemed broader-shouldered, more imposing now that he was not reclined on a stretcher. Then again, Jess supposed this was probably true of everyone.

"I didn't mean to scare you," he said. "I have your pen. I was going to give it back."

She saw that he was watching her to see what she'd do. He'd seen her open the knife. She flushed, uncertain, and tried to shove it deep into her pocket. The blade tore fabric, and she could feel it against her thigh.

His grip tightened around her left hand in a way she didn't know how to interpret. All of her instincts were off-kilter. She could not gauge anyone's intentions anymore. His grin seemed either fond or menacing. She was possibly overreacting. Or possibly not reacting fast enough.

She wanted to be rid of the knife, the burden of its implications, the responsibility of it. It seemed like a curse rather than protection. She wanted her old, vulnerable hopefulness again.

"I have to go," she said, jerking free and running back toward the hospital. She ran the long way, around the sidewalk and back to the old entrance at the dome. There, panting, she climbed the steps, entered, and flashed her badge to the security guard.

It was quiet in the dome, hushed in a way that was churchlike. The octagonal balconies rose above her up to the cupola.

She approached the ten-and-a-half-foot Jesus, looming in marble, his arms outstretched. She'd never really studied his face before: eyes downcast, mouth stern. It was an unfathomable expression. She touched his big toe cautiously before relinquishing the knife. The open blade glinted silver among the drying flowers and heartfelt notes at Jesus's feet.

She looked up at him again, and, of course, his expression did not change. Her pocket felt too light now with the knife gone.

There. Let it be a gift, an expiation, she thought. Let whatever hospital employee was in charge of sweeping up these offerings

ROMANTICS

The Urban Hiker appeared the same day my cousin moved in, and any passerby would have rightly surmised they were both down on their luck. My cousin had rented my basement apartment; the Urban Hiker pitched a tent in the empty lot I could see through my kitchen window. We began to orbit one another loosely, like planets without a sun.

I owned a little place that I could claim was in Roland Park if I were feeling grandiose, or I could admit was actually closer to Charles Village. The basement had been set off as a separate apartment by the previous owners. It was dimly lit with a single, crusty window through which one might view the shoes of people passing outside. That there was a pervasive mouse problem went without saying—every rowhouse had a mouse problem; the creatures crept, steadfast, legion, through the tiny crevices that linked all the structures. They seemed to love my shadowy basement in particular.

But as soon as he saw it, my cousin said the apartment would be perfect. Just what he needed. When I asked what had happened with his previous living situation out in Boulder with a great-aunt, he'd simply shaken his head and muttered, "Big misunderstanding." He referred to my basement as a "garden apartment," which implied, to my mind, azaleas, loveliness, and a willingness to overlook the obvious.

"Thanks, Doc," my cousin said, clapping an arm around my shoulder and pulling me in so tight I couldn't startle and draw away. I was not touched often and so avoided it reflexively. "Together again, right? You need anything, just stomp. I need anything, I'll just tap a broom on the ceiling." He laughed, and though it wasn't that funny, I couldn't help but join him.

My cousin and I had grown up together. He'd taken to referring to himself as my brother, or my *brousin*. We even seemed to share a family face—the same long and thin-lipped visage I'd seen in photos of Appalachian holler-dwellers from the 1930s, though he wore it much better. We looked like people used to weathering hardship.

"Internet?" my cousin asked. This, he had explained, was essential to his business. He was a top-rated eBay seller.

"You can share mine. I'll get you the password. It's finicky, but I keep the door upstairs unlocked if you need to reset the router."

My cousin beamed. He was wearing a crocodile-tooth necklace. His curly brown hair was pulled back into a ponytail, but a fine frizz formed a nimbus around his face. He remained as lean as he'd been as a teenager. When we were growing up, my friends had found him irresistible. *Brousins are off limits*, I would tell them. I was—am, always have been—territorial.

"You okay?" my cousin asked, his eyes gone gentle. He's what my mother used to call a *darlingheart*: kind, solicitous, quick to check on other people's feelings—a scam artist and grifter as well, but I've learned nothing if not that people are complex.

"Fine," I said. "Just fine. Done and done now, so." And I left it there, feeling the muscles of my face stiffen into the protective mask I had perfected. Expressionless, detached even from myself. I had mastered this skill back in my previous life, but it had served me well recently.

"Gotcha. Shit happens."

That was when we saw the Urban Hiker settling in. He was a tall, grizzled man in suspenders. There was a stretch of brush directly behind the houses on my block, and we watched him through the scraggly branches, arranging his meager belongings.

"Well, hello there," my cousin murmured in a speculative way. Admiringly, really. My cousin respected scrappiness and ingenuity. He was the sort of guy who felt pleased when certain people demonstrated a bit of cleverness, but also didn't mind when others tripped up on their own stupidity. "Friend of yours?"

I recognized the Urban Hiker, of course. I saw him in the neighborhood all the time: nursing a bottomless cup of coffee at the nearby café, reading books for hours on end at the Barnes and Noble. He bore an acrid odor, so strong it made my eyes tear, and so wherever he sat, he tended to clear the tables around him. But the café owners, as if bound by some covenant, never said anything. The Urban Hiker was quiet, respectful.

And the Urban Hiker knew me, too, it seemed. I'd been aware of his eyes following me, his little, private acknowledgments—the way he'd nod when I ordered my cappuccino. I could sense his presence in the café or bookstore even before I detected his familiar smell. And if I were to admit it—and this pains me, because it feels like vanity—there was a way his gaze fell on me. It was the way a man observes a woman. Even when I'd been younger, I'd sensed this only rarely, moving through the world with the invisibility afforded plainish women, simultaneously a privilege and an insult. But at thirty-nine, I'd almost completely forgotten that sense of being beheld. Unlike the other women I saw traversing Roland Park with their mesh-paneled workout leggings, I was relatively untended to, a plot gone to seed. I wondered if perhaps the Urban Hiker saw in me the weedy signifiers of compatibility. He studied me like we might share an understanding.

"That's just a homeless guy who hangs around here. He's harmless."

"Living off the fat of the land," my cousin said. "Gotta respect it." With that, he was off to his truck to begin moving his boxes.

The Urban Hiker looked up suddenly, as if, like a hunting dog, he'd caught the scent of something on the wind. We were too far away for him to have heard us talking, but he swiveled, meeting my gaze and offering a little wave.

My cheeks burned. I turned to walk inside.

The new job I'd taken was a long-term sub position at an elite boys' school in the northern part of the city. They had been as desperate as I'd been because one of their teachers needed urgent surgery.

Dr. Elliott, the school director, wore round wire-rimmed glasses and a bow tie. He spoke with long, thoughtful pauses, resting his hands on his neat little paunch. He was sixtyish, balding, with the close-trimmed tonsure of a monk.

"A career change, I see?" he said thoughtfully—or skeptically, because who would not be skeptical upon seeing my résumé?

I sat across from him, trying to exude poise and calm. You see, despite it all, I have no criminal record. That was part of the agreement. A complaint to the board, yes, but no lawsuit, no newspaper headlines. For all Dr. Elliott knew, in every official sense, I remained an upstanding citizen. I truly am, in my heart, an upstanding citizen. I am too timid to be otherwise.

"Yes," I said. "I love English literature. I got my master's in it. I originally planned to teach."

He smiled evenly. "Of course, it's a substantial pay cut."

"Will it sound trite if I say it feels like a calling? I've put my time in elsewhere." I swallowed. "And I felt drawn to this opportunity."

He nodded patiently, whatever questions he had smoothed over with his impeccable professionalism.

"Welcome, Ms. Linke," he said, "to Chalton Academy. Or Dr. Linke? How shall I introduce you to the students tomorrow?"

"Ms. Linke will be very appropriate in this context."

Chalton Academy was a looming Gothic structure in gray stone with all the ornate foreboding of an old Kirkbride asylum, down to the glowering central clock tower. It felt like a place of serious moral instruction. At least half the instructors had PhDs. The boys themselves, the students, wore navy blazers with the Chalton crest sewn to the lapels.

That Thursday, when I arrived at Chalton, it felt like starting a new life. I pictured myself as a solitary governess entering a gloomy, remote manse. I was trembling.

Here is the truth: adolescents terrify me. Boys in particular. The tenth grade class I walked into that morning was filled, as I'd expected, with beautiful, floppy-haired boys, boys of ease and grace and prerogative, boys raised on antioxidants and challenging Latin courses and lacrosse. They loped to their desks with such languid handsomeness it was excessive—decadent, really. I'd gone to a country high school where the boys were no less terrifying, but differently so: rough-hewn and overt, with thick necks and loud voices. These boys, they were more subtle. Polite. Unfailingly polite. They glanced up at me with the gorgeous, sleepy-eyed indifference of grazing animals. Never have I felt so wrong-footed.

"Welcome, Ms. Linke," one of them greeted me as I tucked my leather satchel beneath the desk in the front of the room. "We're so glad to have you."

He was the most strikingly beautiful boy in the room—glossy black hair, black-brown eyes, a ready smile. Samuel Chapman, I would later learn.

I stared at him, prepared for mockery, bracing for insult. But he just kept smiling. The rest of them took their seats, watching me, expectant.

"Dr. Elliott tells us you're a writer," the boy offered, as if his classmates had nominated him ambassador.

This was only partially true. I had once published a poem in a tiny journal few read. I'd mentioned this in my application, and Dr. Elliott had made much of it. Now it felt like a foolish indulgence, like wearing a peacock feather in my hair.

I nodded stiffly to the boys, still waiting for the edges of their laughter to emerge. They, in turn, waited for me: to take charge, to start teaching, to do something. I scanned the room, their faces the faces of noble genetic lineages, these dewy sons of professionals and entrepreneurs—all of them except for the one boy in the very back. He was skinny, underdeveloped, his pale face découpaged with angry red clusters of acne. He stared intently downward at something on his desk: reading a book, I saw. I exhaled. In this boy, at least, I saw a silent ally.

The talkative dark-haired boy stood from his desk and approached mine. "Look," he said, pointing, and I saw there was a red rose lying on my desk. I could feel a heat rising up from my chest, awaiting their snickering. I saw myself before them, nakedly spinsterish, risible. The skinny boy in the back coughed, and I interpreted this as a warning. I tossed the rose into my trash can as if it were a used tissue.

There was an uncertain hush now. If anything, the boys appeared confused. I could feel all their eyes on me, all of them, that is, except for my kindred spirit in the back of the classroom. These were boys unaccustomed to having their charms rebuffed. This unwavering confidence, I thought, was their true gift. They had no need to establish themselves before me, the sub, so fully were they lords of this manor.

"Let's begin," I said, my hands shaking as I pulled out the desk copy of the anthology they were using, "where you left off with the Romantics. I am, as you have already guessed, Ms. Linke, your substitute."

By the time I walked home that first day, it was evening. I'd stayed late to organize the classroom to my liking and go over the syllabus that my predecessor had left. I hummed to myself, pleased at my own bravery, skipping over a dwindling puddle from the last rainstorm. It was still warm out, summery, though autumn.

"Grace!" My cousin waved to me from my front stoop, raising a glass bottle in greeting—nonalcoholic beer, I had to assume. He was sitting next to someone. "Welcome home," my cousin said. "Meet our neighbor."

The Urban Hiker took a sip of his nonalcoholic beer, raising his eyebrows at me, and then he smiled. He had surprisingly good teeth.

"Grace, this is Richard," my cousin said. "Richard, Grace."

I acknowledged the Urban Hiker, Richard, as formally as I could. Splotches were blooming ruddy on my neck, I knew. A terrible tell.

"Richard's a mathematician. Or was. He left academia. Taught at Berkeley, if you can believe it." My cousin whistled appreciatively at his own recital of these facts.

"What did you study?" I asked the Urban Hiker.

"Oh, you name it. Cardinal invariants, determinacy, set theory. All sorts of things." He gestured, drawing a sort of lazy figure-eight in the air.

My cousin nodded eagerly. "Smart guy," he said. "But he needed to step away from it all. Reassess."

"Started to feel inauthentic," the Urban Hiker offered, as if this were an explanation. He tilted his head toward my cousin, lifting his nonalcoholic beer up like he was toasting the ghost of his previous career.

"We may end up doing a little business together," my cousin said.

"I don't want to know about it," I said lightly, as if joking, though I meant it. Better not to know when it came to my cousin.

A silence fell then, followed by the click and pop of street lamps turning on. I could feel the Urban Hiker's eyes, the familiar way they'd started to roam over me.

"Big life change," my cousin finally said. "Grace knows all about that. You two have that much in common."

The history of my profession is not a proud one. Take Nazi Germany, where psychiatrists assisted in planning sterilization and mass extermination. Take the lobotomy. Or the days in which psychiatrists, all men, could involuntarily commit their wives or sleep with their patients with impunity. When homosexuality was, up until fairly recently, treated as a disease. Take the darkest aspects of institutionalization—or, worse still, the darkest aspects of deinstitutionalization.

Take any television show or horror movie or book—rarely, if ever, are psychiatrists heroes. Rarely, if ever, are we even benign. Bumbling phrenologists at best, authoritarian torturers at worst.

The mind is, as ever, a black box. People do what they do. We offer merely hubris and antipsychotics.

There was a time I didn't think this way. Maybe everyone says this after the fact, but I originally went into psychiatry with the best of intentions. Maybe that's always the case.

My fifth week at Chalton, Dr. Elliott called me into his office during my planning period.

"You're acclimating, I trust?" he asked. He wore a new bowtie today, blue check, and I noticed that he had a matching pocket square. His desk was neat, the stack of papers and the stapler arranged exactly ninety degrees from the small vase of flowers. Hints of obsessive-compulsive personality, I thought—not to be confused with obsessive compulsive disorder, of course, as the former is ego-syntonic and unbothersome to the person in question, merely an extreme rigidness of personality with which I am also familiar.

"I am," I said, picking up the pen on his desk, idly, as if without thinking, and moving it. Without breaking gaze, Dr. Elliott picked up the pen and placed it back in its rightful spot.

"Excellent," he said, smoothing an invisible wrinkle from his shirt. "I wanted to speak with you about your experience in the classroom. How are you connecting with your pupils?"

"Very well." This was a lie. I ran the classroom with machine-like efficiency. We had made excellent progress in the anthology and were even further along in the syllabus than we needed to be.

"Here at Chalton, we value intellectual connection. We want our educators to engage with the students as young adults, as individual minds at work. Covering the academic material is necessary, but we aspire to more."

I clenched a bit of fabric from my skirt and twisted it.

He sighed. "The students have reported, umm, a noticeable coolness of demeanor," he said carefully. "And of course I immediately understood that this must be a professional stance you cultivated in your previous career. Things are different here. Certainly you don't need to be overly friendly in the classroom, but . . ." He lifted a hand into the air, a kind of gentle question mark.

"I understand."

Neither of us said anything for a moment.

"I'll try and connect with them," I said.

Already I was rising from my chair, unsticking my skirt from the back of my legs, backing out the door.

"Good," Dr. Elliott said. "Very good . . . And I know how the first year can be." He paused to clear his throat. "If you wanted to have coffee sometime, to discuss, or . . ." A splotchy color like a rash was rising over the bald dome of Dr. Elliott's skull.

"Thank you," I said abruptly, exiting and shutting the door quietly behind me.

Perhaps talking to a great many people has not made me any wiser about human nature, but it has led me to believe certain theories. For example, some people invite cruelty. Their weakness, their oddity, their obliviousness: it sets them apart and inspires in otherwise ordinary people the urge to poke, to shun.

My cousin protected me from this growing up. He was one year ahead of me in school—up to his share of boyish trouble. The sort of guy that everyone liked. He had standing. *When Jacquelyn Dwyer invites you to her slumber party, don't go,* he'd whisper to me. Or *Joshua Brenner is only joking about those tickets to the homecoming dance. Walk by and don't answer him.* Thus I slipped through high school avoiding the greatest humiliations awaiting me. *Don't wear that skirt to school the Friday of the pep rally. Avoid the back parking lot until at least twenty minutes after the final bell. If Chad Rice asks what you're doing Saturday night, just ignore him.* A series of mysterious instructions, oracular pronouncements that no doubt saved me, so I was not picked off from the herd. I was ignored.

But I must still carry it with me, this thing, whatever it is, that invites mockery. An awkwardness of gait? A nervous way of looking up when someone calls my name? I don't know. This must be why, as a student of human nature, I failed.

When I walked back into my classroom after my meeting with Dr. Elliott, I found it waiting for me: my surprise. The young men of Chalton Academy were perhaps not so subtle after all.

On my desk was a note with my name on it, and below it, a sheaf of images that might have, in any other circumstance, made me guffaw or roll my eyes. I am not a prude—oh, no. During my residency I did an entire rotation in a sexual disorders clinic, learning to sit, unperturbed, as I heard everything. But there was a well-chosen meanness here. The way the women's eyes widened, helpless, like frightened livestock, making no pretense at pleasure, the men rearing back bare-chested and wielding implements of discipline, a healthy dollop of coprophilia and pain, the agenda in each image crude yet precise—I knew these images had been carefully selected, for maximum effect.

I sank into my chair, balling everything up and dropping it into my trash can. I could feel a tightness in my chest, just as they'd intended. And yet I wanted to laugh, almost with a sense of relief. Of course, I thought. Whoever he was, whoever they were—I knew these boys. I'd known all along.

When I walked home that evening, I knocked on the door to my cousin's apartment, but no one answered. I knocked again, in case he was napping. Because I had my own key, I opened the basement door and stepped inside.

Already, the basement smelled like my cousin—a sweetish odor of skin and sleep and men's deodorant. I turned on the light. The floor was covered in boxes, shipping supplies, tape. There were heaps of items grouped according to some indecipherable system: dolls, an old accordion, a hat rack carved to resemble a tree, necklaces, a dressmaker's dummy, what appeared to be three brand-new, unopened car stereos.

Walking amongst these items gave me the feeling of being watched, but I continued to my cousin's bathroom, where I opened the medicine cabinet. It was only then that I realized I was searching for something: Xanax, maybe, or Valium. This has never been my style, but there is a time and a place for everything. Or maybe I was simply curious. I knew my cousin was sober now, but I suspected his sobriety might only go so far.

Inside the cabinet I found nothing helpful: lisinopril, metoprolol, ibuprofen. Disulfiram, acamprosate, naltrexone. So he was actually trying, my cousin. Good for him, one day at a time, etc. I closed the medicine cabinet and moved back through the cluttered space, careful not to step on the splayed limbs of a blond baby doll.

"Grace?"

At the sound of my cousin's voice, I sank onto a musty brown couch. "I'm sorry," I managed to gasp. "I was looking for you. I was looking for something."

"Hey, hey," he said. I must have looked worrisome to him, frazzleheaded and faint. He advanced, resting his hands on my shoulders. I let my head drop. I thought, finally, that I might cry.

"I should have warned you," my cousin said. He spoke soothingly, as if to a frightened child. "Selling online means accumulating a lot of crap. You wouldn't believe what people will pay for stuff, though." He gave a low whistle. "The trick is marketing it right. And obtaining it at a discount." He winked.

Then he was kneading my shoulders, because my cousin remains a darlingheart in addition to being a bit of a scoundrel. I felt myself relax into his touch, a shiver running down the back of my neck.

Here is where I admit that the reason I avoid others' touch is not out of dislike, but rather for fear of visibly liking it too much, like a thirsty woman gulping up water. Here is where I also clarify that my cousin is not a true cousin, but rather a stepcousin, the nephew of my stepfather, and there was a part of me that has been in love with him since childhood.

And of course there was the inevitable moment growing up when I walked into our basement and found my cousin there with Jennifer Higgins, my best friend, my *only* friend, a loss that cut me to the quick. And here is where I admit that I stood there at the bottom of the stairs—at first simply because I was too stunned to move, but then I watched them with an almost scientific disinterest, a cool but pressing need to see it all take place.

After that, I stopped returning Jennifer's calls.

"Richard is firing up the grill," my cousin said, pausing, his fingertips still warm and electric on my shoulders. "He invited us to have some hot dogs with him."

"The Urban Hiker has a grill?"

"Well, it's technically your grill. Your veggie dogs, too. I didn't think you'd mind. He's on the back patio."

"Okay," I said, a small sigh escaping me when he lifted his hands.

According to one large survey, forty-five percent of the homeless population have some mental illness. Twenty-five percent have a serious mental illness. I wondered what might be wrong with the Urban Hiker. Mental illness or no, my theory is that we each carry within us, like a fault line, the seam of our own destruction.

We ate veggie dogs on the back patio, the Urban Hiker, my cousin, and I. I got a little bit drunk on cheap Chardonnay. My cousin and the Urban Hiker were singing old Crosby, Stills, and Nash songs my cousin strummed on his guitar. The sky had darkened, and bats darted overhead. I felt a lazy drowsiness fall over me, and I let myself be careless, brushing against my cousin, letting my hands fall on Richard the Urban Hiker's arm. My limbs felt loose and lovely, weightless. I didn't care. My cousin must have let the Urban Hiker shower in my house, I remember thinking before I collapsed into my bed that night, spinny-headed and outside myself. Because he didn't stink anymore. He smelled pleasantly of my own deodorant.

I dreamed that night of my cousin, the Urban Hiker, dark-eyed Samuel Chapman—an innocent dream, really. Chaste. Hands clasped warmly in mine, understanding smiles.

I continued to find things left for me on my desk at work: a crude drawing of a penis with elaborate pubic hair, a photo of a bellowing hog going to slaughter with *Miss Linke* written on it, a large-breasted woman being shocked with a cattle prod, her mouth forming a dainty artificial "o" of surprise. I found these items pleasingly unoriginal, satisfying in their banality. Is the mind of the brutal young male really so predictable? I will confess: I was not put off. Instead, I grew more confident.

As I lectured them, I studied each boy's face when he answered a question. *Was it you, Curtis Walters III? Or you, Oscar van der Sloot? Or you, Samuel Chapman?* I put the rest of them on the spot regularly, but I rarely called on the skinny boy. Sometimes, when I needed an example of an essay done well, I would read excerpts from his assignments anonymously aloud. I wondered if this pleased him, but any time I tried to catch his gaze, he'd look away, inspecting the tip of a pencil, or studying a crack in the wall. Peter Buttersworth was his name—such an unfortunate name it made me like him all the more. Peter never volunteered to answer a question. The other boys seemed to leave him alone. Samuel Chapman was one of their leaders. I was tough on all the boys, but I was especially tough on Samuel Chapman. Relentless. I made him earn every B- or C+.

It wasn't until the Tuesday before Thanksgiving that the culprit made his first original move. I walked into the classroom and found this written on my dry erase board:

IN THE MATTER OF GRACE LINKE, MD, BEFORE THE MARYLAND STATE BOARD OF PHYSICIANS.

My vision grew swimmy as I spied the printed pages scattered on all the desks. My case before the board. I plucked one page, and then another, although I already knew what they would say.

He, whoever he was, had discovered the grounds for my state

medical license being denied. There, in professionally exacting language, was the PDF with all the details laid out against me.

Shall I even say it was not my fault? That I was seduced? Would that matter? If I tried to explain the disjuncture between the way that it happened and the words available to describe it?

EB was my patient. Although she was not exactly beautiful, she was a presence, enveloping everyone nearby in her power, absorbing every particle of light and energy. She wore dramatic makeup, big earrings, scoop-necked shirts, and spoke quietly, her voice husky and warm, so one had to lean in close to hear her. Fine white lines scored her forearms beneath the bangles she wore—she'd been cutting herself since adolescence. She'd struggled with bulimia, pills, what she described as "an addiction to violent men." She'd survived multiple suicide attempts. A failed marriage. On the day I met her, she wept on my couch for the first five minutes of the session, but by the end of the hour, she had us both laughing to the point of tears. She could do this—move from lamentation to laughter—faster than anyone I'd ever known. Of course I recognized that she was borderline, the most charming sort. Of course I knew.

And yet I was drawn to her need. Maybe I had helped others in the past, but rarely before had I felt so indispensable. Never had I known my psychological instincts to be so sharp, my every response so perfectly calibrated and on point.

Still, even after my misstep, I maintain that I helped her. At least, I did at first. She came every week, sometimes more than once. Always the last appointment of the day. And she was charming, even in her moments of misery—quick with a wry observation or a subtle joke. It began to feel (and here is the greatest danger in outpatient psychiatry) that we were friends.

One evening she began weeping again and begged me to hold her. I had never known myself to be attracted to a woman. I had always been a firm, if theoretical, heterosexual. But then she was kissing me, her mouth warm and sudden. I fell back against the couch, and she pressed against me, all the hard and soft parts of her, the jangle of her bracelets obscuring our quiet sounds, the sweet cloud of her breath at my neck.

My recall of all that followed is hazy. It rendered me temporarily sick with love. Something had struck me: thunder and revelation. A giddy bliss.

Things continued like this—a fever, a delirium—for weeks, a couple of months.

Inevitably, however, she turned against me. Maybe it was a medication request that I gently denied. Maybe the luster of my clinical wisdom had worn thin. Maybe, having shucked any mantle of authority, I had lost my peculiar allure. Whatever the reason, when it happened, it happened all at once. She filed the complaint with the board herself.

All of which, of course, resulted in where I stood at that very moment: Chalton Academy, sponging sweat from my forehead, clutching the pile of papers that testified to my notoriety against my chest.

It was still early, well before the students were due to arrive. I had gathered the pages from my classroom, and now I ran with a sinking certainty to the hallway.

Like the mice that bred in my rowhouse, the printouts had multiplied. The hallway looked like the aftermath of a parade, papers taped to walls and lockers, pinned and tossed here and there. One fell and drifted loose to the floor. I grabbed it, almost stumbling. The pages had not been here minutes earlier, which meant the culprit was still at work.

I ran down the hall, turning toward the stairs. I wanted to find this boy, grab him by his arm and wheel him around. I wanted to see terror in his beautiful dark eyes. I would jerk him to the director's office by his glossy black hair—for I knew who it must be. I'd known who it was all along. And I did not care in that moment if it meant that Dr. Elliott would see the pages—not so long as it meant punishment, expulsion for the boy.

There, toward the end of the downstairs hallway, I saw him turning a corner—black hair, red windbreaker. I ran toward him, screeching his name. "Samuel! Samuel Chapman, you stop!"

But the boy did not stop, and I was chasing him down the Gothic corridors of Chalton. I gained on him a few times, but he was fast, changing directions, sliding down a banister. I couldn't quite make out his face, and I wondered if maybe he was not Samuel Chapman after all. The skinny shoulders, the rabbity glances over his shoulder—Peter? Peter Buttersworth? My quiet ally?

The boy seemed to dart down two hallways at once, or was it two boys? Three? Possibly it was a team of them. I was dizzy, no longer sure who my adversary was. I turned right, toward the main administrative offices.

And I ran directly into Dr. Elliott.

"I'm so sorry," I said. I was flushed, panting, holding the papers detailing my shame tighter to my chest.

"Ms. Linke," Dr. Elliott said mildly, as if we'd bumped into one another at a pleasant party. "In an awful hurry this morning, I see?"

"Yes." I gulped. "I forgot something."

Dr. Elliott smiled, almost to himself. He placed a hand on my shoulder, his fingers lightly brushing the curve of my collarbone. It was a professional touch still, just so.

"I spoke with some of your students," he said, his voice dropping, growing honeyed. "They say you've really started to warm up and connect with them. That you are passionate about the material." His thumb stirred over my clavicle, the faintest of movements, dipping ever so slightly toward my chest. "A passionate woman." He spoke so quietly it was almost like he'd said nothing at all.

I stepped away, leaving his thumb flickering there in midair. I nodded as if he'd merely commended me for my good work, walking back slowly to my classroom.

It occurred to me that Dr. Elliott had likely been aware of the circumstances behind my teaching application all along—and that the boys of Chalton Academy had finally made their point.

*   *   *

When I got home that afternoon, I heard voices in my kitchen. The Urban Hiker and my cousin sat at the table, a plate of cheese and crackers before them.

"Grace!" my cousin said. "We thought you might want a snack with us!"

He gestured, generously, to the spread on the table. The cheese was a special favorite of mine—overpriced but delicious. Something I tended to ration in delectable tidbits rather than eating in large chunks as my cousin and the Urban Hiker were doing now.

The Urban Hiker took another bite and leaned back, satisfied, propping his feet on one of the empty chairs. He smiled at me knowingly, like we were old friends. My cousin took a great gulp of sparkling water from the stash I kept chilled in my produce drawer.

"No," I said. A sudden heat rose up in my chest. It had been such a terrible day. My voice grew louder. "No more, Kevin."

"What's wrong?" my cousin asked, wearing a look of genuine surprise.

"What's wrong is you're a thief. That's what you are, Kevin. You steal things. I wasn't going to say anything, but now I can't find Grandma's earrings. For God's sake." My voice cracked a little. "I'm your *cousin*."

It was true: for a while now, I'd been missing things—mostly little things. First it was foodstuff: a loaf of bread almost completely gone, a new carton of orange juice with only a swig left, my favorite crackers. But I hadn't been able to find my little gold clasp bracelet for weeks now. And the pearl earrings from my grandmother? Where were they? Initially I'd assumed I'd temporarily misplaced these items—I told myself this, at least. I knew my cousin occasionally helped himself to my kitchen, and that was okay, but now irreplaceable things, things that had meaning to me, were gone.

"Please leave," I said to my cousin, my voice shaking. "I want him gone too." I jabbed my finger toward the Urban Hiker, Richard, who flinched as if I'd slapped him.

"Grace," my cousin said. "Let's talk about this calmly."

"No," I said. I was crying now. "Leave me alone. And get this bum out of my house. He stinks. You both stink. Now get out."

The Urban Hiker was already rising from his chair, pushing it neatly into the table. I watched him as he took his plate over to the sink, polite, and rinsed it off. He tried to catch my gaze, and I saw that his face was pained, abashed. I looked away.

"Grace," my cousin said again, and it was his placating voice, practiced and smooth. Already, he was handing me a glass of sparkling water, brushing hair from my forehead, running a ticklish finger down the back of my neck. Because I was weak, I was letting him.

"I'm leaving," the Urban Hiker said. "I'm sorry. You're right. I should go."

Later, of course, long after my cousin had disappeared, leaving me with a basement full of boxes and busted laptops and weird costume jewelry—his three months of rent unpaid—an FBI investigator knocked on my door.

"This was the last known residence of Kevin Michael Clarkson?" the man asked. He wore dark Ray-Ban aviators, like an FBI agent from a movie.

That was my cousin's name. At least, one of them. It turned out he'd had several.

I let the investigator poke around the basement while I fixed us both a cup of tea. He sat for a time upstairs, sipping from his cup. He told me things that made me realize I would probably never hear from my cousin again.

I'd found a gold clasp bracelet I was certain was mine listed for sale on eBay. I placed a bid but didn't win.

The following summer, I thought I saw the Urban Hiker once again at my favorite café. He'd disappeared when my cousin had, yet suddenly there he was: the grayish curling hair too long down his neck, his big squareish shoulders, a pack tucked beside him on the floor. He was reading the paper, his back to me.

I approached, unsure what to say: should I offer an apology? Announce to him that we might, at last, be the friends we'd been destined to become? Declare that I'd gotten it all wrong, and that this had become the story of my life: I'd misread everything, mistaken enemies for friends and friends for enemies.

When I tapped his shoulder and he turned, he was someone else entirely, an unfamiliar man wearing a different haggard face. But it was too late then, because I was already hugging him—hugging him so long and hard and with such abandon that anyone who looked at us just then would have thought I'd been waiting for him, and him alone, all along.

WAGES

Eventually, Julia is taking things from the hospital not because she needs them but because it seems like the hospital owes her.

It begins with the good ballpoint pens she finds in the emergency department administrative offices, which are vacant on the weekends and left generously unlocked. She genuinely needs a pen the first time she grabs it one Saturday shift, but afterward, the pens are superfluous—a bad habit.

Next it's an array of hospital toiletries: unscented medical-grade soap and deodorant; bleak unbranded toothpaste; flimsy toothbrushes for people on death's doorstep, people for whom having teeth hardly matters. She discovers a stash of mesh underwear and diaper-sized pads for women who've just given birth, and she takes a few of those too. The compression stockings she accumulates actually come in handy on night shifts. She takes one of every variety of K-cup coffee stocked in the nurses' break room, even though she has no use for dark roast or decaf. She's a collector. She lines up K-cups along her windowsill at home like Hummel figurines. It's like the hospital is paying her back for lost hours of sunshine, lost minutes of freedom. The rest of the weekend world is outside laughing and tossing Frisbees, popping caps off ice-cold beers, but she is trapped here. And she is making up for it in prostate cancer awareness lanyards, pilfered packets of Splenda, and dire all-purpose body wash. She is compensating herself with bluish hospitality candies and pink ribbon key-pulls, with tiny packets of lemon juice and plastic-wrapped graham crackers and squirt packs of French's mustard.

She has neither the time nor the energy to go buy toilet paper, but that's okay. The hospital is paying her back in toilet paper, too. At home, she curls up in front of the fireside light of her laptop screen, streaming online television, wrapped in the bland familiarity of a hospital blanket. Her two worlds are merging, becoming one and the same. The differences are insignificant. The generic medical shampoo doesn't even lather, but she uses it anyway. She has the lank, dull hair of the infirm, and somehow this seems correct. Instead of bedroom shoes, she slides around the cracked linoleum floor of her kitchen in disposable surgical booties. She's collecting hotel flotsam from the world's worst hotel.

Once, Mike comes to her apartment, and seeing the K-cups lining the windowsill, her bathroom stocked with maternity pads, the little bottles of medical toiletries dotting every available surface like sad votives, he looks away quickly, in such a way that she knows it's a kind of sickness. There are framed photos too—photos from Julia's old life, a life during which she laughed and went to weddings and let herself be swept backward into a kiss—and she realizes she doesn't want Mike to see these, either. After that, she doesn't invite him over again.

When her text pager goes off again around midnight, it reads simply: Dr pls come to 5 flr. There's no indication of what's going on, no decipherable tone. Julia sighs and enters the stairwell, which has the familiar chlorine-y smell and bad lighting of an indoor swimming pool. As she climbs, her pockets make a shush-shushing sound because they are, of course, stuffed with individually wrapped straws and mini packets of Oreos.

Lots of patients are detoxing on the fifth floor. Every now and then, someone starts to go into bad alcohol withdrawal. These episodes shouldn't come on unpredictably, but sometimes it seems like they do—the rough-looking guy with rock-solid vitals who was previously sullen and calm is now wracked with chills and fever, vomiting, blood pressure all over the place. When this happens, she is the one supposedly in charge, and it is terrifying.

Opening the locked door to the unit, she sees many of the patients—clad in hospital gowns—are still up, gathered around the TV in the common room. She can hear explosions and a car crash as they gaze into the saintly glow.

Julia makes her way back behind the nurses' station. Several nurses and techs are clustered there.

"Thanks for coming, doc," a large woman in pink scrubs says. She has a Caribbean accent. Julia thinks her name is Marie. "We had an incident. Need to notify the MD." Marie looks to a colleague and clears her throat. "Two patients, were . . . inappropriate."

"The new patient, Jones, gave Hinsey a blowjob behind the trash can," Deirdre, a tech, finishes. Her eyes crinkle with amusement. "In the common room. While everyone else was watching the movie."

"I thought Hinsey was on constant observation?"

"He was," Marie looks meaningfully at her colleague. "Frank here was watching him. Supposedly."

"What should I do about it?" Julia asks.

They all look at her. Marie, with her braids and cheerful pink fingernails, laughs. Julia feels the muscles of her face tighten into a humorless expression. She forces an awkward grimace in response.

"We've already separated them," Marie says. "We just had to let you know. Write an incident report."

"Thanks," Julia says, rubbing her temples with the pads of her fingers.

"Love is strange," Roberto, another nurse, says in a tone suitable for sage advice.

"Blowjob in the common room," Deirdre adds, sighing.

"People get lonely," Frank says, shrugging.

They all laugh good-naturedly, like he's offered a joke.

Julia had been lonely when she'd met Mike. She'd been in a pit of loneliness, a tunnel, a World War I–style trench of it. She'd been dizzyingly surrounded by others during that initial period of stunned grief, but it was the long stretch afterward that got you. It was the week-after-week, the plain old workaday loneliness. That was what built up around you, day after day, like so many shovelfuls of dirt.

That's where she'd been the first time she saw Mike. They were standing in line together at Subway, the only option for food in the hospital after midnight.

Julia had noticed first his smallness, then his quick, thin fingers worrying his pager. He had the delicate, precise features of a pretty girl. He had the pale mustache and buzz cut of a white rapper. He was not her type.

Julia had been aware of herself looming, large and galumphing, in line behind him, all unwashed hair and oily forehead.

At first she'd assumed he was a resident, like herself. But then she saw TRANSPORT written on his ID badge.

He'd looked up at her, as if aware that she'd been studying him. "What kind of sandwich are you getting?" he'd asked.

"I don't know," she said. "Turkey on wheat." She was wondering now about his blue scrubs. There was a whole color-coded hierarchy to the hospital, like the Elizabethan sumptuary laws. Transport wore purple. This was a step above environmental services, who wore light tan.

"Someone threw up," he said as if reading her mind. "And the machine was out. You should try combo three. It's good. Good deal too." He gestured at the menu board.

There was no one else in the cafeteria except for an elderly man with an oxygen tank reading a Halloween issue of *Martha Stewart Living*, even though it was almost Saint Patrick's Day.

"Come sit with me," Mike said.

Julia had been most impressed that night by how artfully he had deconstructed and eaten his Subway sandwich, not getting a bit of oil and vinegar on himself. His fingers were fast and efficient. He didn't use a napkin once. He was studying to be an EMT while working at the hospital in transport. He'd grown up in Frederick. He'd wanted to be a doctor but had to drop out of college when his dad had gotten sick and lost his job. He'd later gone back for an associate's degree at the community college. He had a dog and a half-sister named Sarah who was an ICU nurse. He also had a tattoo he regretted of his ex-girlfriend's name, Cerise, which curled around his biceps like a vine.

When Mike had finished his sandwich, he'd folded the waxed paper into a careful diamond before throwing it away. Julia liked the neatness of this action. Later, when she'd felt those same precise, efficient fingers against her face, her neck, her arms, there in the cramped call room, she'd been struck by his confidence, how different he'd seemed in the darkness. She was at least two inches taller and probably a good fifteen pounds heavier, and yet somehow, there in the gloom, she'd felt smaller. His hands were callused and warm. Somehow—the shock of the contact, maybe, the fact that she'd not been touched by anyone for so long—something about his touch made her cry.

She was grateful for the fact that he did not notice, or pretended not to.

When her pager went off and she had to leave, he'd written his phone number across a Subway napkin and tucked it into the breast pocket of her scrubs.

On the fifth floor, Julia writes an incident note. She substitutes "fellatio" for "blowjob," since this sounds more medical. Then she goes down the hallway to make sure that the two patients are in their rooms.

The TV in the common room is off now. Most of the patients are in bed, asleep. A few staff members on observation sit in the hallway, drowsily playing with their cell phones.

Hinsey is in room 513, a double. The lights are out, and Julia can hear two people softly snoring. The staff observer in the hall nods at her.

Jones is at the end, in 527. As Julia approaches, she can see the light is still on. There's a figure in the doorway—a young woman. Jones.

She is young. Too young, Julia can see, and vaguely familiar in the way that all these too-young, too-made-up girls pushing strollers through the city are vaguely familiar, in an MTV *16 and Pregnant* type of way. Her eyes are ringed in eyeliner. Underneath her hospital gown, her legs are scarred and pale, tinged bluish like skim milk. They seem raw and vulnerable, embarrassing. She leans against the doorframe, inviting confrontation.

"You my nurse?" the girl asks.

"No, I'm the doctor," Julia says crisply.

"Ohhhhh. Am I in trouble?" Jones says with a smirk. "Look, what are you gonna do—I'm already in here. Besides, he asked for it. We made a deal."

She blows a bright pink bubble and pops it, then flashes a lime green iPod mini in front of Julia's face. Julia scowls, feeling like the mean principal of a high school.

"I don't get to keep it or anything," Jones says. "Just borrow. Unless he forgets about it. So . . . am I?"

"Are you what?"

"In trouble?"

"No," Julia says. "Just don't do it again."

Jones laughs. "He's not even my real boyfriend," she says. "My real boyfriend, Ray, he's way hotter. Ripped. Buys me presents just because. He loves me. But Ray's locked up. See?"

She reaches into the room and pulls out an old flip-phone, handing it to Julia. The screenshot is of Jones standing next to a burly guy with gelled hair. They're at some sort of amusement park, and Ray is holding an enormous plush teddy bear. They are laughing so hard their eyes are almost closed.

"He gave me this, too," Jones says, extending her wrist. She's wearing a bracelet, a bit of leather with a silver charm. "Scorpio."

Julia glances away quickly. Somehow the bracelet feels too private. Sad and tawdry and cheap, something not to be shown to others. Like normal people, unglamorous people, naked with each other—nobody wants to see that, not really. She wants to tell the girl this, tell her not to show that bracelet to anybody else. It should be just hers, hers alone.

"That's nice," Julia says instead. "Would Ray want you . . . you know, doing things like that? With other guys?"

The girl turns sullen, her chin jutted. "You don't get it," she says. "You don't know what it's like. He's locked up. Been locked up for a long time. This doesn't count."

Julia digs her nails into the fleshy part of her own palm, but says nothing. Her pager is going off again.

"Small skim coffee and a blueberry bagel," Jones says abruptly, her voice turning curious again, open. "Dunkin' Donuts! You used to come." She smiles, pleased with her recollection. "You and the guy with red hair. With your big dog. You weren't supposed to bring him in the store, but we let you anyway."

Really, it's a small town, this city. And now Julia can place this girl there, too—the Dunkin' Donuts near her apartment, presided over by a crew of teenagers, swearing and bawdy as buccaneers, with all the requisite tattoos and piercings. This mutual recognition leaves Julia feeling strangely exposed.

"A shrink, huh?" Jones says, her nose wrinkling with disdain. "And you seemed so nice. . . . The red-haired guy, he always tipped. How's he doing?" She pauses to pull at a hangnail on one hand. "'Course a few months in, I got fired, so . . ."

"Please. Stop," Julia says, her face tight. *Peter.* Her brain is flashing his name in script behind her eyeballs like a banner ad. Peter. "You should learn to keep your mouth shut." Julia's voice comes out harsher than she intended.

"Jeez," the girl says, rolling her eyes. "Bitch." She whispers the word, her eyes ferocious, daring Julia.

Julia studies her, noting the track marks on her arms, the telltale hollow cheeks and bad teeth. It seems she's lost the heart for this work. She used to root for the underdogs, used to be endlessly ready, ready with chance after chance after ever-optimistic chance for people who'd started off with very few chances to begin with.

Now, though, all she can see is this: some people pour poison into themselves, wear their bodies down hard to trashed carcasses, yet always come out okay, always emerge utterly, utterly alive. She remembers the bitter words of one of her senior residents in an unguarded moment when she'd been an intern: "Watch out for the nice ones. The nice ones get the worst diagnoses. The jerks—they always do just fine."

She has not introduced Mike to any of her friends because she does not consider her involvement with him to be official. The majority of her life takes place in the hospital now, and yet she does not consider the hospital to constitute Real Life. It's like she's existing in a state of suspended animation, a netherworld. Purgatory. An airport departure lounge. She's waiting for her true and rightful Real Life to arrive and pluck her free, sword-from-stone style. But for now, this:

Subway sandwiches in the hospital cafeteria.

Flurried four-minute rendezvous in the call room. (Why not? She doesn't get to sleep anyway.)

She feels vaguely embarrassed by Mike—perhaps because they don't match physically? Or is it because he wears purple scrubs and works in transport and has a white rapper mustache? Possibly she is a snob. Probably. Although technically she is also grieving, and grief can excuse much in the way of bad behavior or characterological flaws. To make up for her discomfort, she kisses him with greater abandon, throws herself at him in great shows of unrestrained passion. She begins to feel like an actor on the set of a very bad soap opera.

"Hey, College Girl," Mike says, stroking her head softly. He's taken to calling her *College Girl* in a way that can best be described as half ironic, though sometimes he says it quietly, like a soothing mantra, for no reason other than to fill the silence.

"Hey," Julia whispers. "Hey, yourself." She looks up at him, then closes her eyes. "I like you a whole lot. I *like*-like you."

"I like-like you, too," he says.

It sounds rehearsed as they say it. The appropriated romantic language of middle-schoolers, twisted into something distancing and adult.

He studies her in the dim light of the plastic desk lamp someone donated to the call room. "I wish I could make things easier for you," he says. "I really wish I could."

She can feel when he turns his face away from her, and Julia shifts slightly. She has found Mike's mechanical pencil and is rolling it between thumb and forefinger. While he is not watching her, she slips it into her pocket.

That same shift, in the wee hours of the morning, Julia is paged to the fifth floor to look at a patient's EKG. Afterward, the nurses are in the back of the nurses' station, eating Flamin' Hot Cheetos and scrolling through Facebook. The unit is utterly quiet, other than the hum and click of someone's IV fluids running when Julia passes an open doorway.

Julia feels the tug of something essential to her. It's unyielding as an itch, this need, this relentless accretion of objects. She slips down the corridor, shadowy and pantherlike, and slows at the end of the hall. Room 527.

She pauses at the doorway, listening. Like most of the doors, this one is ajar. The room exudes a sweet, damp odor mixed with something sour and mammalian, like a hay-filled barn at night. Jones is curled up inside, a hump on the single bed in the darkness.

Julia's hand shoots blindly to the shelf, fumbling quietly. She feels the girl's phone and the iPod and the cheap bracelet lying next to a pack of crackers and two hairbands. She lifts the iPod, tests its slight, cool weight in her hand, and places it carefully back. Then, for reasons she cannot completely explain, she grabs the bracelet and shoves it into her pocket.

When she slips out of the room, she can feel it there, pulsing like a live thing. The bracelet is the first thing she's taken with any pull to it, any presence—the first thing she's taken that will actually be truly missed. Whereas with all the lotions, all the Oreo packets, all the surgical booties, there was still something insubstantial about their cumulative mass, this bracelet burns with the intensity of a talisman. She'd been stuffing and stuffing her pockets and still coming away empty. Until now.

When she is alone, she pulls the bracelet out, holds it before her, inspecting it, and then, like the madwoman she's become, kisses it.

At the more human hour of breakfast, Julia trudges through the different units, tying up loose ends, putting in missing orders for lab work or IV fluids or carb-control diets—all the mundane details that actually go into managing a psychiatric inpatient service. The moment she arrives on the fifth floor, though, Jones pounces from the big chair in the common room. She's been waiting.

"There she is," the girl says, finger pointed at Julia. Her eyes are smeary now. She has the raccoonish look of a party-goer the morning after Halloween. "She took it. My Scorpio bracelet. From Ray."

Julia quickens her pace, walking to the nurses' station. She can sense Jones tagging behind her, still wagging one finger accusingly.

"She took it from me," the girl repeats, looking beseechingly at one of the male techs in pale teal scrubs. "She stole my bracelet."

"Sure she did," he says, his voice filled with amused disbelief but kind still, reassuring. "Sure. Doctor's got nothing better to do than go around taking your charm bracelet from you. Come on now. Back out for breakfast. You'll find it in with your things later."

"But I already looked," Jones says, whiny, ineffectual as a child. "She stole it. I know."

"I heard you. Go on to breakfast now."

The girl huffs, glaring. Julia keeps walking.

Nurse Marie is in the back of the nurses' station drinking a cup of coffee while signing out. She glances at Julia.

"Doc, you got a real fan in Miss Jones. She's been going on about you all morning," Marie says.

"Because I told her she can't give blowjobs on the unit, perhaps?" The nurse scoffs appreciatively as the Scorpio bracelet burns like a coal in Julia's side pocket.

It's fewer than thirty minutes before she signs out to her co-resident, the quiet hour when the nurses are also signing out and the patients still finishing their pancakes, and Julia finds herself texting Mike to meet her. He texts back saying he'll bring breakfast.

"How was your night?" she asks. The animal pleasure of food is intensified by her exhaustion. Every dense morsel tastes better than the last. Her eyes feel like two bruises in her face. She closes them.

They sit together on the sagging call room bed, backs against the wall, licking biscuit grease from their fingers.

"Fine," he says. "Fine. I was on oncology. Mostly quiet until there was a code. They coded the guy for a couple hours before they called it." He wraps an arm, ropy with small tight muscles, around her.

She shivers. Oncology is, unsurprisingly, her least favorite part of the hospital. She pictures Peter being wheeled from there down to radiology for another MRI, then back again, cracking jokes with all the security guards and front desk staff, relentlessly kind, relentlessly good, down to the end. During that period, she had truly never left the hospital, going from work on one side, then to Peter on the other. Work, Peter, work, Peter—an endless repetition. By then, her Real Life had been bled out by the hospital, cannibalized. She'd curled herself against Peter on his tiny hospital bed, breathing in the scent of Purell and applesauce. That faintly sweet, faintly rotten smell of sickness. Those were smells that now conjured him.

She can't even remember his old smell—the scent of original, presickness, normal-clothes-wearing Peter. It has been completely expunged and replaced.

He'd been too polite even to say no to the hospital chaplain who'd wanted to sit with him, hold his hand. When she'd walked back into his room carrying two Styrofoam cups of oversalted chicken soup from the cafeteria, the only thing Peter'd had the taste for, she'd found the chaplain sitting there, so young and sincere and calm, so healthy and alive that it was practically an insult. He'd been saying, *For the wages of sin is death, but the gift of God is eternal life . . .* And that had been when she'd run him out, crying. She'd run out a *chaplain*. She'd run out an ecumenical devotee *of God*, all the while crying and cursing like a devil-ridden witch. Peter had comforted her. He, her sick boyfriend, had comforted *her*.

Maybe that's why God had withheld a last-minute miracle from Peter. *The wages of sin.*

"What about you?" he asks.

"Oh, it was fine. But this place," she says. She hiccups, her body's ridiculous response to intense emotion. "Sometimes I want to . . ." She waves her hands vaguely, unsure of what exactly she's summoning or expelling.

"You know," he says slowly, thoughtfully. "I was admitted once. Years ago. For detox. Oxycontin."

She stares at him, surprised at first, then curious, waiting for more.

"I'd hurt my knee," he continues, "and then, I don't know . . . it was also around the time my dad died . . . That was before I got back into school. Before I started going to NA."

"Oh," Julia says. She's fingering the bracelet in her pocket, playing with the silver charm between thumb and forefinger. There's a crashing feeling in her head, and she knows she's at the dangerous point where sleeplessness morphs into a form of intoxication and all good judgment is lost.

"Oh," she says again, twirling and twirling the charm. Without thinking, she has removed the bracelet from her pocket and is worrying it openly now.

"I didn't know you were a Scorpio," Mike says, ever observant.

"Yeah," Julia, who is not a Scorpio, says. And then, for no real reason, she continues lying. "It was a gift. From my boyfriend. Sentimental value."

She thumbs the charm again, imagining Peter, imagining him big and over-muscled like Ray, swarthy with dark, gelled hair instead of lanky and red-headed, but with the same Peter-y face, waiting in a prison cell somewhere, waiting to get out and come home to her.

"That's the first time you've mentioned him," Mike says, so quietly that she almost doesn't feel the sting. "Your boyfriend."

She searches Mike's face, the pale mustache like a blond caterpillar.

"I'm not an idiot, College Girl," he says, and she realizes then that it's written all over her, in everything she does, everything she says, down to the way she moves. So much so that a stranger in the Subway line can tell it: she exudes loss. "Cancer?" he asks.

She looks down. The Scorpio charm is blurring. She blinks a few times. "Fiancé," she says finally.

"Fiancé?"

"Not boyfriend. Fiancé," she says, which is the truth. But then she continues, "He's in prison." She repeats herself, as if casting a spell or a prayer, lying in the same pointless way she's taken to stealing things, stealing yet again. "He's in prison, and he's coming back."

Mike's brow furrows, and he opens his mouth as if to speak, but Julia's pager goes off. There it is again, that dull, persistent bleat. It's 7:45 a.m.—fifteen minutes until freedom—and she's already cursing whatever request this is, a request that couldn't wait a quarter hour more. She wants to slam the pager against a wall.

She's just about to say this aloud when she reads the message: URGENT. 5 FLR ASAP.

When she gets to the fifth floor, she fumbles her key opening the door to the unit. Finally she enters and scans the common area, which is strangely empty. Rushing toward the nurses' station, she makes out a scrum of nurses down toward the end of the hallway.

158

And she knows already without knowing how she knows.

They are gathered at the girl's room. The nurses spot her and beckon her over, gratefully.

Julia threads her way through and sees Jones, sweating and furious, thrashing on the bed like that girl from *The Exorcist*.

"Xanax," someone says. "She's withdrawing. We must have gotten behind on her taper."

As if on cue, Jones vomits, then bellows like a wounded beast. She is trembling. The room is too hot, the air aspirin-bitter.

"What are her vitals?" Julia asks. "Does someone have Ativan drawn up? Just give it IM. Can we work on getting IV access, please?" Julia swallows. "Call medicine," she continues. "She's going to need to be transferred, at least for twenty-four hours. She might need a drip."

Though Julia herself is near delirious from fatigue, though she sees (or imagines she sees?) this girl glaring at her, she is managing. The techs are checking a finger stick just in case, and she's ordering more Ativan, getting lab work, running through Jones's medical history.

By the time her colleague arrives and starts helping, by the time the medicine resident is also there, Julia feels like she is operating outside herself. The girl, still pale, still sweating, looks calmer. Her blood pressure is a little less elevated, her eyes less wild.

She is watching Julia as the rapid response team moves her to a gurney for transfer to the medicine floor.

"Thief," Jones says. "Thief. Thief." She continues to hold Julia's gaze, eyeing her meaningfully, or else in a delirious semblance of meaning that seems to come only to those in extremis. "Thief, thief." But her voice is distorted from her withdrawal, so instead it sounds like "Grief. Grief. Grief."

As they begin to wheel the girl away, Julia finds herself stepping toward her, mouth open, ready to say something, ready to give back the bracelet.

But the moment passes, and Julia is left just standing there, mouth agape, while the locked doors swing shut.

THE SCARE

Cooperton was the only child in the neighborhood Karina did not like. When Sammy played with any of the other children, she felt just fine, but with Cooperton, it was different. As a mother, she could tell—one of those sudden instincts, a full-body knowledge she couldn't quite articulate—even though his behavior was technically above reproach whenever she was there to witness it. Still, something was off. There was nothing of the traditional bully about him. He was small and wiry, prone to sly glances, dark tufts of hair springing up at odd angles from his head. He had large ears—also sharp ears, Karina had noted with discomfort. He was apt to repeat, with reckless innocence, bits of gossip gleaned from overheard adult conversations. When she was nearby, he was overly conciliatory to Sammy, overly courteous to her. He had a studied politeness she mistrusted. She'd seen the way he maneuvered amongst the other children like a tiny consigliere, how he spoke quietly and they listened, faces inscrutable.

Sometimes Karina felt sorry for Cooperton, encumbered as he was with an unwieldy name, a name one ought to give a town, not a child. His parents were shy, furtive people, both of them software engineers who worked long hours, entrusting Cooperton to the it-takes-a-village oversight of the neighborhood. He was not a beautiful boy either, not like her Sammy, with his expressive face and big soulful eyes and heartbreaking crooked smile. Sammy, who seemed to love and trust everyone in a way she feared would prove disastrous. Karina loved Sammy so fiercely that it actually hurt, a pain delicious in its intensity, like a sore muscle she couldn't stop flexing. That was part of the problem, also. She loved her own son too much. It was the kind of love that was dangerous.

"You're babying him," Robert complained. Robert was her ex-husband, Sammy's dad. No one would ever accuse Robert of babying anything. He taught civics at the local high school, which everyone understood to be a pretext to coach football. Robert's t-shirts were tight in the biceps and belly, and all his students called him Coach. Even as he softened in the middle, he conveyed discipline, strength, relentlessness.

"Sammy's sensitive," Karina always responded. There was too much emphasis on toughening boys, she thought, too much of the residual whiff of retrograde masculinity. She hated the thought of her Sammy on a football field, cowering as coaches barked orders. Besides, weren't the demarcations of gender supposed to be fluid now, every role unfixed and malleable, ready to be donned or doffed as if from a box of dress-up hats? Sammy would be fine now, here, in this more enlightened age.

Robert shook his head whenever she said this. It was hard for Karina to imagine ever having lived with him, ever having been married. He had a brute animal smell, large and equine. Muscles and sweat—a smell she'd once found appealing, like everything else about Robert, until the day rolled around when she didn't. Now it was unfathomable that Robert had ever been part of her life. Motherhood had brought out her monomaniacal streak, her knack for celibacy.

On Tuesdays, she took Sammy to his sensory integration therapy. A nice lady named Miss Beth helped Sammy explore textures and sounds. They used a swing specifically designed to train his vestibular system. Each activity was part of a systematic progression. Karina didn't mind these appointments, though Robert, of course, remained skeptical of the entire premise. Sensory Processing Disorder? Trend du jour. A fancy name for picky, easily overstimulated children. He'd said as much to their pediatrician, who had nodded sympathetically. A constellation of symptoms, yes, merely a descriptive term, but perhaps apt in this case?

Karina had accepted the diagnosis. It fit Sammy, who vomited whenever he heard lawnmowers or leaf blowers, who only wore clothing with all the tags cut out, who'd eaten only certain acceptable foods for years now, avoiding anything too slimy or pungent. Karina had previously understood all this to be mere childhood quirk. Weren't *all* children picky eaters? And didn't the sound of a leaf blower make *everyone* want to vomit, once you thought about it? It really was a viscerally unpleasant noise.

But the pediatrician's diagnosis seemed plausible, at least to her, while Robert maintained that Sammy had just been coddled, indulged to the point of fragility. All he needed was a little toughening up, not special therapy. Maybe Sammy *was* fragile, Karina would admit, but he possessed an artist's soul—one pure membrane of feeling. He'd shown such aptitude for painting already. The art teacher at the elementary school had pulled her aside on parents' night.

"I've never seen work quite like his," she'd said in a tone of genuine wonder, gesturing to one of Sammy's paintings pinned to the wall, which was, anyone would have to admit, entrancing. Sammy's work was like the outsider art Karina had seen—wonderful and wild and filled with hints of naïve, otherworldly wisdom. "He's a very talented boy," the art teacher had added, nodding sagely as if to bestow her fairy godmother blessing. Karina smiled at her—her name was Janet, and she was new enough that Karina didn't know her well, but she liked her for the talent she saw in Sammy. Sammy's occupational therapist, Beth, also remarked how quickly he seemed to pick up on things. Sammy was special: a truth Karina had already known.

"Do you like working with Miss Beth?" she asked Sammy, catching his face in the rearview mirror on their drive to the appointment.

His eyes were closed. He often closed his eyes when riding in the car, a way of blocking out the garish "too-much" streaming past. Karina felt she understood. The onslaught of noisy colors, the giant-font shopping center marquees—it really *was* too much. Yet everybody else, herself included, had somehow calibrated themselves to adapt. Dull but functional creatures. This was what normalcy demanded. Only Sammy, her remarkable, sensitive Sammy, experienced everything at full intensity.

"I like her," he said softly. "She's nice."

Karina smiled. No one could say she wasn't doing her utmost as a mother. They'd go to therapy for years if necessary, but still she'd accommodate him at home. Not to do so would be tantamount to torture. And besides, her accommodations were small: muffling the sounds of household chores, avoiding vacuuming, playing low-volume classical music whenever she ate apples because he could not tolerate the gruesome crunch.

"Can I go outside with Cooperton later?" Sammy asked. They were pulling into the small brick building where Miss Beth's office was. He carried earplugs that he sometimes used as well, which Miss Beth said was okay for now—a reasonable allowance until he advanced.

"We'll see," Karina said, the universal parental dodge for a denial. "It may be too close to dinner time." She paused, eyeing Sammy again in the mirror. "Why do you like Cooperton so much?" she asked.

Sammy's eyes opened, and he met her gaze in the mirror before speaking. "He's very interesting," he said. "He tells me things no one else will."

Karina's best work-friend, Trish, a popular fourth-grade teacher with the exaggerated smile and tinkling voice of a cartoon elf, first mentioned the clowns. They were sitting together at a mandatory all-faculty meeting.

"Has Sammy brought them up yet?" Trish asked before the meeting began. "There's even a term for it. Coulrophobia."

Karina shook her head. As the school librarian, she was often late to hear things. In life, it seemed, she was often late to hear things. This was why she admired Trish, so sure-footed, so able to gauge the tenor of a room. Trish, effortless Trish, always made Karina very aware of how hard she herself was working.

"No, but I saw something online. A viral rumor," she responded.

"Well, the rumor's here now," Trish whispered. "I heard the kids talking at recess. How one of them saw a clown standing near that wooded area by Haw's Creek. And over at the Bi-Lo. All over town, apparently."

"Sammy hasn't said anything."

"He will. They're all talking," Trish said with an authority Karina envied. The meeting began, cutting off any further conversation, and Karina experienced a flash of retrospective understanding.

The day before had been beautiful, a sunny yet autumnal afternoon, and she'd insisted on going outside with Sammy. She'd sat at the small pavilion near the playground, pretending to read a book so Sammy didn't feel like she was hovering while he played with Cooperton.

Cooperton never actually played on the play structure like a normal child. Instead, Karina had noticed, he was always digging at some obscure pocket of dirt, arranging a set of sticks like spikes into the ground, or hacking at the tender trunk of a young tree. If he was near the play structure itself, he was doing his best to dismantle it in some way, peeling off the bright petal of a painted flower or bashing at a bolt on the slide.

She let her eyes follow the boys from behind her sunglasses, behind the prop of her book, and listened to snatches of their conversation. For the most part, it seemed, Cooperton did the talking.

"I saw them this time," Cooperton was telling Sammy. "Two of them, down where the land's been cleared by the creek. They were watching us."

Deer. She had assumed they'd been talking about deer. Their neighborhood, after all, was plagued with them, particularly in the fall, when they sprang out like startled ghosts from the darkness, heavy bodies thudding heedlessly against windshields. Now she felt like a fool. Cooperton had not been talking about deer at all.

"Watching and waiting," Sammy said. His voice was more somber than it should have been, but she'd dismissed this at the time. He was a serious child, a worrier.

"Watching and waiting, then ARGH!" And here, Cooperton had clapped his hands, bellowing so loudly that even Karina had startled. He doubled over with terrible laughter.

She rose to her feet, restraining herself from running to Sammy, scooping him up in her arms. He looked wan. She swallowed, on the verge of issuing some sharp remonstrance to Cooperton. But he preempted her, quiet now, flawless as always, and perfectly correct.

"I'm sorry, Ms. Melner," Cooperton said meekly, straightening to meet her gaze with only the slightest hint of a smirk. "I'm sorry, Sammy. I forget."

A note from the school principal regarding the clown rumors went out to parents at the end of the week. Karina had to admit that it was a measured and reasonable response: the principal reassured parents that, should any actual clowns be sighted in the vicinity of the school grounds, the proper authorities would be notified. Pranks would be taken seriously. The letter also informed parents that children would not be allowed to wear clown costumes to school for Halloween the following week.

Sammy hadn't expressed any concerns, and Karina hesitated to ask him, fearing this might make a laughable threat seem more valid—particularly since he'd been doing so well lately. He was learning to adapt, better modulating his responses to various stimuli. Even Robert had noticed it. On Sammy's night to stay with Robert that weekend—a night that always left Karina feeling aimless and bereft, a night on which she typically started and stopped five different shows on Netflix because she just couldn't concentrate on anything—he'd been able to accompany Robert to a nearby McDonald's, where Sammy had tolerated not only the texture of pickles on his hamburger but also the irate shouts of a frustrated customer who'd requested no onions but got them anyway.

"Little man did great," Robert said proudly, slapping Sammy on the back when he'd delivered him to Karina's door. Sammy was wearing one of Robert's trucker hats emblazoned with the high school football team's mascot. "We had a good time. Right, pal?"

Karina forced a tight smile. Things she disliked included: phrases like "little man," the forced bravado of back-slapping machismo, encouraging your child to eat the dreck they served at McDonald's.

"Good job, Sammy," she said, because Sammy was looking up at the two of them, smiling shyly, the upper portion of his face hidden by the oversized hat. It pained her how badly he wanted his father's approval.

"Maybe the therapy *is* actually helping," Robert said, looking at Karina. She could tell that he very much wanted her to agree with him, to marvel at Sammy's progress toward normalcy, to celebrate a moment of shared delight in their boy. It was easy to forget the secret tenderness with which Robert cherished his only son. Karina experienced a flash of fondness for Robert: his big gruff voice and chummy dad-talk. She could sense his need for Sammy to be happy, to be good at *being*. In this, he too was vulnerable.

"All right, Sam," Robert said, nudging Sammy. "Time to show Mom the battle wound."

Sammy hesitated, lifting the hat so she could see his face in full, his right eye puffy and black, swollen shut.

"My God, Robert," she said. "What happened?" Karina felt the old, familiar fondness shriveling into something small and hard.

"We were throwing a baseball," Robert said. "And Sam took it right in the face. He handled it like a champ. Put some frozen peas on it and then got right back out there."

Already she was kneeling, her hands at Sammy's forehead, brushing back his hair, kissing his cheek. She pressed her shaking hands on Sammy's shoulders to steady them.

"Tell your mom what we talked about, Sammy," Robert continued. "About signing you up for Little League."

She stood up. "Sammy doesn't like baseball," she said.

"He's never tried it. I think it's a good goal," Robert said. "Good bonding for us. Something for Sam to work toward. Right, pal?" He gave Sammy a high-five, then turned to leave.

Robert had driven away before Karina spoke again. "You don't have to do things for Daddy, Sammy," she said gently. "Not if you don't want to. Daddy loves you, no matter what. I love you, no matter what."

"I know, Mama," Sammy said slowly, thoughtfully. "But maybe we all have to pretend a little."

She laughed lightly, something twisting in her throat. "What do you mean, silly?" she asked, careful to keep her voice playful, carefree.

"Oh, I don't know," he said, smiling at her. She knelt, and he kissed her on her cheek, her sweet boy. "Nothing, I guess."

The art teacher, Janet, found Karina in the library the next day just as a class of first-graders was leaving.

Janet waited for the door to close behind the final student before approaching Karina at the circulation desk.

"I wanted you to have these," she said, passing two large sheets of paper to Karina. "We can't keep them in the art room, but I couldn't bear to throw them away."

Karina unrolled the papers, instantly recognizing Sammy's work.

Clowns. Hideous, marvelous, sneering clowns. They grimaced and chortled and leered from the page, their faces super-saturated with color, stretchy mouths limned in white, menacing. The colors alone were enough to hurt her eyes.

"Unnerving, isn't it?" Janet said. "You can see why I couldn't keep them around right now, not with all the talk. But, boy, it produces an effect."

The second picture depicted a single clown who appeared to be laughing in a deranged sort of way as he lurked behind a cluster of unsuspecting children. Karina let the paper drop from her fingers, stepping back reflexively.

"He has a very vivid imagination," Janet continued. "And the gift for translating that into something startling on the page." She hesitated. "I just hoped you might remind him we're not drawing clowns in art class right now."

"Of course," Karina said. "Of course. Sammy's a good boy."

Janet placed a reassuring hand on Karina's. "I know," the art teacher said. "He's not the only one, Karina. Several of the other children have been drawing clowns, too. Sammy's just a better artist."

Karina thought of Cooperton, his crafty smile, the way she saw him leaning close to her sensitive boy, whispering in his ear, insinuating these grotesqueries.

"Thank you," she said as the art teacher walked away. "Thank you!" Karina called again, already rolling pictures up and tucking them away, so that the clowns, smiles bright as blades, were safely out of sight.

That Friday the children and teachers were all dressing up to celebrate Halloween, which fell on the weekend. Karina had already found her witch's costume, the same long black rayon skirt and striped tights she wore every year. Not original, but classic. Didn't all children at some point imagine their teacher, their mother, any female authority figure, really, as a witch? Wasn't this why the witch held such eternal appeal?

When she went upstairs to Sammy's bedroom, pointed hat in hand, she found him sitting on the side of his neatly made bed wearing an ordinary blue shirt and jeans. His plaid shirt and sheriff's badge remained on the chair, his cowboy hat hanging on the bed post.

"You didn't dress up," Karina said.

He studied her in her witch garb. She gave a twirl for him.

"I didn't want to."

"I thought you liked your costume," she said. It stung her to have failed him. "Was the fabric at the neck too scratchy?"

"Oh, no, Mama," he said. "I just didn't feel like it. That's okay, right?"

"Of course," she said. "But I don't want you to feel left out."

"I won't," he said. "Don't worry."

The school, when they arrived, was festooned with orange streamers and pumpkin decorations. Children swarmed in colorful costumes. There were tiny princesses and Hulks and Batmans, butterflies and firefighters and cats. There were, of course, no clowns. Walking beside her, Sammy looked very small and plain. She knelt by the library door to allow her lips to brush the crown of his head.

"Have a good day," she said. "I'm sure you'll have lots of Halloween fun!"

He smiled sadly at her, and she thought not for the first time that Sammy seemed older than any eight-year-old should be. But she flashed a broad smile back at him, then watched as he marched down the hallway to his classroom.

Though the library was quieter than usual, Karina could sense the giddy energy in the school. There was an air of heightened receptivity, the hint that something alarming or thrilling might happen.

It was still midmorning when the administrative assistant from the front office called to tell her that Charlie Ledbetter, the principal, wanted to see her. This was unusual. Charlie was a thoughtful man, a good principal, and he gave her free reign over the library, but they weren't particularly friendly.

Karina walked to Charlie's office with a faint sense of unease—a sense that was confirmed when she saw Sammy sitting in the chair outside Charlie's office, swinging his legs peaceably, hands clasped on his lap.

"Sweetie!" she said. "What are you doing here?"

"Mr. Ledbetter told me to wait," he explained calmly. "He said they were gonna call you."

She frowned, more questions forming, but Charlie was already at the door to his office, holding it open for her. He was smiling what Karina knew to be his professional smile—the kind of smile he offered when there was some difficulty to discuss. She understood then that she'd been summoned not as the school librarian but as a parent.

"Karina, have a seat, please," he said, gesturing to the chair across from him.

Her heart was going too fast, like she'd been pedaling hard in one of those awful spin classes that Trish sometimes dragged her to.

"I hope there's no problem," she began. "I hope . . ."

"There is, unfortunately," Charlie interrupted in a voice of practiced reassurance. "Sammy said some things. He's scared the other children. I'm sorry, Karina. I know you can't like hearing this."

She nodded, her mouth gone dry.

"Sammy told the children he came to school today dressed as a clown," Charlie continued. "A plainclothes clown, if you will." He paused, assessing her reaction. "He told the other children that the evil clowns have gotten smart. That they're disguising themselves in regular clothes."

She almost laughed. She emitted a hoarse sound instead, a desperate gush of air. "But that's ridiculous!"

Charlie pressed the tips of his fingers together one by one, sighing. "We think it's best for Sammy to go home early. In light of our costume policy."

"But, Charlie," she said. "He's not wearing a costume!"

"It's what he said—a conceptual costume."

She rose, uncertain whether it was anger or humiliation that brought on a burning pain in her chest.

"I'm sorry, Karina."

She was already to the door. All the classes were having Halloween parties, parties that Sammy would now miss. She swept out of the office in her witch's garb, grabbing Sammy by the shoulder more roughly than she meant to, and dragged him, stumbling behind her, to the car.

They were silent the whole ride home. It wasn't until they pulled up to the house that Sammy spoke.

"I'm sorry, Mama."

Karina's head throbbed. "Why, Sammy? Why would you say that?"

He shrugged, not meeting her gaze. "I thought it would be scary." She massaged her temples. She could think of nothing to say.

She let Sammy watch TV all afternoon while she stalked through the house, pretending to clean, brandishing her very appropriate broom. She didn't bother to change out of her witch costume, didn't even bother to wipe the eyeliner wart she'd drawn on her nose. The ibuprofen hadn't touched her headache.

When she poked her head into the living room to tell Sammy she was going to lie down for a minute, he barely acknowledged her, mesmerized by whatever he was watching. Ordinarily, she monitored his screen time. Ordinarily, she took such care. And look what good it had done! She would rest her eyes, just briefly, before she started dinner.

When Karina woke, she had the disorienting experience of waking to darkness. A crust had formed at the corner of her mouth where she had drooled. She'd slept hard. It was deep into evening.

Stumbling from her bedroom to the living area, she called Sammy's name. There was no answer. The television was off. She called him again. Her voice disrupted the almost supernatural hush she'd managed to achieve in their little household, having sought out only the most inaudible appliances, the softest rugs, special toilets designed to have the quietest flush. In the daytime, this gave the house the comfortingly familiar quietude of a library; in the nighttime, especially now, there was something sepulchral in the silence. Karina took the steps two at a time, but the lights were off in Sammy's bedroom as well. No Sammy.

She supposed he'd gone to the playground while she slept. Children often stayed even after sunset. The playground was illuminated by several large streetlights. He'd probably gone to meet his friends, expecting her to call him home for dinner.

Her pace accelerated outside, her breath coming sharp and sour. She should have gotten a drink of water. The neighborhood held a strange quiet, and she found herself looking over her shoulder though she'd heard nothing behind her.

There was no one at the playground, not a soul, but she called to Sammy anyway.

"Sammy! Sweetheart! Where are you?"

She worried now that she'd hurt him earlier with her stoniness, her tight-lipped silence. Maybe he was hiding from her, nursing his wounded feelings.

She ducked her head to look inside the tube slide, behind the small pavilion and the little playhouse, even searching the stalks of ornamental bamboo that grew near the sandbox. He was nowhere.

The other houses in the neighborhood seemed to loom around her, strangely elongated and remote, imposing, the smudgy lights from their distant windows containing pleasant domestic scenes that were entirely inaccessible to her.

There was no Sammy. He was gone.

Something rustled nearby, and she whipped around, catching a flash of white through the branches. A human shape. Someone hiding in the shrubs, watching her. *A clown?* She shivered hard down the length of her spine, peering into the blackness. There was another crackle of underbrush, and now she could clearly discern the presence watching her: a deer. He was huge: a solemn-faced buck, staring right back.

She laughed nervously, scolding herself for her stupidity, and the sound scared the buck away. It turned out she was just as prone to hysteria as anyone. There were no clowns lurking, no pranksters, no threat other than the rampant deer population. But still, no Sammy.

He had probably gone to someone else's house. *Where's your mother?* they would have asked, and then, *Let's get you some dinner.*

She headed down the street. She knew her destination now, her steps quick and determined. Turning left, she walked up the hill, through a short cut near the bike path, and over to the adjacent street where Cooperton lived. Sammy would be with Cooperton. It was always Cooperton.

A light glowed from the interior of Cooperton's house. She marched up and knocked decisively, waiting. After several minutes, the door opened.

The woman standing there was small and thin, tired at the eyes, wearing unfashionable wire rim glasses and a green sweatshirt fraying at the sleeves. She squinted at Karina, and Karina remembered then she was still dressed like a witch: the neighborhood witch, aprowl.

"Yes?" the woman asked, hesitant.

They had never really spoken. She hadn't wanted to encourage a connection between the boys. She'd heard Cooperton's mother's name in passing, but she couldn't think of it. Carol? Carla?

"I'm Sammy's mother," Karina said. "I'm looking for him. I thought he might be here, with Cooperton?"

Something flickered across the woman's face. "Oh," she said. "Sammy's mother. I've wanted to speak to you."

"Is he here?" Karina felt suddenly shamed, caught in a lapse in her mothering. "I fell asleep. I had the worst headache. . . ."

"They were at the playground," Cooperton's mother said. "Then your house, I thought."

"No," Karina said. "I was just there."

"Since I've got you," Cooperton's mother said timidly. "I've wanted to talk to you about what your son's been saying to Cooperton. He's been frightening him."

Karina could have laughed; she could have screamed. The world was turned on its head. "Clowns," she said, sighing. She needed to leave and find her boy. She must have just missed them—Sammy and Cooperton were probably helping themselves to the Goldfish crackers in the pantry right now.

"Well, yes," Cooperton's mom said. "Clowns. But other things, too . . ."

Karina did not stay to listen. She'd already turned, racing down the street and the cut-through by the bike path. It was dark now, very dark, only the thinnest rim of moon in the sky. The kind of night that encouraged mischief; a night with cover enough to do all the malicious things no one must ever see.

She flew down the hill so fast it felt she was under some enchantment, like she was truly soaring, her lungs ragged with the cold air. When her foot caught a bit of uneven ground, she almost stumbled but managed to right herself. Everything was clean and chilled and hard. Her mind held a newfound clarity, burning cold as liquid ice: Sammy. She had to find Sammy and—do what? Shake him, scold him, hug him, stare him deep in the eye?

Rounding the corner to their cul-de-sac, she slowed, confused by the noise.

A cacophony of sounds poured into the night, rupturing it. Whirring, grinding, whooshing—the din blending horrifically. An entire discordant symphony of modern machinery. It was loud enough to split her head. Music was part of it, though you could hardly dignify it with the name. Her insides throbbed with bass, the screech of electric guitars tore at her, the whole blitz punctured by someone yelling. Death metal? She could hardly tell.

When the house came into view, she saw now it was ablaze: every light was on, interior and exterior. It pulsed with intensity as the clamor and radiance combined, making it seem almost a living thing, a heart clenching and unclenching. Surely it would soon explode, or erupt. The front door stood wide open. She thought she heard shouts above the racket, what sounded like wild boyish laughter coming from inside.

Sammy, she thought. He would be writhing, vomiting, helpless.

Hearing the laughter again, its taunting quality, she felt that she herself would be sick.

Pressing her hands to her ears, she climbed the vibrating porch-steps. Her eyes watered, an old childish reflex that happened when she was frightened. She would find him now, her genius boy, her clever one, and stop his ears with her fists and shield his eyes. All this brightness and noise, it was positively sinister, their home distorted into a twisted sort of funhouse. She called to him, her Sammy, as she stepped over the threshold, into all that light.

OURO PRETO

The summer before my senior year of college, I spent far too many of my waking hours in the basement of the state natural science museum, rarely leaving, even for meals. During my lunch break, I sat eating red licorice under the yellow orb of a desk lamp, turning pale and flaccid as a mushroom.

"You need something with some damn nutrition to it," my boss, Bill, would say, jabbing a thick finger at me as I chewed plasticky chunks. But he had a MoonPie with Sun Drop for lunch himself, so my eating habits felt like an act of solidarity.

Bill was a geologist whose Twitter handle was @DrRocks and who played in a progressive rock band on the weekends. I was his summer research assistant, having taken the job with little idea as to what it would actually entail but knowing it was the least popular option each year on the university's summer work board. Mostly, I'd signed up as a sort of punishment, knowing there must be a reason no one ever applied. I wasn't a geology major; I'd taken one class as a freshman to fulfill a science requirement: "Rocks for Jocks," people called it. As summer drew near, though, I'd still allowed myself to imagine some possibility of adventure: the geologist and I, hiking over hillsides together, delving into hidden seams of mineral deposits, plundering the earth, the jumble of kyanite and ruby and hiddenite in my hands like cool, disinterested eyes. By the end of such a summer, I'd find myself strong-legged and sun-browned from the fieldwork, restored.

Of course, it turned out to be nothing like that. Bill, or DrRocks, had gotten a new mass spectrometer. He patted it lovingly from time to time, as if it were a trusty basset hound, cajoling it sweetly before each use. We were going through the current specimen collection, reorganizing it.

"Respect the drudgery, Annie," Bill would say, and then, with both thumbs pointed to himself. "Respect the drudge."

He was working on a project involving carbon dating; I'd stopped paying attention the moment I'd understood we weren't going to be swashbuckling our way to gemstones together. Really, I had very little understanding of Bill's methods or aim.

It didn't matter. Bill mostly seemed to want company, a captive audience, and I could provide that. I'd been dumped by my boyfriend and my best friend right around the same time. It felt appropriately punitive to be stuck in a grungy basement all summer, listening to Bill. Most of the specimens were not even beautiful. I felt a little cheated, having imagined that we'd at least be rummaging through boxes of sparkling, candy-colored stones. Instead I sorted hunks of humdrum gray or black or olive-green. Plain old gravel. Penance.

"If they'd give a little more funding to us instead of those damn dino duds," Bill would say, maybe three or eleven or fifty-eight times a day. His perennial plaint was the inequity in funding and attention between the geology department and paleontology. His contention was that paleontology, the damn dino duds, got everything—the money, the glory, the cartoon T-Rex t-shirts in the gift shop. Of all of Bill's rocks—lovingly labeled and identified—fewer than half had made it out for display.

"Damn dino duds," I echoed. Even as hollowed out as I felt, I could be loyal. What I didn't point out to Bill was that dinosaurs were pretty darn interesting, and that's why little kids loved them, and so maybe this was just the natural order of things, an unequal dispensation of gifts—like how some people seem to possess this intrinsic luminosity while others bumble around, dull and uncertain.

Like the difference between Nick and me. My boyfriend, Nick, had broken up with me. I'd met him in one of my English classes, where he'd stood out with his blond dreadlocks, weaponized smile, and effortless, unearned confidence. He'd responded to the professor the very first day of class, September sunlight dappling his shoulders like a mantle of gold, incorporating an appeal to overthrow the patriarchy into his response, his voice actually shaking with passion. After class, the shivery current of my attraction made me bolder than usual, and I'd caught him in the hallway to ask: wasn't he, himself, by definition part of the patriarchy? No, of course not, he'd answered. He was antiestablishment. I laughed. He was too charming to argue with, and I was no arguer. Instantly I loved him in spite of myself.

Later, it turned out that Nick's antiestablishmentarianism included sleeping with other people and getting them pregnant, then using money that would have been his contribution to our rent to pay for the abortion. I preferred not to think about Nick, but I spent a lot of time imagining his new girlfriend, her flaming locks of auburn hair and eyes of emerald green, à la Dolly Parton's "Jolene," a track I was listening to on repeat. I tended to my sad jealousy like it was a small dark creature that writhed inside of me and needed to be fed. The mineralogy collection was a good place for the aggrieved.

"Damn dino duds," I would say at intervals, injecting the silence with this oath of loyalty whenever the lab, with its dull lighting and sharp smell of hydrochloric acid, felt too still. Bill would give me a thumbs up from the mass spectrometer. "Goddamn right," he'd answer. A call and response among the faithful.

Bill had a pierced ear in which he wore an earring shaped like a raven's claw. I could not stop staring at it. He told me anecdotes in which he starred as a hilarious genius, a lady-killer. I imagined women in singles' bars captivated by the earring, just as I was, held in the sort of rapt disgust that does not allow one to look away. Bill wrote long, mournful ballads featuring battles with trolls and orcs for his prog-rock band. Like an ancient mountain king, he wore ten rings, one on each finger, each featuring a different gemstone. They were dazzling. He looked like a madman, but the rings, in their superfluous beauty, constituted a kind of perfection.

"Doomed love," he'd explained that first day, when he'd caught me staring at his hands. "And death. Mostly estate sales. Or jewelry commissioned for someone then sold after a divorce. I reset the stones, of course."

He waggled his fingers before me so that I might better admire. I understood that each gemstone held a tiny tragedy. Wearing them seemed a bit like inviting a curse.

"All right, Annie," Bill said one day, drumming his bejeweled fingers on my desk. We'd made it through May, June, and the first days of July at that point, the two of us grown dusty and parched as tubers in a root cellar. "I've got news."

He paused for emphasis, sticking his index finger with its perfect amethyst, big as a walnut, right into my face. I looked up at him, wondering if he'd caught on to the fact I'd been entering and re-entering the same data tables for the past week. Really, I was worthless at doing actual work.

"And you can't tell a goddamn soul."

I frowned.

"We're going into the field after all. Private land. Diamonds. No one here knows about it." He paused again, stroking his pale mustache with a flourish as he strode to the opposite side of the lab, pressing his hands against the red metal cabinet in which specimens were stored. "When we find the source of these diamonds—natural diamonds, Annie, natural diamonds from *right here*—it'll change everything."

His eyes had taken on the feverish glow of a prospector's. I rose from my seat as if faced with a holy apparition, literally and figuratively moved.

"Where?" I whispered, because this was what I'd been waiting for: a quest, a mission. Meaning. Natural diamonds where none should be: a miracle.

He smiled slyly and wagged a finger at me. "Bring your boots tomorrow."

Instead of Nick, I began to dream of a place a continent away, a place Bill had told me about: Ouro Preto, a small colonial town nestled in the Brazilian hillside. A gem-hunter's town. Bill had gotten a tourmaline there that looked like a watermelon-flavored rock candy. Asleep, I wandered Ouro Preto's sloping green hills and cobblestone streets, trailing my fingers along white-walled buildings with orangey roofs. Along the winding main road were tiny storefronts, dim and unspectacular inside but for a tray each proprietor held, filled with topaz and aquamarine and emerald, crystallized light and pleasure. The jewels of Ouro Preto began to feel necessary, life-sustaining, even. I imagined this was the hunger the gold prospectors once woke with, the same searching need. The hills around Ouro Preto were studded with such magic abundance that my dream-self had only to scoop up a clump of dirt and brush away root tendrils and soil to reveal emeralds as big as goose eggs.

I'd wake, thrown suddenly from my dream town, with a feeling of emptiness in my palms, like they were insufficiently weighted. It was a place I would have described to my best friend, Beau, had we still been talking. But we had not talked since last semester, when he'd turned away from me without a word and walked off. I'd watched him, the sad-angry hitch of his shoulders, that familiar shuffle. He hadn't turned around. Why would he?

It felt like the only thing to do was find diamonds.

"I want you to start at the far end of the stream," Bill instructed. "Goddamn Carolina diamonds, Annie."

We'd driven two hours out from Raleigh to an expanse of private farmland. Bill had made an arrangement with the owner, a gentleman farmer, a friend of the museum. This man had allowed prospectors and amateur gem-hunters here before—one of whom claimed he'd discovered a small diamond—and now he wanted to donate whatever else might be found to the state museum.

"Generous," I said, incapable of imagining such generosity myself. I had been gripped by an appetite for jewels so great, so inexplicable, I can only describe it as an illness. I had never been a person with a taste for luxury. I didn't wear fine jewelry. But the thought of gemstones—something so bright and tangible—made my mouth water. What would I do with them once I had them? I had no idea. Sit upon them like a great greedy dragon, maybe. Eat them until I glowed from within, cup them in my hands like secret flames.

We were standing in the midst of gentle pastureland. Bill had pulled his truck to the shoulder of a dirt road, and we'd tromped through a stand of balding pines down a shallow hill, carrying our spades and pans. Cows grazing along the opposite slope looked up at us with boredom.

"Come on," Bill said, gesturing for me to sift through the silt at the stream's edge as he was doing. I walked downstream from him and knelt and began the process of scooping up spadefuls of dirt.

What was in our favor, Bill had explained, was new construction upstream, just beyond the farmer's land. The upheaval of the earth was to our advantage; who knew what the stream might bear now that bulldozers and track hoes had upended things.

All afternoon, I crouched there, within shouting distance of Bill, sifting and sifting in my little pan. I found olivine and quartz, smoky and rose, as well as a tiny but perfect piece of what I believed to be rhodolite. But no diamonds. There was a crick in my neck, and my knees were damp and sore from kneeling.

Bill and I met under the one large oak that offered shade, where he'd promised lunch. He handed me a MoonPie and opened up another for himself.

"Takes time," he said. "Anything worth finding takes time. People walk past treasure for years."

*　*　*

I ran into Jolene in the grocery store. It was evening but still light outside. Late July. My hands had turned rough from the sun and silt and cold stream water, and I'd developed an uneven tan already. We'd yet to find diamonds, but I could sense their proximity, a feeling of expectation that left me all atingle.

I wouldn't have known Jolene because she was nothing like I'd imagined. In reality, she was small-boned with wary hazel eyes and a slightly beaky face. Her blond hair, her best feature, fell in natural waves to her shoulders. We'd almost collided in the dairy aisle, and she'd sighed softly, apologetically, as she'd backed away to allow me to get my carton of half and half. I had the feeling of having encountered a gentle soul, someone thoughtful and harmless whom I might want to protect.

"Please," I said, gesturing for her to go ahead and make her own selection while I held the door to the refrigerated case open. She reached out, and I saw she had bitten-down nails and grubby, skinny hands. I saw the blink of a tiny gem on her ring finger.

A voice rang from behind me that pained me in its familiarity. "Annie! You've met Natalie!"

I turned to find Nick, all golden skin and smiling eyes. He was incapable of imagining anyone angry at him, and so he embraced me with genuine affection.

Jolene/Natalie, turned to me and smiled shyly. Embarrassed. She, at least, understood enough of the real world to be uncomfortable. Nick had such an unsullied optimism that it almost amounted to stupidity.

"Annie, it's so good to see you. Really," Nick continued, pulling back and inspecting me at arm's length the way you might a long-lost cousin. "You seem great. And I've wanted to introduce you to Natalie so badly. It's funny how well you two would get along."

Again, Jolene/Natalie looked at me, a pained expression on her face. She was wearing a formless black t-shirt and shorts. At ease. Natural, the way Nick liked his women.

"And I wanted to tell you our news." Here, he grabbed Natalie's small hand and thrust it toward me, so that I could better inspect the tiny diamond on her ring finger. "We're getting married! Isn't that wild?" He laughed, a mountain man laugh, unabashed, right there in the grocery store. A lady in a dark coat turned to him, and I saw her eyes instantly soften. Nick was beautiful, and thus the things he did were beautiful. He moved through the world suffused in soft light.

"Wow," I said. My mouth was so dry it was difficult to peel my lips apart and form words.

"Yeah," he said, pulling Jolene/Natalie to his side fondly. "We figured that it's, like, the most unexpected thing we could do. We're reclaiming it, you know? Nobody gets married at our age anymore. We're making it a radical act."

I nodded, bewildered. My older sister had gotten married at our age to a man whose family owned the largest insurance company in my home county. But my older sister, a quiet woman who favored pleats and monograms and Sunday school, was not like Nick.

Suddenly even the chilled dairy aisle of the grocery store felt too warm. Nick's familiar smile—dazzling, malice-free—was far too bright. I was aware then of the girl, Jolene/Natalie, touching my elbow.

"Hey," she said, her voice barely above a whisper. "You okay?" I could see her hazel eyes were worried on my behalf.

"Yeah," I said, waving a hand through the air. "I've been working in the sun all month. Dehydration."

I backed away, stumbling then, almost running.

"Say hi to Beau for me!" Nick called with an easy warmth.

I shook all through the checkout line, shook so hard my teeth were chattering by the time I'd made it to my car.

When Nick had first told me about Jolene, he'd been shame-faced, solicitous, but also a little surprised at how upset I'd been. *I'm sorry,* he'd said. *I just never thought that we had a connection like that, you know? I mean, to be honest, a lot of the time I thought you didn't take me that seriously . . . and I always sort of thought, well—you had*

Beau . . . Bile rose in my throat at the recollection. I wished I could talk to Beau. He would have understood; he would have had the perfect, quick response.

People like Nick were allowed to live in the world with heedless whimsy; the rest of us were resigned to reckon with their own short-comings—Beau had said something like that in the past.

As we entered the month of August without a hint of diamonds, Bill's gruff good humor did not flag.

"My source is reliable," he'd mutter, reconvincing himself, reconvincing me. "He wouldn't give me bad info."

Or, if he caught me rubbing my lower back, sighing, taking a break from our labor, he'd make a little *tsk-tsk* sound and remind me, "Drudges will prevail, Annie. Respect the drudgery."

After a long day sifting, digging, wandering through the pasture-land and dodging steaming piles of cow dung, we'd drive back toward Raleigh in the quiet of Bill's truck. The late summer sun would fall slantwise across us, filling my eyes with such heaviness that I would often drift off while Bill hummed quietly to himself. He was always writing new songs, he told me. For this reason he was never bored, even when performing the most mundane data collection. As I nodded off, my head tilting toward the passenger window, I would catch little whispered snippets of Bill's songs of knights and elves, orcs and wizards, epic battles from some other realm.

When we'd pull into the museum parking lot where I'd left my car, Bill would turn to me, his voice filled with renewed conviction: "When we find them, Annie, I'm telling you: game changer," he'd say. "Finally. The tide'll turn around here. Even idiots appreciate natural diamonds. Even damn dino duds."

"Damn dino duds," I'd repeat, but as the summer went on, I was unable to meet his eyes when I said it.

In the evenings, I'd take very hot showers.

I thought of Beau sometimes. I wondered what he was doing.

* * *

Beau had gone back to his hometown in the western part of the state—a little mountain town, but not one of the touristy, picturesque ones. There were too many charming mountain towns competing, with their little inns and restaurants with seasonal menus and local breweries. His hometown had mountains, and that was basically it. He was helping his dad that summer with geological surveys.

I heard of Beau before I met him. We lived in the same freshman dorm—the honors dorm. Dozens of nerdy, hesitant kids from small towns all over the state co-housed in a cement-block dorm with rooms the size of large bathroom stalls—and word of Beau quickly spread. The night I first encountered him, I'd just walked into a heated debate over some book or band or political event—I don't recall now—in the dorm's common room. Beau was explaining a point softly but with such confidence, I'd paused. As I stood in the doorway, listening to him, the ease and depth of his answer, the lack of showiness, I'd known this guy was smart: so smart that, as he talked, he created a kind of gravitational warmth, and I felt myself leaning forward, willing myself into his radius. I watched the back of his head (chestnut hair, a touch of curl) and followed that voice of his throughout the rest of the discussion.

When the conversation paused long enough for one of my dormmates to acknowledge me, Beau turned. That was when I saw his face. It was knobbed and bulbous, the landscape of his cheeks raised with a series of putty-colored hillocks and cysts. He saw me and held my gaze, and I was thrown by the disconnect between that serene voice, those wonderful thoughts, and his appearance. Immediately I placed him in a long line of kind and gentle monsters—beasts and hunchbacks, lonely in their towers, their libraries, made excessively wise by their isolation.

Later, when we officially met, he'd smiled at me—the weary smile of someone much older, and introduced himself.

"Name's Beau," he said.

"Annie," I said, almost mesmerized by the sight of him.

"I'm going for coffee." He touched my shoulder lightly. "Come on."

I followed him. There was something compelling about his rutted face, an ugliness so interesting I wanted to study it. Beau told me things: smart things, little details he noticed, theories of human behavior offered to me like so many tiny pots of homemade jam. Why people like abstract art. Who gets drawn into cults. Why this person in our dorm was attracted to that one. Beau had also read every book I ever mentioned. And yet he was a geology major himself, following his father's footsteps. Some nights when I couldn't fall asleep, he'd tell me stories of lamproite pipes melted from the earth's mantle, one of his hands floating above my head, not quite touching me, as if casting a spell.

By the time I started dating Nick, Beau and I were the kind of best friends who could communicate our annoyance at a tiresome person by a glance, a slight pressure of a thumb to the other's wrist. I thought of us—and I'd told Beau this—as having a kind of elevated bond—what I imagined had existed between Robert Lowell and Elizabeth Bishop. I'd taken a class on Bishop and fancied myself a newly minted expert.

"The self-aggrandizing romanticism of a young English major," Beau had said, chuckling. "Which one of us ends up in the mental hospital?"

And then, I met Nick. Abruptly, Beau and I stopped spending time together. Rather, I stopped spending time with him. No more dinners, no more late-night walks across the main quad. Nick had filled up the space inside of me like helium, leaving me giddy and high-pitched.

"So you really like this guy, then," Beau observed after I'd arrived late again to our study spot in the library, flushed and exhilarated, the taste of Nick's mouth still in mine. I felt strangely exposed for some reason, but Beau just kept looking at me evenly, the ridge of his brow faintly damp in the hard light of the study carrel.

"It's okay," he said, tucking his chin and shuffling the papers he had before him. "I get it."

* * *

I remembered halfway through that summer the other reason I'd heard of Ouro Preto: Elizabeth Bishop. She had stayed in a little white house, the back porch overlooking a view of lush hillside, with her lover, Lota. This convergence pleased me; I still held a fierce wish for the world to be tied together in neat loops and bows. I imagined Bishop walking along the ribboning streets of Ouro Preto. Did the gem merchants call to her, this odd American lady in their midst? Did she pause, looking into their trays of loose stones, covetous, thirsting for the liquid light thrown from those facets: canary yellow, champagne pink, minty green?

No, I decided. She had a cache of her own, polishing simple words until they glittered like her famous fish. I envied her that. *Rainbow, rainbow, rainbow!* Diamonds refracting light into a hundred hundred colors.

Summer dragged into its final days, and we'd found nothing. I waited for Bill to grow morose, but he maintained his equanimity, ever ready to plod forward. Maybe he sensed, however, my own growing gloom.

"I need a goddamn drink," Bill announced on our drive back. "You in, Annie?"

And because I swear I could hear beneath his cheer a slow creaking in his chest, a mournful sound I didn't want to ponder, I said yes. He nodded. He had a favorite bar, he told me, where he was a regular. Everyone looked for him there. They'd take care of us.

When we walked in, no one turned or acknowledged us.

"Pete! Hey! Great to see you, man!"

The bartender, Pete, looked up with mild interest but said nothing. Bill waved at a couple other older guys sitting on barstools, and they merely glanced at him, nodding as one would to a stranger.

I had a renewed awareness of Bill, the ridiculous figure he cut: large and galumphing, sunburnt, sweaty, his voice too loud, oblivious. As he reached for the beers he'd ordered us, I noticed his hands, their thick clumsiness, the strange affectation of his bejeweled fingers. Dungeon Master chic.

"What do we drink to?" I asked. "Diamonds?"

He paused, closing his eyes and inhaling deeply like he was about to dive into water. "Drudgery." He held up both hands in the universal gesture for *of course*. "Respect the drudgery. Drudges will prevail."

We stayed at the bar too long, Bill and I. I had the feeling I was performing an important task, making some correction to something. As the evening wore on, Bill grew louder, more insistent. He drew in strangers with blustering tales of fieldwork from his grad school days, stories of stolen jewels and lost treasure, the importance of his sample studies with the new mass spectrometer. He'd begun clapping me on the back, like we were allies, and I'd felt something like fondness.

When I finally got home that night, my head spinning and stomach sloshing, there was a new shadow by my apartment door. A figure stood up. I startled. The figure moved forward, and I saw that she was slight. A woman, a girl.

"Jolene," I whispered, then, correcting myself, "Natalie."

"I'm sorry," she said. "I didn't mean to scare you."

I felt lightheaded. I needed to sit down. She sank beside me on my front stoop—Nick's girlfriend. The one he'd chosen over me. The streetlamp cast her face in half-light, and I had the strange impression of her as part ordinary girl, part enchantress, part sylph. I'd been around Bill too long.

"I have to ask a favor," she said, straightening her legs before her and pointing her toes like a child. Across the street, three of my neighbors were returning from one of the college bars, hooting at one another, egging each other on. Frat boys, I thought. Young primates.

"This is weird, I know," Natalie continued. "But I need you to tell Nick for me. I can't do this. The whole thing. It seemed fun at first, this cool, brave idea. Like an adventure. But I can't." Tilting her head back, she sighed. "Here."

She handed me something, and docile, I accepted it. The ring. The tiny diamond on a gold band. It rested lightly on my palm. I made a fist around it.

"Please," she said. "Will you return this to Nick? I'm leaving. I'm driving to my brother's tonight."

I frowned at her, waiting for the ring to incandesce with its own light and heat, or for someone to jump out with a camera, laughing—something.

"Why me?" I asked her.

"You were his best friend. He admired you."

She rose then and walked into the circular glow cast by a streetlamp, as if it were a spotlight and she were going to recite a monologue. But she did not turn to face me.

"You don't have to, of course," she said. "I would understand if you didn't. . . ." She let the sentence trail off and walked away. I heard a car engine start, a block over. Pulling myself up from the stoop, I was aware of how my knees ached, my back, my neck. I stumbled inside and fell onto my bed.

You were his best friend.

I thought not of Nick, but of Beau. My best friend. How I'd driven to his house, weeping, after Nick had made his confession about Jolene, a confession that had, in fact, wounded me even more than I would have imagined. How Beau had comforted me at first, sweetly, patiently, like a good best friend would. And after I'd calmed, after he'd ordered us takeout and turned on a movie, how I'd asked him for one of his t-shirts so that I, a teary mess, could spend the night. How I'd pulled my shirt off right there, in front of him. How I'd known his eyes would fall on me, could not help but fall on me and linger. How I'd undone my bra and turned to him, reaching for the shirt he offered me, daring him, really, to look and keep looking. I was by no means a perfect specimen, but I was young and warm and unmarried. I knew, of course, that Beau was touch-starved.

He'd turned from me, as if from a piercing light.

"Annie," he said. There was new hurt in his voice, something I'd never heard before beneath all his arch jokes and quick humor. "What are you doing?"

"Please," I said, knowing the unarticulated thing I pled for was an act of cruelty.

Shirtless, I moved toward him, to his dear, monstrous face, and I reached out one hand and let it fall, lightly, against the bumpy terrain of his barnacled cheek. I had never touched his face before, knowing instinctively that this was forbidden. But I touched him then, as if we were in a storybook and he might kiss me and be made handsome. He startled like he'd been stung, but I'd felt it: a pent-up electric current beneath his skin, running through my fingers.

And then he was pressing hard against me, something so desperate and urgent in his motions—hands on my waist, his hot, dry lips against my own—that I was frightened. Appalled. He kissed me like a drowning man gasping for air—yet already I was pushing him back gently, pulling away.

"Annie, Annie, Annie," he whispered, and then, he issued a terrible groan, a bellow that shamed me to hear.

"We're like Robert Lowell and Elizabeth Bishop," I whispered, quoting myself as if I were offering an inside joke, undercutting the severity of the situation, inserting a bit of levity. Someone, some day, would read our letters and find us witty and wise.

He made a sound that wasn't laughter and turned away.

"Put a shirt on," he hissed. "I'm going for a walk."

When I took the shirt from him, I saw his hand was quaking.

Beau would not speak to me after that.

In the story I wish I were telling, the story of our nouveau Ouro Preto, Bill and I would have found diamonds by summer's end. One of us, kneeling sunburned by a spot in the stream, would have leapt up, shouting. We would have grasped each other and twirled in celebration, delirious at our discovery.

But as the summer drew to an end, I felt my smoldering jewel-hunger wane and finally dissipate, as if on some level I knew and was preparing myself for the inevitable—the way one learns to kill a longing that will never be fulfilled. I felt clean then, pure, and absent of desire. The act of searching in that field became simply an act that I performed, a ritual in and of itself.

I stopped dreaming of Ouro Preto. I'd remembered a poem by Bishop called "Under the Window: Ouro Preto." Rereading it, I saw its plainness, a poem of mundane observation and small-town gossip—women talking about having their hair combed, people drinking water, an old man passing by with a stick, oil in a ditch. Ouro Preto, merely a place. *The seven ages of man are talkative and soiled and thirsty.*

It had crossed my mind that I could try calling Beau before the semester started, tell him about my summer as a kind of consolation. He would laugh with me, commiserate. Things might somehow be restored. This was my opportunity. I could try it. I could just call him.

But I did not.

I called Nick instead, and we met once more, in a sticky booth at one of the noisy bars near campus. The night ended badly.

Every day until it was time for the fall semester to start, I went back to the farmer's field with Bill. On our last afternoon, when the sun was starting its slow pinkish descent behind the polite cows who'd paid us little mind, their eyes benign, glazed, I told Bill I had something for him.

"Doomed love," I said, producing the ring I'd been carrying around in my pocket. "For your collection."

He looked confused. "I can't take this, Annie."

"Take it," I insisted. "It's a fake. But it sure looks real, doesn't it?" I pressed the little ring into his hand.

"Goddamn diamonds, Annie," Bill said, gazing down at the ring. "We'll find those diamonds yet. If not this summer, then the next, or the one after. We'll find them."

And even now, years later, I see him, the image seared into my brain: standing in the setting sun, ugly-magnificent on that hillside, with his big, clumsy hand outstretched, radiant with want.

EVERY HUMAN LOVE

Sarah had been walking around for weeks with a dead baby inside her. A dead man's dead baby. The baby was no bigger than her thumb, and she'd seen his tiny heart flickering on the screen just a month earlier. Now he appeared as a white, unmoving blob, a moth smooshed against a darkened windowpane.

"There's no heartbeat. I'm sorry," the woman with the ultrasound wand said. "Fetal demise."

Sarah was already crying at that point, and embarrassed to be crying, and embarrassed to be embarrassed. Because it happened, didn't it? She should have known. It was no disaster. Whole families got Ebola and died. This was nothing. Or hardly a thing. She should respond accordingly.

"I'm sorry," the woman said again. "Let's go find Dr. Adler."

Sarah wiped the goo off of her stomach and followed the technician. They went the back way because none of the other pregnant women, smug with their swollen bellies, wanted to see a weeping person with a dead smudge lodged in her uterus. The cruel part, it seemed to Sarah, was that her body hadn't notified her. It had allowed her to go about her business thinking everything was okay.

"Here. Have a seat." The woman pointed to an office chair in a windowless room—clearly an out-of-the-way setting in which to deal with hysterical patients.

Sarah blew her nose and tried to calm herself. She thought of poems she remembered from fat anthologies with tissue-paper pages, poems written upon the deaths of children—she had been an English major once—but this seemed to elevate her loss above what it was. She imagined she could feel the slight mass of the baby stilled inside her, its tiny weight like a stone dropped in a river.

When Dr. Adler walked in, she was tall and no-nonsense. Her hair was dyed an artificial shade of red. Sarah liked her clipped, businesslike manner.

"Do you have someone to pick you up? A partner? A spouse?"

Sarah said yes so as not to be more pitiable, all the while knowing she would end up calling a cab. There was no spouse. She was a single integer now, bleak and autonomous, asexual as a sea sponge. She'd told no one about the baby.

Sarah's husband, her almost-ex-husband, her estranged husband, Will—had he still been living—might have massaged her head afterward, telling her it was all meant to be, that there would be other chances, that this was nature's way. His words might have partially comforted Sarah but also inspired in her the urge to cry, *But I wanted that one.*

She whispered it to herself now, "But I wanted that one," over and over, a verbal compress against the ache—eventually realizing she was unsure whether she meant the baby, or Will, or both.

She was back at work two days later, bleeding any residual out of her and swallowing ibuprofen at scheduled intervals. It was amazing the things you could accomplish while nursing your own inconsequential misery.

"How are you feeling?" Tanea, one of her coresidents, asked, stirring powdered Coffee-Mate into her coffee.

"I'm fine," Sarah said. "A stomach thing." Because why tell others about your small sadnesses? That wasn't the point of the job. The point of the job was other people unburdening themselves to you; you comforting them.

The community psychiatry clinic where they worked was small and drab and cluttered. Her tiny office had previously been a supply closet. The buzzing light gave the room a horror-movie-set vibe. Sarah hoped that her patients had not noticed the glue traps behind the shelves. She hoped the potted plant she'd put on her desk and the photograph of flowers on the wall gave the room a consoling quality that she herself was somehow not privy to.

There was not enough funding for psychiatry; the department didn't generate revenue for the hospital. The new part of the hospital was beautiful and sunlit and clean, with real artwork on the walls and little courtyards with water fountains. The old part of the hospital, the part where the psychiatry clinics and inpatient units were housed, was dismal, with dim lighting and mouse droppings.

"I've got a new one for you," Tanea said, leaning against the doorway with a sheaf of papers in her hand. "A referral from Human Sexuality. Should be interesting." She grimaced and handed Sarah the papers.

"Bestiality?"

"Nope," Tanea said. "Better."

Most of the patients she and her coresidents saw were facing mood or anxiety disorders, schizophrenia, substance abuse. But on Fridays, they also took referrals from the Human Sexuality Consultation Clinic.

Sarah glanced at the facesheet and walked to the waiting room to find Mr. A. N. Butler: age forty-eight, preliminary diagnosis Paraphilia Not Otherwise Specified.

The waiting room was a bleak space of fake flowers and scattered diabetes management magazines. The man sitting in the corner had helmet-like gray hair. He smelled of mothballs and body odor, and Sarah guessed that he had pulled the clothes he wore out of storage.

The rumpled, ill-fitting suit was seersucker, even though it was November. There was a brown stain on the lapel.

"Mr. Butler," she said. "I'm Dr. Daniels. Please. Come this way."

When they'd been trying for the baby, Will had accused Sarah of being overly methodical. There was no pleasure to the process. She'd approached conception with scientific rigor: ovulation test strips, an app on her phone, temperature charting. During one fertile window, she made them try five days in a row, twice a day, their faces grim as marathoners.

Will had fallen against her, his forehead and hairline damp. "I think we've lost sight of the good part," he said quietly.

She had agreed aloud without actually believing him. The thought of the baby so consumed her that the baby *was* the good part. The baby would make her forget to be unhappy. The baby, with its little pink ears and soft, kissable tummy, its laughter like a tiny bell.

"Don't you like it when I touch you?" Will had asked. "I want to do it the right way."

She had nodded earnestly, but maybe there was no right way. What did she know? She worked in a clinic where she recommended sensate focused therapy and mindfulness to people lacking sexual desire, but she had no true understanding of what the execution of these exercises would look like.

It wasn't long afterward that Will was diagnosed with testicular cancer. This was the first irony. They'd postponed their efforts, and he had dutifully filled out the paperwork to bank his sperm. Their lives developed a new rhythm, punctuated by doctor's appointments and trips to the infusion center. They spoke of absolute neutrophil counts and Zofran. And then, after months of treatment, it was over.

It should have been a relief, the end of chemotherapy, but the heightened awareness of mortality had prematurely accelerated their marriage. The experience left them mute, bereft of things to say to one another. Sarah had developed a knowledge of Will's body so intimate as to no longer allow for eroticism. They were wizened survivors, too aware of brutal truths ever to be involved in anything as depthless as sexual love.

They separated shortly after Will was declared to have no evidence of disease. She moved to a one-bedroom apartment across town. Would they get divorced? Probably. And yet they retained an irritable ease with one another. Like old battlemates, they stayed in touch: met for coffee, held their familiar silences over pad thai. All their friends believed they would surely reconcile.

And then Will was killed in a car accident just three months later. Not a cancer cell left in his body, he died pristine, in the full fount of health.

This was the second irony, and possibly also the third.

She was left technically a widow—the youngest widow she knew—left to clean up everything, left to face the facts.

Fact: Frozen sperm can successfully be used in insemination decades after it is first stored.

Fact: The banked sperm of one's deceased spouse is readily obtainable with proper ID and paperwork.

Fact: It can be unexpectedly easy to make a baby, if not to keep it.

Mr. Butler joined her in her dim office, making himself comfortable against the plastic-backed chair. He looked at her expectantly.

"So," she began. "What brings you here?"

He stared, unblinking as a fish, shirt collar tight around his neck. "Sexual incompatibility," he said, then cleared his throat. "No. Human incompatibility."

She swallowed, feeling a strong cramp—an echo of the baby, its absence now a resonant pain.

"To understand my difficulty, you have to understand to whom I'm attracted. It's not acceptable in our society." He studied her face.

She girded herself for him to admit his attraction to children. She had heard it many times—both from the defiant, those who insisted society's standards were wrong, and from the sickened, the ashamed. Or maybe it was something stranger—a fetish involving inanimate objects: safety pins, adult diapers, American Girl Dolls.

"I know what you're thinking," he said scornfully. "Not kids. I'm not one of those sickos."

"What *is* the nature of your attraction?"

"Ghosts. I'm sexually attracted to ghosts."

She looked at him, uncertain of what to say. "You mean you're attracted to people who are deceased?" she finally ventured, careful to keep her voice neutral. Corpses, unyielding in their rigor mortis—she shuddered slightly.

"To the corporeal dead, no," he said. He sniffed with the irritation of a pedant attempting to explain something to someone obtuse. "I'm not a necrophiliac."

"I wonder," she began deferentially, "if you're speaking metaphorically."

"No," he said. "No metaphors. Most people don't understand. My sexual partners are all ghosts. Not living, breathing humans. Ghosts." He sniffed again in such a way that she knew she was among the lesser minds who found his statements incomprehensible. "You can imagine the problems we have consummating our desire for one another."

A flash of an old Patrick Swayze movie poster—one could develop some sort of delusional framework around that, she supposed. "Are these people you knew who died?"

"No," he said. "I can't say I ever knew these souls while they were living."

"It seems impossible," she said, again careful, respectful, inviting him to explain, "to have sex with a ghost."

"Yes, but I've found a way. I've found a way to make it work."

Before they'd separated, while Will was still sick, he and Sarah had gone to a couples' retreat at a resort in New Mexico. Will's parents had paid for everything. It was framed as a healing weekend, a holistic retreat geared for young couples facing cancer. There would be workshops and acupuncture sessions and couples therapists and nutrition classes and reiki—a mix of the practical and what Will called the woo-woo. This would appease Will's mother, a wealthy woman who wore expensive caftans and beaded necklaces and had a generally unshakable faith in all that was woo-woo.

That first evening, they'd befriended another couple, Charlotte and Matt from Washington, DC. Charlotte was a slender beauty with dark hair and thyroid cancer, a classically trained opera singer with something Victorian and doomed in her very voice; Matt was a perfectly healthy advertising copywriter with a sleeve tattoo and a permanent five o'clock shadow. They'd all bonded with the rapid intensity of summer camp cabinmates and began attending all the same sessions.

During the first dinner, Matt's bare knee brushed against Sarah's. The accidental touch sent a current through her, and she admitted something to herself: she was attracted to Matt. She felt a physical pull toward him, a kind of brute magnetism that she had not felt toward Will in years. Maybe it was the sort of magnetism one can only have with a stranger.

She was appalled at herself. It was unseemly. One chair over sat delicate, stricken Charlotte, pretty as an ivory cameo, with a fresh scar at her neck. There was her own sick husband, loyal as a basset hound, beside her.

She watched as Matt took Charlotte's hand in his, adoring, proprietary. Sarah turned away.

Matt's solicitude toward his wife made what happened on the final night of the retreat all the more surprising. After the closing banquet, after Sarah had had one glass too many of red wine and wandered outside, sandalless, to gaze into the big star-pocked New Mexico sky, she'd heard a voice behind her and instantly recognized him. Matt. He was drunk. She could tell. He smelled of bourbon.

"It's you," he said, his voice smeary and jocular, faintly mocking. "Sarah from Baltimore."

"It's me," she said, and then, "Where's Charlotte?" which was a stupid question in that moment, socially transgressive in its clumsiness, a crude question that made things more awkward. It was like asking about someone else's prognosis—something they'd all quickly intuited was verboten at the beginning of the retreat. This information might be volunteered, but never sought outright.

"Tired," he said. "She's always tired now. In bed. " His voice trailed off. He did not ask Sarah where Will was.

There was a wooden split-rail fence around the perimeter of the resort, and Sarah held the top rail, tilting her head back as if to swallow all the stars.

Matt shifted toward her, slowly, like this had all been rehearsed. His mouth was against her throat, tasting it, kissing her, his warm, broad hands against her back. She stayed as she was, head tilted back, perfectly still, as he moved his lips up her neck, tasting her earlobes, her clavicles, her chin.

He did not kiss her on the mouth, as if by some predetermined agreement. She remained motionless as a statue, the sound of blood rushing in her ears, not daring to move lest he stop.

When he finally stepped away from her, he brushed his hands together as if he'd just completed a task, and she knew that this had been a confirmatory test of something—some central principle—to which she was quite peripheral and unnecessary.

And then Matt, with his angular shoulders and sleeve tattoo and angry devotion, had walked back inside. The thought of him kissing her throat filled her with a kind of stomach-lurching thrill and a deep sadness.

She did not speak to Matt or Charlotte again. They had already disappeared the next morning for an early flight without any goodbye. She'd been careful to avoid finding either of them on Facebook afterward. She did not actually want to meet up with them for drinks or dinner, even though they had promised each other this at the beginning of the retreat.

Later that last night in New Mexico, after that kiss, she had clung to Will in their luxurious king-sized hotel bed and felt the same sadness. She'd clung to him with something that, if not love, if not spousal devotion, was something desperate and pained enough to be close to it.

Mr. Butler had long, big-jointed hands that were somehow still strangely elegant, the knuckles large and faceted as gems. He clasped his hands loosely in his lap like a respectful child.

"Please," Sarah said. "I'd love to understand how it works."

"There's a place I go," he said, "where the spirit world is accessible. With the help of a medium—she summons them. It's more intense, more sensual than if I were to touch you right now."

She flinched unintentionally at this. The great boundary violation in psychiatry was, of course, the touching of one's patients beyond a proper handshake. She felt a wave of revulsion at the thought of Mr. Butler's hands on her.

"And how does it compare to—" she almost said *the real thing*, but thought this might offend him.

"Intercourse with a living human?"

"Yes."

"I wouldn't know." He looked down at his big hands, and for a moment she thought he might be embarrassed, but when he looked back up at her, his face was strangely open. She considered his stiff monotone and awkward formality, his odd affect.

He tore a sticky note from the pad on Sarah's desk and wrote something down, sliding it across the desk to her.

"You could come and see what I mean."

It was an address outside of the city, a commuting suburb. She imagined a séance from another century, weeping women in ruffled, high-necked period garb clustered at a table, desperate for a thump of communication from a lost loved one. But no, this wouldn't be like that. She imagined instead other people like Mr. Butler, men with stilted speech and stained clothes, a self-proclaimed psychic/spirit-medium ready and eager to take their crumpled twenties.

"It doesn't look like much," he said, tapping the address with his index finger. "But décor doesn't matter." He tilted one palm up, gesturing to her grim little office. "It's a place of porous borders."

She studied the address as if it might reveal something, then realized he was gazing at her.

He stood up then, smoothing his pants and pushing the chair back. The session was over, but she hadn't indicated this. Ordinarily, she had to make some concluding remark.

Rising, she escorted him to the door.

"Congratulations on your pregnancy," he added, glancing at her flat midsection as he exited. There was a note of something in his voice, and understood she had gotten the whole thing wrong from the start: it was he who pitied her.

The rest of the afternoon, it was impossible to concentrate on what her other patients were saying, and she found herself answering automatically at the wrong moments.

She knew she needed to leave her office, its claustrophobic dark. She wished she could call someone—the right person—and tell the whole strange story. She felt somehow that Mr. Butler had unfairly implicated her, involved her. Folie à deux.

She needed to get out of there, to be somewhere else.

Typing quickly into the search bar on her internet browser, she began clicking through results. Matt. Matt, a copywriter in DC. She thought of the warmth of his lips on her throat, the terrible exhilaration. She thought of the way he had looked at Charlotte, a look of resigned longing, as if Charlotte were already a ghost.

There was something beautiful about that. To love someone beyond the bounds of the flesh. Something transcendent. She needed for someone to need her like that.

She would find Matt. She would get in her car and go.

The address listed was near U Street, and she knew there were good bars and restaurants nearby. It would be too much just to show up at his door, but if she happened to be nearby . . . She would call him, and he would laugh with delighted disbelief, offering to meet her. And then what? She dared not imagine further.

The traffic to DC was only moderately awful that evening, but by the time she parked off Florida Avenue, her hands were clammy and she had two damp crescents beneath her arms. The pad she was wearing was cumbersome. She felt dull and lumpy, bloody and unbeautiful. Unfeminine—her body inhospitable to any new life that should try to inhabit it.

She dialed the number, chest tight while the phone rang.

"Hello," a familiar voice said.

"Matt?" she yelped. "This is Sarah. From the retreat? In New Mexico? Gosh, was it five years ago?"

There was a silence, and she felt a pang. He didn't remember her. The silence lasted a few beats more, but then he responded with a voice as warm and familiar as she remembered. "Sarah! Wow," he said. "It's great to hear from you. Seems like a lifetime ago."

"I know," she said. "It's really good—really weird—to hear your voice again." She massaged her temple. "I called because I happened to be in DC." She paused for a second, unused to lying. She was speaking too loudly into the phone, shrill and giddy. "For a meeting. And anyway, I'm at this place just off U Street. I was going to grab a drink or maybe something to eat, and I thought, why not? Why not call Matt? And Charlotte? It'd be so good to see you! Both of you!" All this poured out of her, hollow-sounding and desperate.

There was another silence. She could picture Matt frowning in thought.

"Oh, wow," he said. "I mean, I'd love to. But I've actually got a project due tomorrow. . . ."

"Maybe a drink, then?" she asked, her voice filled with false cheer. "I have to get back, too. One drink's better anyway."

"Maybe we could plan something in advance? Look at our calendars? I'm also on kid duty tonight."

She winced at his apologetic tone, the caution in his voice. Something rose up in her throat, almost a sob, or wild laughter.

"You've got a kid!"

But of course—it was good and to be expected. They'd had a child. Matt and Charlotte. Of course they had.

"Yeah," he said kindly. "Violet's eighteen months old. The boss of everything."

"Wow," Sarah said, her voice higher and higher pitched, as if she'd been sucking helium. "I can't believe you and Charlotte have a kid! That's so great!"

"No," Matt said, with a trace of reluctance now. "Not Charlotte. I'm married to someone else now. Elizabeth. You'd love her."

Sarah sucked in a deep breath but did not answer.

"Charlotte died, Sarah," Matt said quietly. "She was dying when we met you. I thought you knew."

Sarah nodded into the phone like he could see her. She had known. Of course she had known. Or should have known. Just like she should have always known there would be no reprise of that moment under the stars in the New Mexico desert. Never.

"Listen. I'm sorry," he said with the practiced calm of someone used to backing away from unreasonable people without antagonizing them. "Rain check, okay?"

She did not answer because she had already hung up, her eyes burning.

Shame mixed with disappointment was a quick-burning fuel, and it seemed to exhilarate Sarah, to grant her a newfound clarity. She wasn't tired at all. She was not hungry. She buzzed with a clean energy that seemed to feed on air alone. She drove back toward home, but she was not going home. She was following her GPS to the address in the suburbs on the yellow sticky note Mr. Butler had given her. It was not out of the way on the return trip. She gripped her steering wheel at ten and two, as if someone might come along and divert her from her mission.

What she wanted was to see Mr. Butler. What she wanted was to see him and give him a piece of her mind.

She saw his disdainful face again, sniffing like he smelled bad meat as he rose to leave her office. Acting as if he were above the fray. When he was the pathetic one. *Find some internet porn like all the other lonely losers*, she would tell him, *and quit pretending you're so superior.*

Imagining herself saying this granted her a kind of relief. Obviously this was a boundary violation. Obviously this was an awful idea. And yet she drove. The tiniest part of her was curious. The tiniest part of her—dumb vestigial hope—wondered if there might be something more.

When she pulled up to the address, it was a small, brick house in a neighborhood of unassuming houses. She parked in the drive behind an old Buick. She was here, and it wouldn't make sense to turn back now. She felt light-headed with anticipation.

She walked up the drive, noting the grass needed cutting. There was a cement birdbath with a crack running up the base. She paused at the door before ringing the bell.

It took a moment for someone to answer. The woman who opened the door was older, her brown hair threaded with gray. She wiped her damp hands on the t-shirt she was wearing and eyed Sarah curiously.

"I'm here for the ghosts," Sarah announced.

"You're wanting Becky, then," the woman said, unfazed, gesturing toward the side of the house. "She runs her little operation around back. You got to walk around to the basement door." She looked Sarah up and down. "You sure, honey? You don't seem like the type."

Sarah turned, following the slope down to the back, where sure enough there was a door to the basement, one with a sign on which Madame Marie, Psychic and Medium was painted in curling font.

She raised her hand to knock, but then thought better of it. She pushed the door open.

The interior of the basement was so dark that Sarah couldn't see much. There was a mildewy smell. Quiet music—something Middle Eastern, maybe?—was playing from an old CD player. Her eyes adjusted as a woman, Madame Marie or Becky, moved toward her, frowning, her finger to her lips.

Sarah hit the light switch, and in that crude and sudden brightness, several semi-recumbent nude men blinked up at her. They were engaged in what her mind first construed to be the act of strangling hideous pink mole-rats jutting from their crotches. Otherwise the basement was plain and ordinary, with shag carpeting and only a few nods to the occult scattered throughout (a crystal ball here, a pentagram there). The men propped on pillows on the floor stared at her, flesh in hand, stricken, vulnerable in their nakedness. One, two, three, four . . . five, six . . . She counted their waxen faces.

"Turn the lights back off!" one shouted.

"You've ruined it!"

"Fuck off!"

Madame Marie clucked and shook her head. "Oh my. You're here on the wrong day, honey. I do readings on Thursdays."

"This is all?" Sarah heard herself say softly.

She spied Mr. Butler. His slight paunch, pale as an unbaked loaf, and his thin legs and skinny shoulders made him seem even older than he was. His face was slick with exertion. He stood, wrapping a thin brown robe around himself, and approached her.

"This is all it is?" she repeated, almost to herself.

He seemed to hear this and absorb it, as if seeing for the first time himself the fake wood paneling, the tired-looking crystal ball, a purplish lava lamp, and the soft bodies of the other men reclining on the floor.

"I didn't think you'd actually come," he said, lifting his hand to her cheek, almost but not quite touching it, as if he had conjured her. His eyes were welling up, and he wiped them with the sleeve of his robe.

Her righteous tirade had long left her. He was just another soul trapped in his own awkward spacesuit of muscle, skin, and skull. The right thing to do would be to comfort him, to let him bury his face against her shoulder, to pat his back gently while whispering nothings to him as if she were soothing him to sleep.

Lay your sleeping head, my love, Human on my faithless arm. As she drew Mr. Butler into a stiff embrace, these lines returned to her. They were from a poem she'd once read and loved in an undergraduate class, back when she'd had the capacity still to be moved by beauty. Auden, she thought, continuing to shush Mr. Butler, stroking his coarse gray hair.

"Turn the lights off!" someone yelled again.

She felt suddenly very tired, even dizzy, the whole afternoon and evening now seeming surreal.

"Oh, honey," Madame Marie/Becky said, reaching behind Sarah to the light switch. "You're bleeding. You've got blood all over your backside."

The next thing she knew, Sarah found herself gazing up at the purplish-red hair of Dr. Adler. *Retained products of conception,* the doctor was explaining. *Good thing your friend drove you here.*

She hazily recalled having ridden in the passenger seat of her own car, Mr. A. N. Butler at the steering wheel, his Greco-Roman nose sharp in profile.

Words slid through her brain, disjointed, so slippery she could not grasp them. *Proves the child ephemeral.*

He'd helped her, his large hands proving capable, guiding her into the emergency room, and she was grateful.

"Humans," he'd said flatly. He swept his arm around the ER waiting room, which was crowded and smelled of vomit and sweat, the musk of many bodies passing through the premises.

Mortal, guilty, she whispered silently to herself, letting the words roll over her tongue like lozenges, *but to me The entirely beautiful.*

"Look at them," he said.

ACKNOWLEDGMENTS

Thank you to the editors and magazine staff who first published these stories, and a huge thank you to Nicola for helping edit and strengthen this collection. Thanks also to Rae and Sara for being writing accountability buddies for several stories (#writingchurch). Thank you for the endless support of my parents, grandparents, and my incredible siblings, Lane, Alex, and Adrienne. Thank you also to all my wonderful in-law family—I'm lucky to have y'all!

Biggest thank you of all to my true writing partner, Matthew. And hi, Josie! Hi, Ellie! You actually make writing, like most things, a little bit more difficult, but you're also the source of my greatest delight, and I hope someday you'll like seeing your names here.

These stories originally appeared, sometimes in slightly different form, in the following publications: "Changeling" in *Blackbird*; "The Private Collection" in *Shenandoah*; "Fox Foot" in *Mississippi Review*; "Rumpelstiltskin" in *Copper Nickel*; "For the Dead Who Travel Fast" in *Memorious* and *Best of the Net 2016*; "The Undead" in *New Madrid*; "Higher Things" in *Alaska Quarterly Review*; "Gifts" in *Carve Magazine*; "Lucky" in *Tupelo Quarterly*; "Romantics" in *Kenyon Review* online; "Wages" in *Big Big Wednesday*; "The Scare" in *Joyland*; "Ouro Preto" in *Ecotone*; and "Every Human Love" in *Hopkins Review*.